DATE			

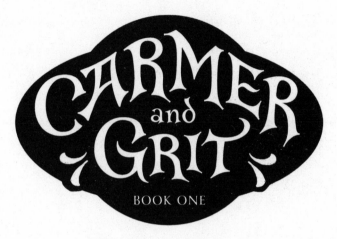

BOOK ONE

The Wingsnatchers

SARAH JEAN HORWITZ

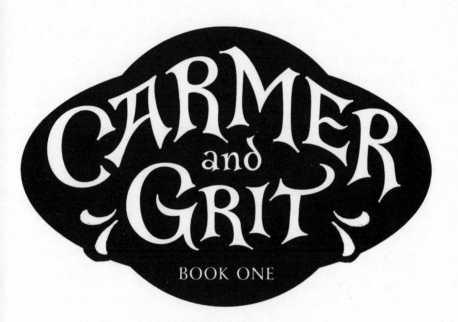

BOOK ONE

The Wingsnatchers

ALGONQUIN YOUNG READERS 2017

Published by
Algonquin Young Readers
an imprint of Algonquin Books of Chapel Hill
Post Office Box 2225
Chapel Hill, North Carolina 27515-2225

a division of
Workman Publishing
225 Varick Street
New York, New York 10014

© 2017 by Sarah Jean Horwitz.

Printed in the United States of America.
Published simultaneously in Canada by Thomas Allen & Son Limited.
Design by Carla Weise.

LIBRARY OF CONGRESS CATALOGING-IN-PUBLICATION DATA
Names: Horwitz, Sarah Jean, author.
Title: The Wingsnatchers / Sarah Jean Horwitz.
Description: First edition. | Chapel Hill, North Carolina : Algonquin
Young Readers, 2017. | Series: Carmer and Grit ; book 1 | Summary:
Aspiring inventor and magician's apprentice, Felix Carmer III,
is aided by Grit, a fiery, flightless faerie princess, in winning a
magic competition, in exchange for him helping Grit investigate
a string of faerie disappearances.
Identifiers: LCCN 2016043933 | ISBN 9781616206635
Subjects: | CYAC: Magicians—Fiction. | Fairies—Fiction.
Classification: LCC PZ7.1.H665 Wi 2017 | DDC [Fic]—dc23
LC record available at https://lccn.loc.gov/2016043933

10 9 8 7 6 5 4 3 2 1
First Edition

For Mom and Dad,
for never laughing at me
for wanting wings
of my own

THE CAT ON THE TRAIN

THE RELERAIL CAN TAKE THE CAT ANYWHERE, EX-cept where it wants to go.

Something funny happens to machines when they get near the city's oldest and largest public park, Oldtown Ar-boretum. Most either stop working completely or go a bit haywire. Gears turn the wrong way, buttons push them-selves, spring mechanisms unfurl like wet noodles. It's why the elevated railway travels *around* the Arboretum instead of through it, and why even the closest platform is at least two blocks away from its wrought iron gates.

Below, the streets of Skemantis are a churning mass of steam carriages, bicycles, velocycles, and pedestrians all jockeying for space on the evening journey home, and the

1

Relerail isn't much better. Yet despite the cramped quarters, the passengers give the cat a wide berth. It even has its own seat.

It's not a real cat, of course. This cat is an Autocat—a mechanized clockwork creature—and an impressive one at that, even in a city accustomed to seeing shiny brass automata marching down the streets. Yet there's something *different* about this Autocat with the glowing orange eyes that people can't quite put their finger on. If the cat could, it might suspect a few people even switch cars to avoid it. Silly humans.

The train spits the Autocat out with a crowd of dusty, soot-blackened factory workers who have much farther to go on foot than the Relerail reaches, but they hold little interest for the cat. It doubles back toward the Arboretum, paws clicking lightly on muddy cobblestones.

The lampposts just inside the Arboretum's gates flicker as the Autocat approaches. It makes no move to go inside—at least not yet. The cat simply sits, cocking its head to better hear the soft whisper that could be the wind in the trees, but is not.

The whisper travels up and over the hills and around the frog ponds, shuddering through cattails and briar patches and finally reaching the base of the oldest tree in the Arboretum, an ancient willow with roots wide enough for a man to sit on. The grass rustles. The whisper cartwheels up through shaking leaves, up and away to the very, very top, where the last listener pauses to hear it and frowns.

At the South Gate, just outside the winding iron bars, the Autocat waits. Its jeweled eyes gleam in the darkness. It watches as each golden lantern on the pathway blinks out, one by one, and it growls—a rough, scraping sound like metal on metal, a sound never heard in the garden before. The creature slinks off into Skemantis's black night, its mission accomplished.

For now.

1.

PREPARE TO BE AMAZED

"AND NOW, LADIES AND GENTLEMEN, FOR MY LAST
and final trick! I will be performing the unimaginable, the
grotesque, the miraculous! What you are about to see may
shock you, but fear not. We will all come out in one piece,
after all."

Antoine the Amazifier clapped his bony hands together, relishing his own dramatic pause.

"Prepare to be amazed."

Surely, sawing his lovely assistant in half would earn
him a shriek or two from the women in the crowd. If not a
shriek, then maybe at least a gasp. The Amazifier couldn't
be too picky these days.

His audience did not look particularly amazed. A handful

of underfed mill workers and dirty children, tired after a long day's work, gathered around him in what passed for the town square. The men wore stony glares, the women deep lines in their faces, and a few of the younger ones eyed the magician's tip collection in a way that made the Amazifier nervous—not that there was much in there to begin with.

This was the blessing and the curse of running the country circuit. Far from the pressures of pleasing over-entertained city audiences, who were used to all manner of marvels and delights, country crowds were a simpler folk. More often than not, they were pleased that any sort of show had come to town at all. Then, of course, you had years when the harvest was bad or when a mine shut down, and the grandest tricks in the world couldn't get them to crack a smile—or open their wallets.

Resigning himself to another mediocre showing, the Amazifier gestured for his assistant, Kitty Delphine, to step forward. There was no response. The Amazifier cleared his throat.

"With the help of the lovely Miss Delphine!" hinted the Amazifier loudly. Kitty snapped out of her bored reverie and shimmied over to his side, the little golden bells on her costume jingling as she walked. One of the men in the crowd whistled.

The Amazifier instructed Kitty to lie down in a large black box in the center of the square. As he explained the process to the audience, brandishing a fearsome-looking saw, the third and heretofore unseen member of his entourage prepared to complete the trick without the audience ever knowing. Or at least, that was the hope.

There was a boy in the big black box, and his name was Felix Cassius Tiberius Carmer III. We'll call him Carmer, or this book will be much longer than any of us would like.

What looked like one box to the audience was actually two. As Kitty Delphine settled herself into the first half, Carmer shoved his own skinny legs—stockinged and high-heeled, to look like Kitty's—out of the foot openings in the second. To the audience, it appeared as if one whole girl was about to be sawed in half.

Carmer did not particularly like being stuck in a box wearing stockings and ladies' shoes, but he knew it was necessary. Carmer was Antoine the Amazifier's apprentice, and if he hoped to become a great magician himself one day, he had to pay his dues. Even if those dues included shaving his legs.

Carmer heard the grinding noises against the box and Kitty's scream of pretend shock that signaled the "sawing" had begun. He wiggled his feet a bit for dramatic effect.

A few muffled, disgruntled voices echoed from outside, and Carmer tensed. If the show was going south, it would be best to wrap it up quickly before things got ugly.

"The old man's full of it!" a teenaged boy sneered. Murmured grunts of assent followed.

"That's a boy in that box!" cried another.

Perhaps the wiggling feet had been a bit much.

Splat. Carmer heard the distinct ooze of rotting fruit hitting the side of the box, just near his head. He cringed at the Amazifier's tremulous protests as the crowd grew more impatient.

"Now, just a moment, ladies and gentlemen!"

Splunk. A tomato, this time.

"Boo!"

Sploosh.

"Get outta here!"

Squish.

"Take your sorry excuse for a magic show somewhere else!"

And finally—mercifully—the sound of retreating footsteps. The Amazifier stood alone in the dirty little square, picking bits of spoiled lettuce off his velvet cloak.

Carmer shook Kitty's shoes off his feet and shimmied out of his box. He took a moment to pop his favorite hat, an old and bedraggled top hat, back onto his head. It was too big for him, and only his large ears kept it from sliding down completely over his face.

Carmer looked at his mentor—old, hunched, and abandoned by his audience—and thought of what it must have been like when the Amazifier was in his prime, when hundreds gathered to see his every performance. Those times were long gone now.

But Carmer owed the Amazifier his life and his freedom, and he was resolved to help in any small way he could. He wished he could have done something to stop the hecklers, but cleaning up after the fact would have to do.

"We'll pack everything up, Master Antoine," Carmer assured the old man.

"We?" asked Kitty Delphine. She appeared to be taking a nap in her half of the box. Carmer shot her a look, and she sighed.

"You go on, just like he says," said Kitty resignedly. She hoisted herself up and jumped down, careful to dodge the moldy cabbage in a mud pile by her feet. She pecked the Amazifier's cheek. "Head back to the Moto-Manse and put the kettle on. We'll be right behind you."

Their steam-powered house on wheels, built by the Amazifier himself, was parked at the town limits. Its tendency to take up the entire road did little to endear it to most locals.

"Oh, well . . . yes, dear. All right." The Amazifier nodded absentmindedly and tottered off. He was always like this after a bad performance.

"You think he'll be all right?" Carmer asked once the Amazifier was out of earshot.

"Even if he's not, we'd best shake a leg," said Kitty, looking around nervously, "I don't fancy it'll be long before those folks come back wanting a double refund."

Carmer nodded and started to wipe the grime off their

9

box with a spare rag. The wind picked up, scattering bits of rubbish everywhere and making it hard to see through the dust. Carmer and Kitty ducked their heads against it.

Smack. A piece of paper flew right into Carmer's face. He yanked it off and was about to toss it aside when something caught his eye. He unfolded the flyer and read it aloud.

"'SKEMANTIAN INTERNATIONAL EXHIBITION— October 15—For the scientifically inclined, the technologically talented, or simply the curious! Featuring the newest cutting-edge technology from Titan Industries and beyond. Presented by the one and only Titus Archer himself!'"

An illustration of a stern-looking man shaking hands with a brass humanoid automaton looked up at Carmer. He grinned back, all thoughts of the disastrous magic show forgotten.

"Kitty?" he called across the square. "How would you feel about a trip to the city?"

THIRTEEN-YEAR-OLD FELIX CARMER had been interested in "how things worked" since he could babble and point (talking having never been a strong suit of his). His inventions and the various mishaps and minor injuries they caused had made him notorious throughout the orphanage where he spent most of his early childhood. He earned his first caning from the headmistress when he borrowed a wealthy donor's watch, though he protested again and again that he'd only wanted to take it apart and put it back together again.

The Amazifier, at least, understood Carmer's penchant for tinkering, even if he didn't encourage anything too adventurous. By the time he was ten, Carmer knew the ins and outs of nearly every magic trick and illusion the Amazifier performed, and even more besides. The Indian rope trick, the bullet catch, the levitating linking rings—Carmer picked up on them all. He even convinced the Amazifier to try a few of his enhanced smoke bombs, flash strings, and other magical supplies.

Carmer made other things besides contraptions for the magic show, of course: self-winding bobbins for Kitty's sewing machine, a relay system to send messages through all the wagons in a caravan, and other small but (arguably) useful machines. His most prized possession, however, was a miniature automaton soldier he'd built entirely by himself. It was this project that had first led Carmer to discover Titan Industries.

Helmed by the formidable Titus Archer, the company was at the forefront of modern scientific discovery, specifically automaton technology. Clockwork creatures that could walk, work in assembly lines, play musical instruments, serve a table, or even cut the grass were all the rage from the manufacturing sector to the homes of the wealthy, and they endlessly fascinated Carmer.

Titan Industries' base of operations was Skemantis, a

gleaming metropolis lauded by many as the "city of the future." Carmer had never set foot inside it, though he'd traipsed through nearly every one-horse town within fifty miles. Skemantis was no longer part of the Amazifier's circuit, and convincing his mentor to go off the seasonal schedule for a few days would be no easy feat. But Carmer just *had* to meet Titus Archer and learn whatever he could.

"Spirits and zits, Carmer, I sure would love to visit Skemantis!" said Kitty on the way back to the Moto-Manse. (The undead and a poor complexion were the only things worthy of exclamation in her book.)

Carmer hoped he'd be able to convince the Amazifier with Kitty on his side, even if all she wanted to do in the city was look at new dresses.

"But you know Master Antoine'll never go for it," she said, shaking her head. Beside her, their ancient horse, Eduardo, let out a soft whinny. The weight of their big black box was clearly getting to be a bit much for him.

"Besides," Kitty added, "I don't think this beast would survive the trip."

Eduardo snorted into her hair.

THE MOTO-MANSE WAS one of Antoine the Amazifier's proudest accomplishments. A three-story motorized house on wheels, with a small trailer for Eduardo hooked onto the back, it provided nearly every comfort of modern domesticity—a flush toilet, a working stove, and even a shower, just to name a few.

The cab of the Moto-Manse looked much like the front of any steam car, except that it was nearly double the size and was steered by a giant ship's wheel. Driving the Moto-Manse was a precarious business, as it had a tendency to tilt rather wildly from side to side if anyone dared push the accelerator to more than ten miles an hour. This did not make it a popular vehicle on the road.

But to Carmer, Kitty, and the Amazifier, who had no other place to call their own, the Moto-Manse was home. It was with a relieved sigh that Carmer and Kitty sat down to the tea the Amazifier had ready for them. Carmer clutched the flyer for the Titan Industries expo in his pocket.

After a few minutes of Kitty's chatter about their day, Carmer finally got up the courage to speak his mind.

"Sir, I was wondering . . ."

"What the square root of six thousand five hundred and sixty-one is?" The Amazifier was clearly in a better mood, as he had reverted to his favorite habit of turning everyday conversations with Carmer into Teachable Moments.

"Well . . ."

"The origin of the carrier pigeon?"

"I, um . . ."

"The melting point of magnesium oxide?"

"Two thousand eight hundred fifty-two degrees," answered Carmer automatically. He looked down at his tea.

13

"I've told you time and time again, Carmer," said the Amazifier. "If it is knowledge you seek, you need only ask."

Carmer extricated his hand from the depths of his pockets and smoothed out the International Exhibition flyer on the table. The Amazifier put his monocle to his eye and surveyed it critically.

"And I suppose you want to go to this . . . exhibition?" asked the Amazifier stiffly.

Carmer nodded.

"To poke about with experimental engines and hazardous chemicals and whatever else I won't let you get your hands on, with a bunch of other addle-brained young men?"

"Y-yes, sir."

The Amazifier gave Carmer a long, hard look and peered down at the flyer again. "As it happens," he said, gathering up their empty teacups, "I had plans to bring our little show to Skemantis anyway."

Antoine turned to bring their cups to the sink and Carmer and Kitty exchanged looks of surprise. What could the Amazifier want in Skemantis?

The old magician answered their question by placing an advertisement of his own on the table. It featured a colorful drawing of a dashing magician in a spotlight, surrounded by pretty dancers and flying hawks.

"The Seminal Symposium of Magickal Arts," declared the Amazifier grandly, puffing out his chest.

Carmer tried and failed to hide the skepticism on his

face, and he knew Kitty was doing the same. The Seminal Symposium of Magickal Arts was the most prestigious magic convention in the United States. Magicians from all over the country traveled to compete against each other for the grand cash prize. Kitty and Carmer knew that the Amazifier, while great in his heyday, was hardly competition material now. And the biggest one in the country? They didn't stand a chance!

But if this Symposium was what Carmer needed to get to Skemantis to see Titus Archer, he'd grin and bear it. He was concerned, however, that the city folk might have even *more* rotten tomatoes to spare than their usual audiences.

"Also, it's eighty-one," added the Amazifier.

Carmer looked at him questioningly.

"The square root of six thousand five hundred and sixty-one, of course!"

2.

AN IMPOSSIBLE THING

IN THE PRICKLY SHELTER OF OLDTOWN ARBORE-tum's famous blue roses, a flame was born. It came to life with a breath and a wish and the rubbing together of two tiny palms. It was no bigger than a candle flame, but that was sort of the point, really. A forest fire was *not* the goal of the exercise . . . at least not today.

The teardrop of a flame floated up and out, willed on by the tiny hands that guided it carefully around delicate petals of cerulean, indigo, and turquoise. It came to the edge of a frog pond, plucked up its courage, and glided out over the water. It caught one of the last of the sun's rays and grew a little larger, like calling to like, before the hands coaxed it small again. The pinprick of light descended ever so gently into the open blossom of an expectant water lily. Nearly a dozen floating flowers already glowed on the pond's smooth surface. Not a single petal was singed.

The rosebush rustled. A casual passerby would have expected a squirrel to dart out, or perhaps a small bird, but the face that peered out between the thorns was most certainly neither.

It was a very small face; that much was obvious. The tiny features were those of a girl in miniature, though upon closer inspection, one could not help but notice the pointed ears and impossibly dewy complexion, and come to the conclusion that this face was not altogether human. The little face with the wide eyes that seemed too big for her head was neither human nor animal, but fae—a fire faerie, to be exact.

Like all fire faeries, her eyes were a warm golden yellow. She had bits of red in her hair, though it was mostly a frizzy mess of dirty blonde tresses piled on top of her head. She was dressed in a fitted green vest and well-worn brown leggings tucked into deadly looking lace-up boots with spurs of thorns. A shiny hatpin dangled from a sheath belted around her waist, ready to be drawn at any moment. All in all, she cut quite the intimidating figure for five inches tall.

Such an imposing costume undoubtedly warrants an equally imposing name, and so this faerie was called Grit.

Grit crept to the edge of the pond and surveyed her flaming flowers with a satisfied smile. She almost wished a human would walk by to see it, but the chances of that were slim. It was nearly dark, and if all the talk around the Arboretum was true, there would be no faerie lanterns to light the paths tonight. Few humans, especially the city folk of Skemantis, would venture into the park in total darkness. The Queen of the Seelie Court had summoned all her subjects to the castle at the Great Willow for the first time in ages, and even the lamplighters were expected to be there. *Everyone* was expected to be there.

Grit, for one, wasn't planning on going. In fact, if things went her way, she'd be far away from the Arboretum before all the boring serious talk about jewel-eyed spies and the portents of death and destruction the old crones were seeing in their tea leaves started. They were always moaning about something—the encroaching iron world, the antics of the Free Folk, prophecies unfulfilled, doom and gloom and aching feet when it rained. Grit didn't know what made this time any different.

Like most evenings, Grit was preparing for an adventure. She breathed in the October breeze hungrily, savoring every smell it brought from the city beyond, and looked toward the South Gate with longing.

The flames in the lilies dipped and flickered. Grit swore and lifted them back up with a flick of her wrists, but a few of the flowers wilted and sank into the pond's murky depths. A surprised frog leapt out of their way and glared at her reproachfully.

"Sorry," Grit said. "I don't have many places to practice!"

She let the flames fizzle harmlessly into the water, but the frog hopped farther away with a pointed *ribbit.*

A second faerie darted out of the rosebushes, this one with a mop of spongy green hair that looked like a broccoli floret, with light green skin to match. Her furry eyebrows gave her a look of constant anxiety, which wasn't far from the truth.

"Gretti—" she started to whine, but Grit clamped a hand over her mouth and dragged them both down under a nearby willow's roots. The green-haired earth faerie let out an *oof* as they tumbled into the soft soil. "What was that for?" she complained, shaking dirt out of her gossamer wings.

Grit flushed and picked a water beetle out of her hair. "First of all," she seethed, "how many times have I asked you not to call me that? It's Grit or nothing, especially when we're outside!"

"Sorry, Gretti—Grit," corrected the earth faerie, smoothing out her leafy skirts.

"Do you want my name to bring the whole guard down on us like a flock of pigeons on a sandwich?"

The other faerie looked puzzled. "On a *what?*"

Grit threw her hands in the air and paced. "This is why you can't come with me, Bressel. I can't have you slowing me down with . . . with your lack of sandwich knowledge!"

Bressel backed away. "I was just asking where you were going," she said quietly.

Grit's anger faded as swiftly as it had come. She sighed, deflating like a tiny balloon. "It's human food," Grit explained. "You know, like the old women leave out on their doorsteps for the garden faeries sometimes? You'd like it."

Bressel looked doubtful. She peered up through the roots of the willow. "Bring me another time, then, and I'll try all the sandwiches in the city. But please, Grit, don't sneak outside the gates tonight."

"Why ever not?" asked Grit, though she knew full well.

"Because there'll be no lights tonight, Grit! The queen said so at court! Everyone will be at the meeting." Bressel rubbed her hands together nervously; small green vines sprouted from between her fingers. She shook them off without thinking.

Grit only grinned. "All the more reason to slip away, then. It'll be easy!"

"But they *never* bring the lamplighters in, you know that! There might be something out there, Grit, something even more dangerous than humans, and you want to run out after it in the dark?"

"I can handle myself, Bressel," Grit insisted, putting one hand to her hatpin sword. "The Free Folk aren't afraid of everything outside their own briar patches."

"I don't like those street fae," Bressel said.

The Free Folk, or the street fae, lived outside the park's

gates in Skemantis, braving humans and iron and alley cats and all of the dangers of the city. They were a rough bunch, and Bressel knew Grit's mother would never approve of Grit associating with such riffraff.

"Besides"—Bressel hesitated—"how . . . how are you going to get there?"

Grit stiffened and ceased her pacing, face turned away from her friend. Bressel let her eyes wander, just for a moment, to Grit's back, and immediately felt guilty.

Grit was not like most faeries, you see. She might have been the toughest fairy in the Arboretum but for the one thing that separated her from all the others: she could not fly. Grit had been born with only one wing.

A faerie without flight was like a hornet with no sting, or a mermaid without a tail. It was an impossible thing, and yet it had happened—to Grit. There was no ignoring the whispers behind her back, or the pitying stares as Bressel gave her a boost up to a too-high branch. Grit was the best climber in the Arboretum, even better than some of the squirrels, but a faerie domain was designed for flying.

Grit whipped around and crossed her arms, regarding Bressel imperiously. Bressel recognized the look and groaned.

"You're to take me as far as the Whispering Wall, of course," declared Grit. "As usual."

"No, Grit." Bressel shook her head. "I shan't, not when the queen's ordered *everyone* to stay inside until they investigate whatever's in the city. Especially you!"

"You will fly me to the Whispering Wall," said Grit, "or I shall tell your sproutsitter you've been neglecting the leeks because you think they smell funny."

Bressel blushed. "Oh, Grettifrida, that's not fair! You don't like them, either!"

"Bressel."

"Sorry, *Grit.* I'm sorry. I just don't want anything to happen to you." Bressel reached out and took Grit's hands in her own.

Grit kissed Bressel on her fuzzy green cheek. Her heart was in the right place. "You're a good friend, Bres," Grit said. "So I know you won't tell!" Grit vaulted up from under the roots, ignoring Bressel's protests, and shot off toward the birch path, running much too fast for her friend to catch up with her.

The earth faerie stomped on a mushroom in frustration. She didn't *want* to get her friend in trouble, but if something happened to Grit out in the city . . .

Bressel took a deep breath. There was no other way for it; she had to call the guards.

They only had one faerie princess, after all.

GRIT BOUNDED THROUGH the garden as fast as her small legs could carry her, eager to get out of view of the Great Willow. She felt bad leaving Bressel behind, but there was no way she could stay cooped up tonight, not with almost the entire kingdom taking refuge there. Her mother would be in Seelie council meetings around the clock, leaving Grit at the mercy of the other noble faeries' children. She hated the way they whispered about her—as if she couldn't hear, as well as fly!—and their insipid chatter about dewdrops and silk spinning was so boring that Grit felt like falling asleep (as she often did, much to the queen's chagrin).

Most of the things she did were to the queen's chagrin, when she came to think of it. Grettifrida "Grit" Lonewing was the sole child of Queen Ombrienne Lightbringer, the only living heir to the faerie kingdom of Oldtown Arboretum, and a future Seelie queen. This was *not* something of which Grit liked to be reminded.

Fortunately, nights like this were perfect for forgetting.

Once she was certain no one was following her, Grit poked her head above the grass. Quieter than any human could hope to hear, she put two fingers to her lips and whistled.

After a few seconds of silence, a soft *hoot* sounded in reply. Grit heard the flutter of wings and ducked out of the way just in time. A small gray owl landed before her, eyeing her with a curious expression. (Perhaps this was just its face, but you could never really tell with owls.) Grit smiled and silently thanked the stars. Contrary to the superstitions of humans, owls were actually anything but wise, and she hadn't been certain that this one would come when called. It had taken ages for her to train Dusten to respond to her signal at all, and another year to get him to fly to any one destination reliably.

"Cheers, Dusten," whispered Grit, reaching up to scratch the owl behind the ears. Dusten leaned in to her touch and cooed. "You up for the gate tonight?"

She usually only flew Dusten as far as the Whispering Wall and made the rest of the way on foot or on squirrel-back, but even she was leery of getting all the way to the South Gate without the steady light of the lanterns to guide her. The lamplighters were accustomed to turning a blind eye to her escapades by now; their chief responsibility was keeping danger out of the Arboretum, not keeping faeries in. But they were all at the Great Willow, and the Arboretum seemed a stranger and scarier place in total darkness.

Grit scurried back to a hedge a few yards away and over-turned a small stone with a long white scratch on it. The owl's saddle was hidden underneath. Grit had made it herself after studying the contraptions humans put on their horses. Built with bits of leather, wire, and twine scraps collected from her adventures in the city, it was hardly beautiful. But it kept her on Dusten's back, and that was good enough for her.

Grit secured the harness around Dusten's head and wings, ducking here and there as he playfully snapped at her for treats. She fished a dried beetle out of her small satchel and held it out, but the owl turned up his beak.

"Sorry," she shrugged. "Last-minute change of plans. It's all I've got tonight." She swung herself onto Dusten's back, taking care not to pull his feathers too hard or prick him with her spurs.

"Okay, Dusten," she said. "Let's try for up and not down, all right?"

Dusten hooted cheerfully and lurched into the night sky.

Grit grasped the reins and let out a whoop as they reached full height. Her hair whipped in the wind, coming loose out of its messy bun and flying around her head in a dandelion cloud of yellow and red. She was leaving the Arboretum behind, leaving behind her mother's disappointment and frilly gowns and all of the expectations that came with them.

Dusten soared through the gardens. He was confused about the absence of the lanterns, and Grit had to steer him more forcefully than usual to keep him on course. The lampposts, usually filled with the faeries' golden glow, stood dark and empty. The wind whistled through the holes in the Whispering Wall, skittering around the tiny rolls of paper scrawled with Skemantians' deepest wishes that were shoved between the stones. Dusten was nearly there when Grit heard the call: the Royal Guard was on her trail.

She looked down to see dozens of dark shadows racing behind her on the ground, reaching amazing heights as they leapt across the grass. Grit was too high up to see their pointy feelers or probing eyes, but the armored crickets' screeches echoed through the night with unmistakable clarity. Dusten noticed the guards chasing them and hooted with alarm. Grit clenched the reins to keep herself upright. She willed the owl to fly faster as they approached the wall, but Dusten began to descend.

"No, no, no, no, no!" pleaded Grit, pulling on the reins with all her might, but Dusten landed resolutely on top of the crumbling stone wall. Grit lurched in her seat and felt her face plant into his neck. He hooted proudly. Owls really *were* the dumbest birds in the kingdom.

"*Argh,*" Grit groaned. She kicked at the owl's sides, jumping up and down in the saddle in a futile attempt to keep him going. The guard closed in below, their clicking and chirping growing nearer every second.

The crickets reached the base of the wall. They latched on to the vines that covered the stone, sharp armor glistening in the moonlight. Grit knew if they caught her, it would be straight back to her mother and the lecture of a lifetime. She didn't stand a chance against an entire platoon of armored crickets.

"Dusten, I will personally find you the juiciest worm in the kingdom if you. Just. Move!" cried Grit. Desperate, she made perhaps the best, the worst, and the only decision: she pricked the owl with the thorn spurs of her boots. Dusten shrieked and shot straight up with an indignant flurry of wings that strained against his harness with an audible squeak. He bucked and twisted in the air, spinning Grit around in nauseating somersaults that left her clinging to the saddle for dear life.

But they soon left the guard behind, the crickets scrambling up the Whispering Wall and chirruping in anger. Grit allowed herself a brief moment of triumph and pumped her fist in the air. With any luck, Bressel had told the guards that Grit was missing, but not the queen. The crickets, though excellent muscle, had no true powers of speech, and could hardly deliver a report of her flight to the queen. If she planned the night just right, her mother would never even know she'd left her hollow in the Great Willow.

Grit guided Dusten to a hasty landing on the South Gate, where he must have looked a curious sight — a lone, tiny owl balanced precariously on the wrought iron bars. Grit slipped on her leather gloves and tucked her leggings deeper into her boots, careful not to leave any skin exposed; iron is toxic to faeries, and not only did she need to climb the fence, but the city would be full of it as well. She'd learned that tip the hard way in her early years of exploring.

"Good boy," Grit praised the owl and hopped down. She smoothed his wrinkled feathers and pecked him with a quick kiss between the eyes. She'd make good on her promise to fetch him the juiciest worm she could find.

"Who needs Bressel, anyway?" Grit muttered as Dusten flew back into the Arboretum. No doubt he had his own nightly adventures to pursue.

"We were starting to think you weren't coming," said a smooth voice to her left. Grit whipped around to see

Ravene, a sleek-haired street fae, standing with a hand on her hip. Ravene was tall for a faerie—nearly six inches— and her silky black braid fell to the backs of her knees. The razor blades she wore tucked into her hair weren't visible, but Grit knew they were there, and so did everyone else.

"You know Grit," said another street fae, floating down to meet them. "She likes to make an entrance." It was Remus, one of the few male faeries Grit had ever met. He looked rather dashing in his red leathers, with wavy brown hair and tanned skin. His trusty slingshot, which he was teaching Grit to use, hung off his belt.

"Just a small delay," Grit replied with a toss of her head, "but I *may* have roused the crickets." Ravene made a face, and Grit added hastily, "They hardly ever leave the gates. They might be seen."

"As we will be, if we dawdle out in the open for much longer," said Remus.

Grit smiled at him gratefully. She could always count on Remus to have her back. "Where to?"

Ravene and Remus exchanged a quick look that didn't escape her notice. Something, as the humans said, was apparently *up*.

"It's a surprise," Ravene finally said with a smile.

"What a coincidence," said Grit. "That's my favorite place."

3.

A MAD, MAD WORLD

IT WAS TRUE THAT PERHAPS THE FREE FOLK WERE a bit rough, as Bressel had said. Most faeries were naturally inclined to live in kingdoms in forests, mountains, and other places far from prying human eyes. Yet such swaths of natural resources were growing scarcer by the year. Humans had overrun many faerie lands, chopping down their trees and polluting their rivers and streams. The Oldtown Arboretum faeries were a rare example of faeries and humans coexisting in a mutually beneficial relationship. With a little help from some persuasive magic, the humans unconsciously left the Arboretum untouched, and the faeries provided light and safety for the humans to enjoy it by.

But a few faeries went a step further. Rather than simply

tolerating human expansion, they embraced it. Some earth faeries began helping humans in small ways—keeping the bugs out of their gardens or their milk from going sour—in exchange for small tokens of appreciation, like a thimble full of sweet cream or a shiny brass button. These faeries soon left the wild kingdoms altogether for the comforts of human hearths and homes, becoming brownies, domoviye, nisse, and other household spirits. Yet even so, these faeries stayed mostly in the country and open air, far away from the hustle and bustle of human cities.

Then there were the street fae—or the Free Folk, as they preferred to be called. The Free Folk were not part of any kingdom, swore allegiance to no faerie court, and made their own hard living in the very hearts of the most populated cities and towns. They scavenged for food and supplies from the land around them, living in the nooks and crannies of attics or the rafters of abandoned factories and repurposing human trash for their own treasure.

Free Folk like Remus and Ravene didn't seem to care that Grit had only one wing. All of the street fae were outcasts, without court or kingdom, and any fae who could fend for themselves—in whatever way suited them best—were welcome to join them.

Ravene, Remus, and Grit rode on squirrelback through the streets of Skemantis, dodging the occasional human on his way home and teasing stray dogs too slow to catch them. But as Grit rode alongside her friends, she couldn't help but notice they were quieter than usual. Remus's brow was furrowed, and he checked over his shoulder so often it made Grit nervous. Had the street faeries felt the gaze of those glowing orange eyes as well?

Ravene stopped abruptly at a drainage grate in the street subtly engraved with a snake-haired woman. Her steel eyes opened at their approach, wide and gray and unseeing. Ravene flew off her squirrel's back and tapped his rump, sending him off into the night; the animals could come no farther.

Apparently, they were going to the Green Goddess, a popular street faerie pub in the tunnels underneath a brewery. Grit was surprised. They hardly ever took her to the Green Goddess; it was where the Free Folk came to discuss serious business, and it was not uncommon for the occasional brawl to break out before the evening was over. The owner, the ancient and cross-eyed Abby Absinthe, never seemed to buy the story that Grit was Ravene's cousin visiting from the border towns.

"Let's go, Princess," teased Remus, spreading his arms wide.

Ravene rolled her eyes as he lifted Grit off of her squirrel and into his arms with ease. "Why not just shout her name from the rooftops?" Ravene asked flatly, fluttering over the grate. Her wings moved faster and faster, like a purple and black hummingbird, until a fine cloud of golden dust rose into the air around her. Ravene slowed her wings and shook them over the grate, spilling more of the shining powder down into the hole. Only faerie dust was accepted as proof of identity to enter the Green Goddess— something Grit could never produce on her own, since she couldn't fly.

A melodic three-tone whistle rose up from the darkness below and Ravene answered it with one of her own. Then she and Remus, Grit in his arms, began their flight down into the tunnel. They all switched their lights on, the soft golden glow from their bodies just enough to see by. Their tiny feet were still far from the damp floor when a hiss came out of the darkness.

"Foolish little faeries, with their lights on so bright," a deep whisper scolded.

Grit looked down and saw the floor wasn't just damp, as usual, but totally submerged in water. It lapped at the tunnel walls, inky black in the moonlight. The fire faerie that usually greeted them was nowhere to be seen.

Ravene and Remus slowed their descent.

"Just announcing our presence, friend," said Remus lightly, though he dropped his voice as well. "How about you do us a courtesy and do the same?"

The deep voice chuckled—a sickly, wet sound like a mucus-choked cough. Grit gripped Remus a little tighter. The black water danced under their feet, little waves jumping up to lick their boots.

"Oh, I think I'll stick to the shadows, *mon ami*, as should you. They're a much safer place to be in times such as these."

Ravene and Remus shared another look, and Grit suddenly wished for nothing more than to be on solid ground again. What could possibly be so threatening that the Free Folk had such an unscrupulous Unseelie fae guarding their local meeting place?

Grit's friends shut off their lights, but she stayed aglow, still wary, and sat up as straight as she could in Remus's arms. "Says who?" she demanded, not bothering to whisper.

Tendrils of black water snapped up quicker than lightning, lashing at their ankles, but Remus and Ravene darted out of the way just in time. The water churned and rose higher, frothing and angry.

"Says I," croaked a gravelly voice behind them.

It was ancient Abby Absinthe, one of the toughest and oldest of the Free Folk in Skemantis. With scraggly gray-green hair, withering wings, and skin as leathery as a tanned rat hide, Abby was just about the ugliest faerie Grit had ever seen. Her faded blue dress hung loose on her frame; it was covered with spiderwebs (and the occasional spider) and was tattered and brown at the hem. Abby's eyes were cloudy and crossed, but she hovered just inches over the water without a hint of fear.

The tip of Abby's dandelion walking stick lit up with

a dull greenish glow. She slammed the stem into the water, sending the waves rearing back. The kelpie let out a sound that was both a neigh and a scream, the waves sloshing and roiling until the vague shape of a horse's head emerged at the far end of the tunnel. The kelpie's dark eyes narrowed and he let out a sulky whinny, tossing his mossy black mane.

At another fierce look from Abby, Grit extinguished her light without question. Only the faint glow of Abby's staff kept them from total darkness.

"Abby, *ma chérie*, what's with all the fuss?" the water horse complained. "I was only . . . horsing around!"

His crackling chuckle was the only sound in the tunnel.

"Mind your methods, kelpie," rasped Abby. She raised her staff again in warning, and the horse head shied away.

"Ah, you run a tight ship, old Abby Absinthe, " said the kelpie, "but you should be glad of the extra security! Especially on a night like tonight!"

"Why a night like tonight?" prodded Grit. "What's going on here?"

"A very good question, little lone-wing," said the kelpie, beady eyes flashing. "And one I hope we learn the answer to soon enough. But I know when I'm not needed. So alas, back to the shadows I go. *Au revoir*, little faeries . . ."

The horse's head shrank, becoming more and more indistinct as the waves retreated, until there was nothing left but a shallow stream of murky water winding its way along the grimy floor. Remus, Ravene, and Grit gave it a wide berth as they landed.

No one spoke until the last trickle wound around the bend and out of sight, though they knew the kelpie wouldn't be far.

"I need a drink," Ravene said finally, shaking a few water droplets off her wings. "Preferably one that doesn't try to drown me."

Abby nodded. Everyone seemed to agree that she was blind, but the old bat could still mix potions like nobody's business. Abby beckoned them forward and they followed her along the tunnel in silence. Grit was bursting with questions, but the elderly faerie placed a finger to her lips and shook her head.

Around the next corner, the usually lively bar held a grim scene. Despite the excitement at the entrance, Grit had expected the normal evening crowd—street faeries swapping forage stories or dancing to the beat of the wooden tumbler drums in the corner, sipping Abby's hair-curling concoctions all the while. Any occasion, however small, was usually cause enough for a party, and the faeries would sing and dance long into the night.

Yet what awaited them was not a celebration, but a tragedy.

A water faerie lay on the long middle table, half-conscious and shivering. Her seaweed hair was knotted and torn, bits of it ripped out at the roots. She was filthy, as if she'd been dragged through an oil slick, and her breathing was labored. A small crowd of street faeries were gathered around her, conversing in low voices.

"Her sister?" Ravene asked shakily. She did not look surprised to see the injured faerie.

"It came for the both of them," growled old Abby. "She's the first to get away."

The first to get away? thought Grit. *From what?*

"Far's we know," Abby continued, "the other one wasn't so lucky."

The crowd parted to let Abby through, some greeting Ravene and Remus with supportive embraces. They regarded Grit suspiciously, and she couldn't blame them. She had no idea what kind of mess she'd gotten herself into, or what mysterious ill had befallen the poor faerie on the table.

"What's going on?" Grit asked. "What's happened to her?"

No one answered. Then the crowd backed away and Grit saw the full extent of the damage.

The water faerie's right wing was torn nearly to shreds. Someone—or *something*—had snatched at it viciously, piercing the upper membrane. The faerie's panicked struggles to free herself may have saved her life in the short term, but the resulting tears in her wing had likely done even more damage than the initial blow. Thin branches of cartilage were snapped clear through in several places. To Grit, who had studied wing anatomy religiously in hopes of understanding her own, it was clear that even faerie magic could not salvage what was left of the wing.

"We thought you'd know what to do," said Ravene quietly.

Grit felt hot tears forming behind her eyes and angrily blinked them away. "Why?" she demanded. "Because I was born this way, so I should know *everything* about living without a wing? Or maybe you thought some royal faerie magic could save your friend. Well, I've got news for you. I *don't* know everything, and I haven't got any special magic!"

A stunned silence followed. Some of the Free Folk backed away, nudging each other and whispering. Grit glared at them.

The faerie on the table let out a long, keening cry that echoed eerily throughout the tunnel. Her breath came in short gasps, the ruined mess of her wing fluttering weakly.

Grit pushed Ravene and Remus out of the way and leaned closer to the wounded faerie, gently wiping her forehead with a wet sponge from beside the table.

"Shh, it's all right," Grit said softly. She looked into the faerie's pained eyes. "What's your name?"

Remus opened his mouth to answer, but Grit held up a hand to silence him. It would be better to keep the water faerie distracted while Grit examined her wing. The injured faerie whimpered and her eyes fluttered closed.

Grit gripped both sides of her face, forcing her to look up. "I need you to listen to me, sweet pea. Can you do that?"

A weak nod.

"Good. My name is Grit, and I'm going to help you." Grit ran her fingers gently over the base of the faerie's wing. It didn't look good. "What can I call you?"

"Echo . . ." mumbled the water faerie. "Name's . . . Echolaken."

"Nice to meet you, Echolaken," said Grit. She'd seen enough. Stroking Echo's hair with one hand, Grit turned to Abby. "Can you give her something for the pain?"

The old faerie nodded, detached one of the many pouches and vials tied around her belt, and popped the cork with her teeth. She poured a cloudy powder into her palms, motioned for Grit to stand back, and blew the powder over Echo's face. Almost instantly, the water faerie ceased shaking and fell into a deep but troubled sleep.

Abby rinsed her hands from a leaky pipe behind the bar.

Grit waited for her to return before breaking the rest of the news. "You'll have to cut it off," said Grit flatly, loud enough for some of the other faeries to hear. They gasped.

"As I thought," replied Abby, hardly batting an eye.

"She's . . ." Grit took a shaky breath. "She's expending too much energy trying to heal herself, but the top membrane is all but severed at the shoulder."

"There's got to be another way!" protested a fire faerie. Several others murmured in agreement.

"She'll never fly again. The stress on her body is too

much. If you don't get it over with and patch her up soon, she'll die."

Grit was surprised at the coldness in her own voice, the detached way she could speak of another faerie's life or death. She was disappointed, though not surprised, at the awkward silence that followed her proclamation. The unspoken sentiment was clear: better off dead than unable to fly. She saw the thought on each face, replaced quickly by embarrassment.

"The girl is right," Abby addressed the crowd, all traces of her usual addled air gone. "Pippalit," she said to another fire faerie, "cauterize the wound once we've finished. Remus, you'll need to hold her steady. This isn't going to be pretty. Grit—"

But Grit was gone.

She ran blindly through the tunnels, unsure if she was running up or down, left or right. She was too distracted to care and unwilling to let herself feel anything more than her hair whipping at her face. Grit was thirteen summers old, and she'd seen more horrible things in one night than in her entire life.

Bressel had been right. She shouldn't have gone with the street fae—not tonight, not when the lanterns were dark and the whole world was going mad.

A few minutes passed before Grit slowed down, breathing hard and blinking back tears. It was only then she heard the footsteps following her.

The soft pitter-patter stopped when Grit stopped, but not fast enough. Faeries have keen ears, and the tunnels amplified even the smallest drip of water. She started walking again, slower this time, fighting every instinct to turn around, and was unsurprised by the soft shuffling that moved with her.

Grit drew her hatpin sword in a flash and whipped around, but there was nothing there except darkness.

"Hello?"

Hello-ello-ello-lo-lo-lo, the words echoed back to her out of the gloom.

"If that's you, kelpie," Grit warned, "just know that I'm a *very* good swimmer."

But no gurgling laugh or richly accented taunt responded.

Grit brandished her sword. "I know you're there," she said, taking a step toward the last corner she'd rounded. "So you might as well tell me . . ."

Another few steps . . .

"Why exactly it is . . ."

Almost there . . .

"That you're following me!"

She ran the last few steps around the corner and caught a glimpse of small running feet clattering against the stone floor, just before they slipped away into another sprawling tunnel.

The hunter became the hunted. Grit took off in hot pursuit, following the click-clacking of the feet—was that the sound of *wooden* shoes? — through the winding tunnels, but her quarry remained infuriatingly out of sight. Small feet they may have been, but they were bigger than Grit's by a considerable margin, and they outpaced her easily.

Grit needed more light, but she didn't have the time to stop and concentrate on a proper spell — not to mention that she was surrounded by water — so she had no hope of conjuring a flame. She snapped her fingers as she ran instead, sending little clusters of bright sparks shooting out of her fingertips and toward the running figure. In the brief flashes of light she saw it was shaped like a human, curiously small but distinctly *not* childlike. It moved with the jerky motion of the metal machines the humans some-times paraded down their streets, but Grit couldn't detect a whiff of iron. Was the creature actually *made* of wood?

"Stop!" Grit yelled. "I just want to talk to you!" *And possibly chop you up for kindling, if it comes to that*, Grit thought, but kept that part to herself.

It was no use. The thing was much too fast and getting farther away by the second, and Grit was forced to stop running when she stumbled into a puddle of muck that nearly covered her knees. She doubled over, gasping for air. The sludge only grew deeper as she stepped forward, and she could hardly remember the way she'd come. She couldn't hear even an echo of the running feet.

Grit thought of the kelpie's control over the water in the tunnels, and small seeds of panic settled in her stomach.

She was just about to turn back when a light illuminated the corridor.

Ravene hovered in the passageway behind Grit, a cloud of faerie dust in her wake. She too was out of breath.

"I thought I'd lost you," Ravene said, wiping strands of hair from her eyes. "You run almost as fast as I can fly, Grit."

"Did you see it?!" demanded Grit.

Ravene's head whipped around. "See what?"

"There was something in the tunnel with me," said Grit. At Ravene's alarmed look, she added, "It didn't attack me or anything! But I couldn't get a good look at it."

The pounding of Grit's heart was starting to slow, replaced swiftly by exhaustion. She felt like sinking down into the mud and never getting up.

"You need to be careful down here, Grit," said Ravene. "Now more than ever. Now come out of there before some snake decides he has a taste for faeries."

Grit sloshed out of the mud toward Ravene's light. Furious as she was, the dark-haired faerie was her only way home.

"What *did* that to Echolaken?" asked Grit. "What isn't everyone telling me?"

Ravene sighed and lowered herself onto a pile of loose bricks against the tunnel wall. Grit clambered up to join her.

"Free Folk have been going missing, Grit," confessed Ravene. "It's been happening for a few months now. At first, we didn't notice anything out of order. The Free Folk move around a lot. It's not unusual to see a traveler in the tunnels one day and hear they've flown on to bluer skies the next. But more and more of us started to disappear in the night, without warning. We were just about to appeal to your mother for help—"

Grit raised her eyebrows. The Free Folk and the Fair Folk did not mix. This was an unspoken rule of their co-existence. Grit couldn't remember a time when the Free Folk had *ever* approached a royal court, Seelie or Unseelie.

"When we heard reports that she'd summoned in all the lamplighters, we knew the Wingsnatchers had come to you, too."

"The Wingsnatchers?"

"It's what we started calling them." Ravene shrugged. "It seemed to fit."

"But Echolaken got away. From these Wingsnatchers."

Ravene nodded. "We think so. That's all the fae who found her were able to understand before she went un-conscious. That, and that whatever attacked her took her sister, too. It's made everyone paranoid."

Grit thought of the kelpie who had blocked their en-trance; for all his posturing, he was just as scared as the other faeries.

"You should have told me, Ravene," said Grit, feeling her temper rise again. She clenched her fists to her sides.

Ravene's expression immediately closed off, ever the calm and unruffled street fae. "No, I shouldn't have," she said coolly, jumping down off the bricks. "We may let you tag along for a few larks, Grit, but our business isn't your business, and it never will be."

"How . . . how can you say that?" asked Grit. "You just shoved a dying faerie in my face, but it's *none of my business?*"

Ravene was unmoved. She shook her head. "Not all of us have a castle to run home to when the sun rises, Grit. You think being a Free faerie is all foraging for bottle caps, moonlit revels, and chasing cats, but it's not. It's facing the iron world with nothing but your wings and your wits. And you . . ." She trailed off, her gaze wandering to Grit's back. "You're just not one of us."

For the first time in a long time, Grit was speechless. True, Ravene and Remus were a few years older, and certainly wiser in the ways of the human world outside the Arboretum, but Grit had thought the street faeries *accepted* her for exactly who she was. But Ravene had just made it perfectly clear that as a princess of the Seelie Court—and a grounded one, at that—Grit would never truly fit in with them. And if she couldn't do that, Grit was sure she would never fit in anywhere.

4.

IT'S ELECTRIFYING

CARMER, KITTY, AND ANTOINE THE AMAZIFIER HAD arrived in Skemantis just the evening before, but Carmer already thought he could get used to the place. Hardly anyone stopped to stare at his patched suit and oversized hat like they did in the small farming towns the Amazifier frequented. Carmer had already walked past a set of identical twin old men in matching lederhosen, a woman smoking a pipe nearly as tall as herself, and a ballerina marionette performing for a delighted crowd without any visible strings attached, and he'd decided that the people of Skemantis were very used to the unusual—especially around the time of the Magickal Symposium. Someone like Carmer was hardly worth making a fuss over.

He was surprised to see so many people out and about this early in the morning, but he supposed Skemantis was one of those cities that never really slept. It was a different pace of life than he was used to, and all the people and steam carriages and trams rushing about were rather overwhelming for a boy who spent most of his life on the open road. He could study and tinker all he liked, but actually being *in* the technology capital of the coast, with the Relerail zooming over his head, airships and steamboats alike docking by the river, human factory workers and automata working side by side—that was a new experience entirely.

Carmer stifled a yawn and watched Kitty do the same on stage. It really was quite early. He would have more time to explore the city later, but for now they needed to rehearse. Thanks to a late and hasty entry into the competition (relying mostly on the Amazifier's dwindling reputation to get them in the door), the Amazifier had been saddled with one of the first rehearsal slots of the day: seven o'clock in the morning. It was going to be a long day.

The Seminal Symposium of Magickal Arts was held in the Orbicle, a grand theater known just as much for its magicians as its ballets and plays. Unlike the smaller and shoddier vaudeville houses often frequented by illusionists, the Orbicle was just as large and decadent as the state opera house down the street. Only the best talent headlined there, and every week saw regular performances by the greatest magicians from all over the world.

Carmer had been able to see the Orbicle's roof before they even reached the city, a great circular dome that shone like a fabled golden egg. Once inside, looking up was dizzying; chandeliers the size of carriages hung from the frescoed ceiling, where nymphs, gods, and goddesses Carmer vaguely recognized from his lessons played out their timeless scenes above the audience's heads. The three tiers of seats could fit almost three thousand people, Carmer had heard, though now they faded into blackness under the brightness of the stage lights. He imagined six thousand critical eyes trained on him and gulped. Carmer spent more time backstage than on it to facilitate the Amazifier's illusions, but he couldn't help feeling nervous.

While the Amazifier talked with the stage manager about the next lighting cue, Carmer ducked away from the wings to look for the entrance to the trap room; he would need to be very familiar with the underbelly of the stage before tonight. He was hurrying along the crossover to the prompt box to ask someone where he should go, when he ran straight into someone striding around the corner.

"Ah, sorry!"

"Do watch where you're going," snapped the boy Carmer collided with, rubbing his shoulder. He was finely dressed in a tailored black suit, with long blond hair pulled back in a sleek braid. Carmer saw a flash of silver metal underneath the boy's cuff when he raised his arm—

probably an expensive timepiece of some sort, judging by the rest of the boy's costume.

"Sorry," said Carmer again, shrinking back a little. Though the blond boy couldn't have been much older than Carmer, he walked like he owned the place, and he definitely wasn't dressed like a stagehand. "I don't know my way around here too well."

The boy looked Carmer up and down. "Clearly," he said. "Here for the competition, are you?"

Carmer nodded and fidgeted. He didn't fancy standing there making small talk with someone who looked at him like he was an unpleasant bug they wanted to squash.

"Can you point me toward the trap room?" Carmer asked.

The boy gestured lazily to his right but said nothing.

"Thanks," Carmer said, resisting the temptation to bump the boy's shoulder again as he walked past.

"Good luck to you and your master, Carmer III," said the boy to Carmer's retreating back. "You're going to need it."

Carmer whipped around. "I never said my—"

The boy was gone.

"—name."

It took Carmer another five minutes of fumbling around in the dark and a missed cue before he realized the boy had sent him off in the entirely wrong direction.

Good luck, indeed.

. . .

AFTER REHEARSAL AT the Orbicle, Carmer spent the day at the International Exhibition, listening to lectures on mechanics, steam engines, electrical wiring, and all manner of gadgets until his head was swimming with facts and figures and his folder was overflowing with hastily jotted notes—but it was finally time for the main event that he, the other scholars, and the people of Skemantis had been waiting for.

Titus Archer was much different in person than Carmer had expected. Though the posters for the Titan Industries expo showed a stern, confident, and adventurous-looking man, Archer cut a slightly less impressive figure in the flesh. The face that Carmer had pictured as angular and imposing was actually long and flat, with a rather weak chin and a hint of flabbiness around the jowls. Though it was hard to judge height at this distance, Archer could hardly be considered tall.

Fortunately, Carmer quickly recovered from his mild disappointment. Who cared what Archer looked like when his inventions spoke for themselves? Carmer was hardly one to judge by appearances, and it couldn't be denied that Archer had a commanding presence. Every eye in the audience was glued to the stage—or, in this case, the altar.

Well, what used to be the altar. The main event of the Skemantian International Exhibition was held, strange as it might seem, in an old cathedral. It was just one part of a parcel of such buildings in the area, collectively known as Theian Foundry, which formed Titus Archer's personal research and development facility.

Not all events in the expo were open to the public, but this one — the unveiling of the Titan Industries' newest invention — was plainly welcoming to the average people whose lives it might one day improve.

"Now, I know I've kept you gentlemen waiting," said Archer teasingly. When a not-so-subtle cough interrupted him from somewhere in the audience, he corrected himself, "And ladies. What we've already demonstrated today shows the progress we've made with current technology. How to make our airships fly faster, our Relerail more efficient. All very valuable in the present. But what I am about to show you, this . . . this is the *future*."

The stained glass windows of the church cast rainbow shadows over a towering dynamo that took up most of the altar — or, at least, it looked like a dynamo, with two thick pillars and a heavy iron base surrounding the copper-wrapped rotor. A ring of unlit streetlamps surrounded it. Yet there was no steam turbine, boiler, water inlet, or exhaust in sight. What would start it spinning?

"As most of you know, Titan Industries is one of the leading producers of coal and natural gas on the East Coast. It's our gas that lights the streetlamps of Skemantis at night to keep our city safer, to keep our factories open longer and our homes bright and warm."

"And you who sets the prices," someone muttered. There was a small chorus of amused assent.

Instead of ignoring the heckler, however, Archer looked the man square in the eye. "Yes, sir. I'll be the first to admit that gas has its drawbacks and inconveniences. Both to ourselves and to this planet we call home. No doubt many of you have been following the recent developments in electric lighting. But even the most sophisticated dynamo to date still needs a steam turbine to spin it, and a furnace and a boiler to power *that*. How many of you, your employees, or your comrades are forced to breathe in coal dust every day? How many lost a fortune or a friend in the disaster at the Vallows?"

Carmer had no idea what the Vallows were, but it didn't sound good. More than a few hands went up.

"What if I told you that Titan Industries has recently patented a previously untapped energy source, one that is both clean and unlimited? That we have refined a method of producing electric light that cuts down on nearly half the machinery required and all of the waste?"

Mutters of disbelief cut through the crowd as they peered at the new dynamo.

"My friends, I present to you: the Hyperion."

Archer stepped back and flicked a long switch at the base of the dynamo.

Prepare to be amazed, added Carmer silently. Archer was certainly a showman.

Carmer's amusement was cut short by the dynamo roaring to life. The rotor began spinning of its own accord, a strange glow emanating from the copper coils. Silver sparks skittered across the surface, crisscrossing each other in wild patterns. The streetlamps around them burst on, enveloping them all in a light that was more like sunshine than any artificial light Carmer had ever seen. A chorus of *oohs* and *aahs* rose up from the gathered crowd. Inside each lamp, Carmer could just make out the silver sparks behind the frosted glass globes, dancing and crashing into one another with such speed it was hard to tell they were moving at all.

Though beautiful, there was something unsettling about the machine. Once he could tear his eyes away from the lamps, Carmer looked at it more closely. The sparks along the rotor hissed and snapped and made the air around the machine crackle with energy. There was something rather . . . violent about it.

Questions from the crowd soon peppered the awed silence.

"How does it work?"

"When will this technology be hitting the streets?"

"Is it compatible with existing electric wiring?"

Archer held up a hand to silence them and grinned.

"All in good time, my friends! On a most basic level, the core of the Hyperion is a synthesis of the energies that already run throughout the earth. Some of you, particularly our alchemists, have worked with telluric currents before. The combination of magnets used in the Hyperion, in addition to my own special composites, amplifies these low-frequency currents that already run just below our feet and transmutes them into usable electricity."

More hands shot up in the air to have their questions answered, but Carmer was already wandering closer to one of the lamps. It would be more helpful for him to take a closer look at the Hyperion than to listen to Archer dodge questions about it, and he wanted a chance to explore before the rest of the crowd descended on the machine. The faintly pulsating globe seemed to beckon him forward, and before he realized what he was doing, he'd reached out a hand to touch it.

"Careful, lad!"

Archer's voice cut through Carmer's reverie and his hand froze in mid-air. A hundred pairs of eyes turned to look at him at once. He snapped his hand back down to his side.

"The globes can get rather hot," explained Archer. His expression was friendly, but there was something hard behind his eyes that Carmer hadn't seen before. "I'll kindly ask all of you to keep your hands to yourselves, as difficult as that is for curious minds."

Carmer nodded. A few of the other spectators looked disappointed, too, but held their tongues.

"We wouldn't want anyone to get hurt, now, would we?"

5.

FRIEND OF THE FAE

AFTER SPENDING THE NIGHT IN THE SEWER TUN-
nels, lost and alone, Grit was more than a little on edge.
She'd left Ravene behind again, and this time, the street faerie didn't follow. It was well into morning by the time she
found an outlet close enough to the surface to attempt the
long and slippery climb up. Bressel had been right about
Ravene and the street fae after all. And after seeing the
poor fae they'd made her examine . . .

Grit clamped down on the thought and pushed it out of
her mind. She had to keep her wits about her, here on the
ground level of the streets. She scurried along in the shadows of a dingy alley, constantly on the lookout for humans
and wild pests who were unlikely to think much of her

royal status. She was craning her neck as far as it would go, searching for any sign of the way to the Arboretum, when she felt it—the presence of fae.

The surge of power entered her consciousness so suddenly it made her dizzy. There were at least half a dozen faeries behind it, Grit was sure. Her heart leapt; her people were near, and a small part of her dared to hope a few Seelie Court members had come to take her back to the Great Willow—though she would never admit that to *them*.

She tracked the presence of faerie magic doggedly, heading west, but her progress was slow on foot, and her sense of it began to fade as swiftly as it had appeared. Grit ran as fast as she dared in the crowded streets, but only minutes later, the energy disappeared altogether. It was as if a giant iron door had slammed in front of whatever magic was being cast.

Grit skidded on her heels as she rounded the next corner, desperate to find the source of the magic, and stopped dead in her tracks. Four human boys were blocking her path in the alley ahead, and by the looks of things, at least three of them were itching for a fight.

"LOOKS LIKE WE'VE got him now, boys," said the head goon, grinning. There was always a head goon.

Carmer should have known that things wouldn't change in Skemantis, not really. After the Hyperion demonstration, he'd lost his way in the maze of the city's cobblestone streets and soon found himself being followed by a group of less-than-savory-looking characters. This time, as was usually the case, the aggravating party was a group of local boys who had come to the decision—Carmer wished he knew how—that the magician's apprentice was a funny little chap, much too stuck up for his own good, and was therefore in need of a good pounding by fellows made of far sterner stuff. They were all too happy to provide this service to the community in a swift and brutal fashion.

"Whatchya doin' with that fancy hat . . . fancy boy?" taunted another, apparently unable to come up with more than one adjective at a time.

Carmer almost wanted to laugh. Yet he couldn't stop his hand from self-consciously reaching up to adjust his tattered top hat. He stood up straight and tried to meet his tormenter's eye.

"It's a magician's prerogative to present himself in a manner befitting his profession," he wanted to say, astounding them all with his eloquence in the face of adversity. Yet all that came out of his mouth was a few mumbled words that vaguely expressed the thought, "'S a magic hat."

The boys spat at him and edged closer, ready to come to the end of their game. Defeated once again by his own traitorous tongue, Carmer prepared for the inevitable.

The leader picked up a broken fence post lying in the mud and slapped it against his hand with a wet *thwack*. Carmer flinched and forced himself to think.

The magician's apprentice currently had five small

smoke bombs in his jacket pocket. They were supposed to be for that night's performance, but they might also be his chance at escape.

Traditional smoke bombs, Carmer found, left an acrid smell in the air after they deployed, like the bottom burned out of a cooking pot. With a few chemical alterations, Carmer had developed a serum to counter this effect: when the bomb hit the ground and the release mechanism was deployed, it also released his counteragent. (He was particularly fond of the one that smelled like cinnamon.)

Well, it *should* release his counteragent. He'd been testing them along the road by dropping them out of the Moto-Manse's windows until the Amazifier groused that Carmer was going to suffocate Eduardo with all of his "arcane vapors." Carmer hadn't had a chance to try them out since they arrived in Skemantis.

There's no time like the present, Carmer thought ruefully. He took a deep breath, set his eyes on the mouth of the alley, and shoved his hands into his pockets. Before the bully could even raise his weapon, Carmer tossed the small metal cylinders out in front of him. The other boys backed away in surprise.

The smoke bombs seemed to fly in slow motion toward Carmer's adversaries. He could only imagine their surprise when the billowing smoke would explode outward, catching them sputtering and coughing while Carmer sped off, victorious at last.

He held his breath as the smoke bombs descended, clattered on the cobblestones, and remained stubbornly, terribly, and totally intact.

The surprise was wiped from the boys' faces as quickly as it had appeared. The sausage-shaped cartridges rolled harmlessly into the gutter. Carmer could only watch, bewildered and helpless, as his grand plans joined the refuse of Skemantis. The head goon began to laugh, clutching his sides; the others joined in until they were all but crying with mirth.

"What was *that* supposed to be?" asked their leader between gasps of amusement.

"They look like turds!" declared another boy, rolling over one of the bombs with his toe. It landed in a puddle at Carmer's feet.

"That the best you've got?"

Carmer bowed his head in defeat, but the blows he expected never came. Instead, the boys shouted in alarm as a sharp *crack* sounded. The street lamp at the end of the alley had burst. The globe fell to the ground with a smash, bits of glass exploding against the cobblestones. Carmer's head snapped up at the noise as the other boys shied away in alarm, cursing and shielding their eyes.

Seizing on their moment of distraction, Carmer lunged for the gutter and retrieved his smoke bombs before the other boys knew what was happening. With only half a second's hesitation, he lobbed them straight at the head goon's bottom.

This time, the forcible impact was just enough to trigger an explosion. And explode they did, enveloping the bully in a cloud of purple, cinnamon-scented smoke and leaving two well-deserved scorch marks on his pants. The boys shouted and bumped into each other in the confusion.

"Let's get out of here!"

"He ain't worth it, Billy!"

"Don't think you're safe, fancy boy!" warned their leader, apparently named Billy, clutching his bottom. "Come on!"

Billy and his two accomplices retreated to the mouth of the alley and ran off, wisps of purple still training behind them.

Carmer let a small, relieved laugh escape his lips as he watched his tormentors run away, coughing and sputtering and smelling of burned cinnamon. He could hardly believe his luck with the lamp, and his invention had worked! He would have to tell Kitty and the Amazifier about it when he got back.

When he got back! Carmer had forgotten that the first show of the competition was tonight. He dusted himself off and prepared once again to find his way back to the camp when a small cough, so quiet he barely heard it, caught his attention. Carmer looked around uncertainly.

"*Ahem*," coughed the small voice again, a tad impatiently this time.

Carmer's gaze finally rested on the broken streetlamp, where a very tiny something—someone?—was perched at his eye level, its minuscule limbs entwined in the filigree of the post. It regarded him with an imperious stare.

Carmer's first thought was that she was a windup doll, perhaps ignorantly left behind by someone at the exposition, but she was so . . . lifelike. No, not lifelike. *Alive.*

"Friend of the Fae," said the creature, eyeing him with suspicion as he took a few steps closer, his mouth agape, "I am Princess Grettifrida Lonewing of Oldtown Arboretum and sole heir to the Seelie faerie kingdom of Skemantis—"

"You can talk!" interrupted Carmer delightedly. Clearly, she was some sort of advanced automaton. He stepped closer, and the little eyes widened under her shock of red and blonde hair. She looked quite taken aback.

"Of course I can talk!" she shot back at him. "I don't know which king or queen made you a Friend of the Fae, but whoever it was must have been a few thorns short of a rosebush!"

Carmer laughed, the grin spreading across his whole face. He had no idea what a "friend of the fae" was, but he did know he'd just been insulted by a mechanical doll that was five inches tall.

"What is your name, human, and where are the faeries you've been consorting with?" She did not look pleased at being laughed at. "They can't have gone far."

"Um . . . F-Felix Cassius Tiberius Carmer III, miss. They call me Carmer," he said. "And I don't believe I've been consorting with anyone."

The doll blanched at that, her big yellow eyes widening even farther, but she recovered her haughtiness well. Her little mouth twisted into a thin line. "A Friend of the Unseelie Court, are you?" she snapped. "You should tell them to be a little more careful, concentrating so much power in the middle of the city like that. And where were *they* when you were about to eat dirt just now?"

"Um . . ."

"No matter," she said, rolling her eyes. "Your secrets are yours to keep as you wish."

"Er, thanks?" said Carmer.

"Well, Carmer, they call me Grit, and I suppose you'll have to do."

"Do? For what?"

"For taking me home, back to the Arboretum and the boundary of my kingdom. As you can see," Grit said, hesitating, "I cannot fly, and am thus in need of your assistance. As an apparent Friend, you are obliged to help."

Grit stuck out a dainty foot from the lamppost, still hanging on with her other side, and Carmer saw it. "Lonewing," she'd called herself, and now he saw why. While one wing shone and fluttered like no material he'd ever seen, the other was plainly missing.

Two warring halves of Carmer's intellect were coming head to head. On one hand, his very first instinct had been that this . . . Grit . . . was a living, breathing thing. In fact,

Carmer didn't think he'd ever seen anyone, or anything, so *intrinsically* alive—so bright and practically pulsing with energy.

Yet the rational part of Carmer's brain, the part that built mechanical soldiers and smoke bombs and memorized the periodic table when he was eight, knew better than that. *She's only an automaton!* it assured him. *She's been broken, and now she's transmitting some kind of signal to get herself back home and repaired.*

That was the logical explanation, and therefore, the only explanation. And yet . . .

As a magician's apprentice, Carmer knew there was no such thing as real magic. It was all smoke and mirrors, levers and pulleys and sleight of hand. Carmer knew this better than anyone. There was *no such thing as magic.*

And yet, in his heart of hearts, Carmer knew this little girl . . . this faerie, he supposed, was altogether quite magical. The proof was right in front of him, looking rather like she'd fancy boxing him around the ears, if she could.

"Well?" Grit asked impatiently, still holding out her foot.

There was only one option; she *had* saved him, after all. Carmer held out his hand and watched bemusedly as the faerie jumped deftly into his open palm. They looked at each other for a long moment, Grit sizing him up with a critical eye.

Uncomfortable with being stared at, Carmer swiftly deposited her in his breast pocket and set off down the street.

"Hey!" The muffled shout was followed by a sharp pointy object poking into his chest.

Carmer cried out and clutched at it, jostling the faerie around even more. "Ow! What was that for?"

Grit's dandelion head poked out of the pocket and glared up at him. She clutched a long hatpin in one hand like a sword. "What do you think you're doing?!"

Carmer nudged her head back down.

"Who do you think you are?" she shrieked.

"I'm making sure you're not seen, for a start," whispered Carmer, reluctant to look like he was talking to himself on a crowded city street. "And apparently, I'm a 'Friend of the Fae.'"

Carmer neglected to mention he hadn't the slightest idea what a Friend of the Fae even was.

6.

THE PUPPET MISTRESS

IT TOOK GRIT A GOOD PART OF THE AFTERNOON
to steer Carmer in the general direction of the Arboretum,
hampered as they were by Carmer's unfamiliarity with
the city. The altered perspective of being at human height
threw Grit off as well; she was used to either soaring above
the city on one of Ravene's birds or making her own way
on foot or squirrelback. Carmer received more than a few
pokes and prods with the hatpin.

After the fourth time Carmer squashed her head down
into his pocket, Grit had had enough.

"What are you *doing* that for?" she demanded.

"Someone will see you!"

"Please, do you think I'm daft? My magic's been diverting their attention since I appeared to you in the alley." *Really, he should have known that from the start*, Grit thought. *How does this boy think the fae have survived for thousands of years? It certainly hasn't been by letting every bumbling human in the world see us plain as day.*

"You mean like . . . filtering their perception?" Carmer asked. "You're not invisible, but . . ."

"But when people glance our way, they suddenly remember something very important they've forgotten to do, or an appointment they have to make, or what have you. And they forget all about us. To be honest," Grit continued, looking out at the harried and distracted faces they passed, "most of them won't even look at me. For the most part, humans only see what they expect to see."

Carmer was quiet for a moment. As far as Grit could tell, they were approaching the western side of the Arboretum. With any luck, she wouldn't be at the mercy of this dimwitted boy much longer. The Unseelie could have him forever, for all she cared.

"And you're doing all of this? With your . . . magic?" Carmer asked, eyes wide.

"Of course! Though it took me a while to learn without faerie dust." Truth be told, Grit wasn't supposed to be doing magic at all. Her mother had forbidden it except in small, controlled practice sessions in the Great Willow and in dire emergencies, fearing that it would "tax her health" even further. Almost all the magic Grit had learned, she'd taught herself.

"Faerie dust?!"

"Well, I can't very well make my own dust without two wings, can I? And most faeries use their dust for magic, so—" Grit stopped, suddenly gripped by doubt.

They passed an old stone church, its arches and gargoyles with cold gazes and slavering mouths hovering above their heads.

"You should know all of this," she said, suspicion creeping into her voice. "Why don't you know all of this?"

Carmer looked down at her guiltily. Before she could protest, he ducked behind the church's garden gate and into the empty courtyard, away from prying eyes.

"I . . . " He trailed off.

Grit tried to conceal her growing panic. "You're not a Friend of the Fae, are you? The presence I sensed, that had nothing to do with you at all!"

Carmer shrugged.

"Put. Me. Down!" exclaimed Grit, stabbing Carmer with her sword and kicking his chest with the thorn spurs on her boots.

"Wait! Grit! Ow!"

"No! You're a *liar* and a—"

"I've just never seen anything like—"

"Oh, I'm a *thing* now!"

"Just hold still, then!"

Carmer thrust his hand into his pocket, careful of Grit's flailing sword, and set her down just in front of the fountain in the middle of the garden. It gurgled pleasantly, the cool water utterly indifferent to their fight. Grit scrambled to her feet and glared at him with a mutinous expression.

"Look, I'm sorry. I've never met any*one* like you before, and . . ." The boy couldn't seem to find the words. He rubbed a hand across his face and through his messy black hair, making it stick straight up.

Grit would have laughed if she hadn't been so angry. She marched off in the opposite direction, only to realize after a few steps that the garden was walled in on all sides but the entrance. She doubled back as gracefully as she could.

"Where are you going?" Carmer crouched down and scurried after her, though a single stride of his was worth about ten of Grit's.

"Home," spat Grit, head held high.

Carmer watched her helplessly. "We've got a quarter of a mile until the edge of the Arboretum. You said so yourself. Think you're going to make it there at your pace before dark?"

Before dark. The words sent a shiver down Grit's spine. She knew what unnamed horrors might find her on the open streets in Skemantis after dark. Echolaken, and whatever the Wingsnatchers had done to her, was proof of that.

A second shiver ran through her, and Grit noticed a change in the air. A shadow passed over her, disappearing in the next instant.

"Don't move," warned Grit, her eyes darting around the garden. She silently cursed the tall grass and shrubbery around them, providing cover for *something* that had obviously caught their scent.

Carmer obligingly froze; he must have sensed something wrong as well. "Do you . . . smell that?" Carmer whispered, and Grit realized she did. The heady, unmistakable smell of—

"Oil?" They both guessed simultaneously.

And then the thing pounced.

Grit saw only a metal monster, legs outstretched as it leapt over her from behind.

"Grit!"

She dodged just in time, the air next to her still humming from the sharp *snap* of the creature's jaws. The claws came next, paws striking at her with ferocious determination. She didn't even have time to draw her sword, though she doubted it would be much use against this beast.

"Hey!" Carmer shouted. The creature stopped in midswipe, distracted. Carmer had picked up a large stick and was waving it back and forth in front of him. "Here, kitty kitty," he said tentatively.

As Grit scrambled backward, she saw that Carmer was right. The thing that had attacked them was a cat, but a cat unlike any other Grit had ever seen. Twice the size of a normal house cat, it was made entirely out of metal, with no skin or fur to speak of. Grit could see every tangled nest of wires, gears, and springs that made up its insides and connected its limbs. It even had a tail, silver and sleek, with a nasty-looking barb on the end that Grit was sure no real cat ever possessed. Just before it turned around, Grit caught a glimpse of pointed, razor-sharp teeth and glowing orange eyes.

The cat—for Grit could think of nothing else to call it—watched Carmer curiously. It seemed almost confused, as if it were not sure what to do with Carmer there.

Carmer cautiously tapped the stick on the ground. "You, uh . . . you want to play, huh?" he asked the creature, tapping the stick again. "You want the stick?"

The cat licked its lips, making a metal scraping sound that set Grit's teeth on edge.

"Then go . . . get it!" Carmer threw the stick in the opposite direction and the cat bounded after it. In a flash, Carmer was at Grit's side. He hurriedly scooped her up, and this time, she didn't protest. He ran for the garden gate, their only means of escape—

But the cat was ready for them. Carmer's distraction hadn't lasted long enough, and the cat was already blocking the exit. It growled—a horrible, grating sound—and lunged right for Carmer. The force of the beast's attack sent Carmer's feet out from under him. He fell flat on his back, the breath knocked out of him, Grit still clutched in his hand.

The cat's full weight pressed on his chest, rows of gleaming teeth gnashing and hissing in his face. It went straight for Grit, but Carmer rolled to knock the creature off balance.

And so they fought, in a dizzying back and forth: Carmer, dodging the cat's claws and gaping maw as best he could, and the cat, pushing Carmer back down again and again.

"What . . . is this thing?" Carmer panted, holding Grit out of harm's way. The oil lubricating its joints dripped into Carmer's face, dark and sticky.

Grit glimpsed something silver and shining inside the cat's writhing body. It was moving too much for her to tell, but she was pretty sure she knew faerie dust when she saw it.

"We've no chance!" Grit shouted to Carmer. "It's using fae magic! I don't know how, but it is!"

Carmer dodged another swipe from a vicious claw. His coat, already bedraggled, was getting torn to shreds.

"And what about you?" Carmer asked plaintively. By sheer luck, he managed to land a good kick. The cat flew backward, giving Carmer just enough time to get to his feet.

"What about me?"

"*Your* magic. You made a lamp explode!" Carmer said breathlessly. "Explode *that*!"

The *that* in question was circling them again. Grit felt her cheeks burn. How could she tell him—this silly human boy—that her magic wasn't strong enough to defeat this powerful a foe?

Before she had a chance to answer, however, the cat jumped again—straight for Carmer's head. He threw up his arms in self-defense, prepared himself for the worst, and—

SLAM. Something tackled the cat to the ground in mid-leap. A miniature soldier jumped to his feet beside it; for a second, Carmer thought it must be his own automaton, but this figure was nothing like his. He noticed the waxy, painted skin and wooden joints, and he realized their savior was not an automaton at all. It was a puppet.

As Carmer pondered this strange new development, more puppets emerged from the garden's shadows until the cat was entirely surrounded. The marionettes were a strange lot. Some of them were clearly soldiers and knights, outfitted with wooden swords and shields, while others seemed less suited to impromptu battles; a ballerina, a milkmaid, and a pointy-capped wizard. But they advanced on the cat all the same, herding it away from the garden gate. It swung its barbed tail and yowled with impatience.

The milkmaid approached Carmer. "Well, what are you waiting for?" it asked crossly in a low, gravelly voice that clearly belonged to someone else. "A magic carpet service?"

Carmer didn't need to be told twice. He shoved Grit

in his pocket—*Again*, Grit sighed to herself—and took the puppet's proffered hand. As they ran past the cat, it yowled pathetically, batting at the marionettes now harrying it from all sides.

Grit shook her head at the puppets, eyes wide. They didn't look any less terrifying than the cat.

"This is madness!" she yelled, kicking Carmer's chest.

"Would you rather stay back there?" he asked, and that was the end of that.

THE CHEERFUL ATMOSPHERE of the circus camp seemed a different world compared to the perilous streets they had just left behind. Out of danger for the moment, Grit looked curiously at the strange specimens of humanity around her. She saw fire-eaters juggling knives, men beating on drums that lit up with all the colors of the rainbow when struck, and snake charmers covered head to toe in writhing serpents. Carmer hardly batted an eye.

The Seminal Symposium of Magickal Arts was more than just an official competition; it was a chance for entertainers of all kinds to get together and show off. Only the wealthiest alchemists and first-billed magicians could afford the limited and luxurious accommodations in the city proper, but the sprawling circus camp that now stood in the valley of Skemantis rivaled even the best hotels for entertainment.

It was as if a small town had suddenly sprung up out

of the marshland. Large, round circus tents and impressive moto-mansions stood side by side with cloaks propped up on sticks and brightly painted Romani vardos. A few local peddlers were selling lemonade, pastries, and beer from their stands, sounding the last call before they packed up for the evening.

Ignoring Carmer's protests, Grit clambered up onto his shoulder and hoisted herself onto the brim of his hat. It offered her the best view of the camp (Grit was beginning to deduce that Carmer was quite short, for a human) and would have been perfect if he didn't lurch like a lily pad in a rainstorm with every clumsy step.

"I'd take cover for a bit, if I were you, girl," said the milkmaid marionette in her strange, hoarse voice. "There are more folk here as can spot you for what you are than you'd think."

Reluctantly, Grit rapped on Carmer's hat to be let down. After a moment, he scooped her right under it and placed that hat back on his head.

"Hey!" Grit was engulfed by darkness and a furry mess of boy hair that she had no choice but to grab on to in order to stay upright. "I can still stick my pin in you!" she warned, but Carmer was already talking to their puppet rescuer.

"Not to offend you, uh . . ." Carmer hesitated. How *did* one address a wooden milkmaid? He finally settled on "miss" and paused again. "We're very thankful for your help, but . . ."

"Who are you and where are you taking us?" demanded Grit. She had cut herself a small hole in the already shabby hat to peek out of.

Carmer, who was not quite as accustomed to magic and automaton cats and talking puppets, cringed at the faerie's directness.

"Patience, daughter of Lightbringer," growled the puppet. Carmer felt Grit tense. They walked the next few minutes in silence, making their way to the very edge of the camp.

There, where the valley was at its most marshy and deserted, was a faded gray vardo that had clearly seen better days. The paint was peeling, the wheels needed aligning, and the mollycroft roof had several broken panes. A skinny black horse munched on the few blades of grass still struggling to survive in the mud. Carmer followed the marionette inside. The door creaked ominously and shut with a definitive thud behind them.

Carmer removed his hat. As his eyes adjusted to the dim light, he heard Grit gasp above him. A second later he realized why.

The inside of the vardo looked nothing like its ramshackle exterior suggested. The room they were standing in was about four times the size it should've been. Hardwood floors shone under a gigantic crystal chandelier that sent prisms of rainbow-colored light scattering around the room. Tapestries hung from every wall embroidered with fantastical scenes—leopards lunging at hunters, a unicorn with its head in a maiden's lap, a three-faced man with eight arms and legs. Beaded curtains separated the lavish sitting room from the rest of the house. Carmer couldn't understand how all of this could fit into one tiny wagon.

Dozens upon dozens of marionettes, much like the milkmaid, were mounted on wooden shelves all over the walls. Carmer had the distinct impression he had just interrupted their conversation—and then dismissed the thought as a figment of his imagination. But he was definitely *not* imagining their beady glass eyes that followed his every move.

"What *is* this place?" Grit wondered.

Carmer shook his head, nearly shaking her off in the process.

"It's about time," said the gritty voice of their savior. But it didn't come from the milkmaid, as they expected, but from an old woman who had suddenly appeared on a divan in front of them. She was ancient and wrinkled, but the intricate braids that wound around her head and down her shoulder were dyed all the colors of the rainbow. She wore enough bangles and beads that Carmer was surprised her thin frame could bear the weight. Her ears were stretched low with equally impressive gold chandelier earrings. She gave a great sigh and heaved her feet onto a fur-covered footrest, which promptly jumped up with an indignant yowl and scurried away.

"Time for what, exactly?" demanded Grit.

Carmer was suddenly thankful for her forthrightness. His own meager conversational skills seemed to have escaped him somewhere between meeting a real-life faerie and being saved by a talking puppet.

"You two have been showing up in my cards for months now!" groused the old woman. "Though of course, I couldn't be sure if it was really you at all. It's easy enough to tell the customers, 'You'll meet a tall, dark stranger' and leave it at that—everyone likes a little mystery—but when the existence of Faerie hangs in the balance, well . . ." She fanned out a yellowing set of tarot cards on the table before her; they looked almost as old as she did. "Most folk'd have the decency to turn up by now."

Carmer plucked up his remaining courage. "Pardon me, ma'am, but . . . who exactly are you?"

The crone sat up straighter, pushed her half-moon spectacles up her crooked brown nose, and tossed her rainbow braids over her shoulder. "I am Madame Euphemia de Campos," she declared, "Possessor of the Second Sight, the finest puppet mistress in the New World, and"—she dropped her voice and winked at Grit—"Friend of the Fae."

In a flash, Grit hopped down to Carmer's shoulder and scurried down his arm like a spider. She vaulted onto the table and stared unblinkingly at Madame Euphemia. "Are you *really*?"

Carmer could hardly blame Grit for her suspicion, after the events of the day.

"I was named Friend by your grandmother, Princess Grettifrida. Back before Oldtown was Oldtown, when the Arboretum was still trees as far as the eye could see. Queen Willowright ruled then with her paramour, the Thorn with Wings."

Willow whites? Thorns with wings? *Paramours?* Carmer's head was spinning. He took a seat across from Madame Euphemia without being asked.

Grit, on the other hand, looked somewhat mollified. "It was your puppet that was following me last night," she said. "Wasn't it?"

"These old bones don't move like they used to, that's for sure," Madame Euphemia said with a wink. "When my faerie friends started whispering about these Free Folk disappearances, I sent out my extra eyes and ears to keep watch where they could."

"Thank you for saving us," Grit said. The milkmaid, who until now had stood as still as stone, curtsied. "But how did you —"

"Well, now all the apple polishing is out of the way, it's time to get down to business," interrupted Madame Euphemia, all traces of her brief mystical air vanishing.

Grit's eyes looked like they might pop out of her head. A red flush crept up from her neck to the roots of her fiery hair.

"I would appreciate it," Carmer said plaintively, "if someone would tell me exactly what is going on here?"

"Don't get your knickers in a twist, Carmer III," said the old woman.

Honestly, it was starting to seem like *everyone* he'd never met before somehow knew his name.

She waved her hand, and a puppet butler appeared carrying a tray of tea and snacks. "Have a cookie."

Suddenly, Carmer remembered the old stories they used to tell the children in the orphanage about little boys and girls trapped forever by old witches in gingerbread houses. It was with great trepidation that he took a small wafer from the proffered plate.

"Now, it seems that Princess Grettifrida—"

"*Grit,*" Grit said through her teeth.

"—has mistaken you for a Friend of the Fae. That is to say, a human given the privilege of open knowledge of the fae."

"And their magic," said Grit pointedly, looking askance at the rows of puppets.

"But even though she was mistaken," continued Madame Euphemia, "fate has thrown you two together for a reason. I've seen great changes coming to Skemantis, as fast as its train in the sky, but my cards tell me I'm not the one to bear witness—not this time. Perhaps *that* honor belongs to you."

The look Grit gave Carmer said just how much stock *she* put into fate.

"Or," said Madame Euphemia, "You just happened to

be in the wrong place at the wrong time. That happens, too. At any rate, you're in the weeds now, as they say!" She chuckled.

Grit ignored her. "But what does that have to do with the thing that attacked us?" she asked. "What even *was* it?"

"An automaton," Carmer answered. Finally, a question he knew the answer to. "It had to be. But . . ."

"Powered by faerie magic," finished Madame Euphemia, "I saw it clear as day."

"No faerie could build those . . . auto-whatsits on their own." Grit shook her head. "And they'd never make a Friend out of anyone who would. At least . . . not willingly." Grit thought of Echolaken's shredded wing and suppressed a shudder. "Those cats have been attacking the street fae," she continued. "But why?"

"Who are the street fae?" asked Carmer.

"None of your business, human boy," snapped Grit.

"These automata are undoubtedly the 'Wingsnatchers' that have been taking the Free Folk," Madame Euphemia agreed. "Though to what end is a mystery."

It was probably none of his business—why should *he* get involved with missing faeries?—but both Grit and the old woman seemed to be missing something very important.

"But . . . someone must be *behind* the cats," Carmer told them. "Even if these things do run on . . . magic, like you say, someone needed to build them in the first place.

And I doubt they'd let machines like that out into the world without looking after."

Madame Euphemia looked at him appraisingly. Carmer tried his best to hide behind the lock of hair hanging in front of his face.

"The *human boy* is right," she said, with a small smirk at Grit. "To stop these Wingsnatchers, you've got to find the proverbial man behind the curtain."

The man behind the curtain. Carmer's stomach nearly dropped out from under him.

"The magic show!" he exclaimed, jumping up. "Tonight's the first round of the competition, and I'm going to be late!"

7.

THE MASKED MAGICIAN

WITH ONLY TEN MINUTES UNTIL CURTAIN, IT seemed like every one of the Orbicle's three thousand seats was filled. In the closest sat Skemantis's elite in their evening finery, along with the thirteen judges who would be scoring each magician. The members of the more average populace lucky enough to snag tickets took up the higher tiers. It was a veritable sea of humanity. Carmer had never even imagined himself performing in front of an audience this large in normal circumstances, never mind with an angry faerie under his hat.

"Take! Me! Home!" Grit had raged at him as he sprinted to the theater a few minutes before. "You promised!"

"And I will," Carmer assured her. "But I can't miss this show for anything!"

Much to Carmer's surprise, Madame Euphemia had refused to take Grit home herself. She only chuckled and muttered something about not being much of a "welcome face" in the Arboretum. Carmer had a feeling that much like her magical vardo, the old woman was more complicated than she appeared. So despite Grit's many protestations, she was in Carmer's custody until the evening's entertainment was over.

Carmer thought of leaving Grit in the dressing room during the performance, but decided against it. The Amazifier would be sharing the space with several other magicians, and the idea of Grit being spotted under some assistant's powder puff was not an appealing one. He rushed through his own preparations with great haste, sparing only a few seconds to brush the dust off his suit. He raced from the dressing room, taking great care to keep his top hat firmly upon his head; Grit was still clinging to his hair like he was an unruly horse she couldn't tame. He bumped into several performers on his way backstage, whispering apologies and asking whether anyone—*anyone*—knew where Antoine the Amazifier was waiting.

Backstage left, a slender hand shot out and gripped Carmer's shoulder so hard he felt the nails dig in.

"Ow!"

"SPIRITS AND ZITS, FELIX CARMER." Kitty Delphine stood between a snake charmer and a dwarf giraffe, looking murderous. One of the stagehands who dared to shush her received a death glare of his own and quickly backed away. Carmer wished he could do the same.

"You, uh, you look nice, Kitty," said Carmer. It was true; she'd spent the afternoon sprucing up her shiny gold costume with the better materials the city had to offer, and her hair was a more startling shade of white blonde than he had ever seen it.

She clocked him over the ear. "Where have you *been*?" she hissed, pulling him in line to straighten his tie with much more force than necessary. "What were you *thinking*? Of all the times to—"

"I'm here now, all right?" Carmer was beginning to sweat with nerves. This was *not* the way he'd pictured starting the most important performance of his life.

The snake charmer was called onstage. He pulled the miniature giraffe on a short bejeweled leash behind him. Kitty shuffled out of the way, still glaring daggers at Carmer. Above him, Carmer heard Grit let out a small, self-satisfied snort.

"Keep quiet," warned Carmer. He realized his mistake a second later.

"*What* did you say?" Kitty looked ready to smack him around the head again.

"N-nothing!"

"Two minutes, Amazifier and company!" the stage manager whispered from just inside the wings.

"Thank you, two," replied Carmer automatically. He thought he might vomit all over the audience. He squinted to the other side of the stage and could just make out the Amazifier's worried, wrinkled face waiting in the wings. But the Amazifier wasn't looking his way, and there was no time for Carmer to race all the way around to the other side.

He rushed off to the trap room, where a young stage-hand handed him a black box labeled "Amazifier" that Carmer had prepared earlier, filled with props he'd need for the act. He could hear the audience applauding for the snake charmer. Apparently the dwarf giraffe, whatever its purpose, had been a success. For a brief, mad second, Carmer considered revealing Grit to the audience during the routine — a miniature *person* was surely more impressive than a tiny giraffe — but dismissed the thought just as quickly. Grit hadn't chosen to be here, and she'd just as likely make herself invisible and leave him standing there with an empty hat, looking the fool.

In no time at all, the announcer was calling their act onto the stage.

"Thank you, thank you, to Kernzi and his little friend, Giovanni the Giraffe. And now, may I present the legendary Antoine the Amazifier!"

GRIT HAD ABSOLUTELY, positively no idea what was going on. They had entertainment in the Seelie Court, of course—seed singers and minstrels who played the bluebells or the reeds and such. Faerie revels were legendary; Fair Folk and Free Folk alike just couldn't resist showing off when they got together. But as far as she could tell, there was nothing *magical* about this magic show at all. From what she could hear from the footfalls above, it was mostly just standing about and gesturing grandly.

Grit peered out from the hole she'd carved in Carmer's ridiculous hat. They were under the stage in a poorly lit compartment barely tall enough for a man to stand in. Carmer crouched underneath a trapdoor that lead to the stage above, ready to aid in whatever silly sleight of hand these people thought passed for magic.

"Prepare . . . to be amazed!" declared the Amazifier above them.

"Not if I can help it," Grit muttered. Just as Carmer lifted the latch on the trap door, Grit dug her fingers into his hair and pulled with all her might.

"Argh!" grunted Carmer. He stumbled and failed to catch the handfuls of billiard balls tossed down from above. They clattered and bounced along the staircase with merciless little pops that surely echoed to at least the front of the theater. Grit was pretty sure *that* wasn't part of a successful magic trick.

"Not to worry, ladies and gentlemen!" covered the Amazifier as a murmur swept through the crowd. "Oftentimes the energies around us react unexpectedly when manipulated!"

Carmer whipped his hat off and clamped it over some of the rolling billiard balls, scrambling to catch the rest before any more sound could leak out. He pried Grit off his head like a stubborn leech and hung her by the back of her vest from one of the pegs in the wall. She waved her fists ineffectually at him, swaying to and fro.

"Don't," Grit whispered savagely, "mess with a faerie princess!"

The next few minutes seemed interminably long as the Amazifier tried to salvage his routine. When he finally ended the performance in an admittedly pretty shower of coppery sparklers and peppermint-scented smoke, Grit was relieved. Kitty and the Amazifier took short bows and hurried off the stage. Carmer yanked Grit off the peg with a little more roughness than necessary.

"Master Antoine, I'm sorry—" Carmer pleaded in a whisper once they were all backstage together.

But the Amazifier held up a hand to silence him, shoulders stooped in defeat. "Of all the days, Carmer . . ." He wandered off into the hallway beyond, leaving Kitty behind to glare at Carmer.

"I can't believe you, you know!" she said, her eyes full of tears. She scurried off after the Amazifier.

Carmer didn't follow. "Are you satisfied?" he asked,

and even under the hat, Grit knew he was talking to her. Suddenly, her vengeance didn't seem quite as sweet.

"Take me home," Grit replied, "and I will be."

SOMEONE INFORMED CARMER they'd be receiving their scores by a posting in the camp the next day, but Carmer was barely listening. He took a cage of doves and the Amazifier's other instruments from the harried props master without comment, unsure of what to do with himself. If he went back to the dressing room, Kitty and the Amazifier would probably still be there, and he wasn't sure he could face them again just yet. He made do by retreating to the stables, where Eduardo was waiting, looking doleful at the prospect of being loaded up again.

Grit had been mercifully silent since they left the stage. Carmer looked around and found the stable empty. He placed Grit on the edge of the pen, where Eduardo sniffed at her curiously.

"Are you going to feed me to it?" Grit asked, shying away from the horse's wet nose.

"As much as I'd like to, no." Carmer sighed and began loading his supplies into the carriage. His anger at Grit was slowly redirecting toward himself. "I made a promise that I'd get you back, and I will."

He didn't mention that he was just as likely to foul up when there *wasn't* an angry faerie under his hat as when there was.

"He talks to himself, too! So you're a nutter on *and* off the stage, Carmer III?"

The finely dressed boy Carmer had run into at the rehearsal lounged in the doorway of the stables, the moon big and bright behind him. Carmer glanced quickly at Grit, but she had already ducked into the shadows.

"How did you know my name?" asked Carmer.

"I make it my business to know my master's competition," said the boy with a shrug. "Not that I'd count you as such, after tonight."

Grit snorted; Carmer hastily covered the sound with a cough.

"You should watch our performance, Carmer," the boy continued. "Perhaps you'd learn a thing or two." He took a few steps toward Carmer and looked him up and down, a disdainful sneer spreading across his fair face. "On the other hand, perhaps Skemantis is a bit out of your league." He spun on his heel with the grace of a dancer and strode away.

Grit stepped out into the moonlight once more, looking contemplative. She stuck out her tongue in the haughty boy's direction.

Carmer laughed despite himself. "All right," he whispered, "I should have enough time to run you back to the Arboretum before the show's over."

Grit hesitated, still staring after the other boy. She bit her lip in concentration. "The Arboretum may have to wait," she said, as if she would rather admit to anything else.

Carmer raised his eyebrows in surprise.

"There's something not right about that little git— something I'm sure I've felt before. I want to know what it is." Grit hopped up onto his arm and looked at him expectantly. "Well," she said, "do you think we'll be amazed?"

CARMER GRABBED A program out of a bored-looking usher's hand in the back of the third tier and snuck into a group of miraculously empty seats in one of the back rows. Grit perched once more on the brim of his hat, thorny heels crossed under her, assuring him that she was hardly likely to be noticed in a darkened theater with everyone's attention directed at the stage. He finally conceded the point, and they settled down to watch the show.

Carmer scanned the program until he found the Amazifier's name, wondering how many sets he'd missed and who the snooty boy's master might be. The master of ceremonies, a reedy man in shiny midnight blue tails and an oiled goatee, cleared his throat as the applause for the previous act died out. A woman in a red sequined gown hurried off the stage, patting a gloved hand at the blackened remains of an elaborate peacock feather fascinator in her hair that was still smoking. Carmer got the feeling he wasn't the only one who'd dropped the proverbial ball that evening.

"Thank you, Madame Mystique, for that *electrifying* performance!" declared the announcer, whose name the program said was Conan Mesmer. "And now, for our final performance, an expert illusionist who has graced this stage on more than one occasion. He has all of Skemantis in his thrall, and we can't get enough of this fresh face in the magic scene—that is, if we could see his face at all! Please join me in welcoming the marvelously modern masked magician . . . the Mechanist!"

The audience burst into expectant applause.

"Have you ever heard of him?" Carmer asked Grit, but before she could answer, the crashing sound of thunder rumbled all around them and the theater plunged into darkness. Several women screamed.

"What's going on?"

"Someone's cut the gas!"

"Anyone got a light?"

In the moment before true panic set in, the chandeliers overhead started pulsing with a faint glow. The light faded in and out, getting brighter with each pulse, casting eerie shadows over the theatergoers' faces. One moment Carmer could see the whole theater illuminated in ghostly half light; the next, he could barely make out his hand in front of his face. A violin in the orchestra struck up a plaintive tune. The strings swelled with each pulse of light, weaving a spell that kept all eyes transfixed on the ceiling.

There was a strange *whooshing* sound, and the entire

audience shielded their eyes, blinded by sudden light. Quite a few more people screamed this time. Carmer was one of the first to lift his head, and when he did, he gasped. The stage lights were back on, along with some of the house lights, giving him a decent view of the whole theater. The chandeliers were completely obscured by giant clouds of pure white. Something soft floated down toward him, and he reached out to grab it, but Grit was faster; she caught the first feather in her hands and stared down at it, eyes wide.

They're birds, Carmer realized, and it seemed everyone else did, too. There were gasps and smatterings of shocked applause. Hundreds of white doves circled overhead.

The birds came together in a giant swarm, flying here and there across the theater, skimming ladies' hats and making everyone in their path dive for cover. Carmer, for one, stayed upright, and caught a strange silver gleam in a bird's eye as it flew close enough for him to feel the flutter of its wings. Doves didn't normally have silver eyes . . . did they?

In one swift motion, the swarm of birds dived toward the stage, flying so fast Carmer was sure they had no choice but to crash into it with a sickening crunch of broken wings. But as the white cloud made contact with the stage, the doves disappeared, leaving nothing but showers of silver sparks in their wake. With a swish of his cloak, the man they had all been waiting for emerged from the shining deluge of silver: the Mechanist.

Carmer's first thought was that the Mechanist's cloak was the most beautiful fabric he'd ever seen; he doubted even Kitty could make something so splendid. It shimmered with the colors of a thousand tiny rainbows, changing colors with even the slightest movement, refracting and reflecting the light around him and casting eerie shadows upon the stage floor. Grit gasped, but Carmer hardly heard her.

The Mechanist was masked, as Conan Mesmer had promised. A delicate silver clockwork contraption covered the top half of his face and reached all the way up under his shining silk top hat. It was shaped perfectly to his facial features, like a second skin, and his eyes looked unnaturally bright staring out between almond-shaped slits. There was no disguising his smile, however. It was as bright as the light around him, and Carmer imagined he could see the sharpness of his teeth even from the cheap seats. It was a smile that knew he already had the competition in the bag.

The last of the silver sparks dissipated, and the Mechanist bowed with a sweep of his mesmerizing cloak. Carmer saw a familiar flash of silver at the magician's gloved wrist; he was too far away to be certain, but the thick band reminded him of the one he'd spotted on the blond boy earlier.

The audience erupted in applause, clapping and cheering until their hands hurt, and it was only then that Carmer came back to himself. It was like awakening from a dream. He remembered the Amazifier and his own disastrous performance, and found he didn't have much energy for clapping at all. What chance did they stand against *that*?

"Thank you! Thank you, ladies and gentlemen. I am," said the magician, "the Mechanist."

While the applause continued, the blond boy from the stables brought out a large birdcage on a stainless steel table on wheels. A quick glance at the program told Carmer the boy was called Gideon Sharpe. At least now he knew his tormentor's name.

The Mechanist spread his arms, purposefully showing the crowd the silver bands this time. A billiard ball–sized silvery blue orb was embedded on the inside of each. With a flick of his wrists, the doves appeared over the audience once more, and the music picked up. The Mechanist threw his cloak over the cage and the birds flew into it, hundreds of them seeming to fit impossibly inside. He withdrew his cloak and the cage stood empty.

The audience applauded again, but Carmer knew the trick was far from over. Once again the cloak fell over the cage. The doves streamed out the other side and flew another lap around the theater. The Mechanist urged them back to the cage, the stones at his wrists flashing along with the birds' eyes. They pelted toward it as they had dive-bombed the stage earlier, but again, the expected crash never came.

Real birds flew into one side of the cage, but real birds did not fly out.

Hundreds of gleaming white-painted automata streamed out over the audience, each a perfect mechanical facsimile of the living thing. Carmer reached out and brushed his fingertips against a cold metal wing as it fluttered by. He shivered at the touch. Amazing as the birds were, Carmer didn't want to see what feats the rest of the show would bring.

Apparently, he wasn't alone in this opinion. Grit suddenly swung down in front of his face, her tiny fingers clutching the brim of his hat. Her expression was bloodless.

"What's the matter?" Carmer whispered under the *oohs* and *aahs* of the enraptured crowd.

"That man. The Mechanist."

"I don't like him much myself," said Carmer bitterly.

"No," said Grit, and for the first time, Carmer saw true fear in her eyes. "You don't understand. That man is using faerie magic."

8.

A DEAL IS STRUCK

"BUT HOW CAN *HE* BE USING FAERIE MAGIC?" CARMER asked again. He was just beginning to process the idea that magic was even *real*, and now a grumpy faerie princess was telling him someone was stealing it. Grit sat on Eduardo's head, absently scratching the horse between the ears, while Carmer waited for Kitty and the Amazifier to return.

"I told you, I don't know. There weren't even any faeries *there*. I would have known," Grit insisted.

"But Madame Euphemia uses magic, right?" he asked. "She's a Friend of the Fae, like you said. Maybe the Mechanist is like her?"

Grit shook her head. "Being a Friend of the Fae doesn't actually *give* you that much magic. It just makes you more attuned to it. Madame Euphemia is . . . different, I know, but she's also not parading her puppets around in front of half the city! The one thing I know for *sure* is that the Mechanist is no Friend of the Fae. We would never allow someone to exploit our talents like that. It attracts too much attention."

"I could see that," Carmer agreed.

Outside, the stable boy wished someone a pleasant evening and the doors creaked open. The show must have ended. Coachmen were suddenly waiting at the ready for their wealthy employers. Assistants and apprentices began loading up carts and revving engines, and gossiping all the while. Carmer held out his hand, and Grit hopped up to be put under his hat.

"Did you see the way those birds flew? It was better than the ballet!"

"How did he make all those lights appear?"

"Sent the chills right down my back, though, didn't it?"

Carmer spotted Kitty on her way in, chattering animatedly with a team of identically costumed acrobats. She caught Carmer's eye and her expression soured. She turned back to her acrobats, ignoring him. Carmer sighed.

"She'll come around. I daresay I will, too. No sense in crying over spilled ammonia, even if the scent is rather pungent." The Amazifier stood in front of them.

Carmer couldn't bring himself to meet his mentor's eyes.

"Is there something you want to tell me, Carmer?" the Amazifier asked, not unkindly.

Carmer tried to keep his face blank. Somehow he felt the reply "Why, yes, there was actually an angry mythical creature under my hat for the entire performance!" would not be suitable. He shook his head.

"I'm sorry, Master Antoine," Carmer said instead. "I just . . . I understand if you need to let me go now."

Eduardo whinnied softly in the silence that followed.

The Amazifier reached over to pat the horse on the head. "How long do you think I've kept Eduardo here, Carmer?"

"I . . . I don't know, sir."

"Longer than you, that's for sure." The Amazifier winked. "And I supposed you've wondered why I've never gotten rid of him. Retired him to a kindly old farmer somewhere, or even sent him off to the glue factory. But the truth is, I'll stand by this old horse as long as he sees fit to stand by me, because we've learned from each other, and taken care of each other, and traveled the world together. And that might not sound like very good deductive reasoning to scientific minds like ours, but that's the way it is. There may be faster horses in this world, but there's only one Eduardo."

The Amazifier flicked his hand in a graceful gesture, and a shiny apple appeared in his palm. Eduardo happily gobbled it up. "You really thought that after one bad night,

97

I'd toss you out on the street, boy?" The Amazifier looked slightly hurt at the suggestion.

What Carmer couldn't say to his mentor was that he'd thought exactly that. Enough people had given up on Felix Cassius Tiberius Carmer III in his short life that he still expected it as a matter of course. "I thought you'd be angry with me for costing us the competition."

"Oh, I'm about ready to toss you into a vat of liquid nitrogen," admitted the old man cheerfully. "But we'll figure something out. There is, after all, only one Carmer III."

Carmer knew this was supposed to make him feel better, but it only made him feel worse. He'd done nothing to deserve the Amazifier's continued affection.

"Master Antoine, why did we come here?" Carmer asked, though he already knew the answer.

For the first time, the Amazifier looked abashed. "I entered this competition, my boy, so that I could keep you on with me, and Kitty as well."

"That's why you stopped me from keeping the books a while ago, isn't it?" Carmer said. "We're in trouble."

"I'll be frank with you, Carmer," said the Amazifier heavily. He suddenly looked as old as he was. "If we don't win this competition, I'm afraid that Antoine the Amazifier and his traveling companions can be no more. Even if there is only one Carmer III."

Carmer had suspected as much, of course, but to hear the Amazifier admit their dire situation aloud gave weight to his greatest fear. If the Amazifier could no longer afford to keep up his act, what would they do? Would Carmer go back to an orphanage? And what about Kitty? Would she have to sell all her beloved costumes and go back to the small mining town she once called home?

Carmer knew the Amazifier disliked the city, knew the old magician was far past his prime. Yet his master had tried so hard to keep their little misfit family together by coming to Skemantis. And now Carmer had ruined everything.

"We'll make it to the next round," Carmer found himself saying, though he didn't believe a word of it. "I've got some new inventions that'll really spice up the act."

"Not literally, I hope," chuckled the Amazifier, stepping up into the wagon. "Last time, we all smelled like paprika for a week!"

"ONLY A LITTLE longer," Carmer said quietly as they followed the caravan of carriages, both steam and horse-drawn, out of town. The Amazifier and a still-sulking Kitty Delphine were discussing the Mechanist's standout performance in detail as they bumped along, leaving Carmer free to whisper a comment or two to Grit. "I'll sneak you out of camp first thing in the morning."

Carmer mumbled something else about looking like he was talking to himself, but Grit was hardly listening. She was thinking about the conversation in the stables between Carmer and the Amazifier and all the strange things she'd seen since she'd left the Arboretum the night before—Wingsnatchers and mechanical cats and Friends (or foes) of the Fae. The minute she stepped back into the Arboretum, her mother would lock her up in the highest branch of the Great Willow. She might never have a chance to discover who—or what—was attacking the faeries, or how the mysterious Mechanist was using his powers. This Felix Carmer, strange and uneducated in the ways of the fae as he was, might be her only chance to explore the city and get to the bottom of things.

"No," said Grit from her seat on the brim of his hat. She swayed from side to side with the movement of the wagon. "I have a better idea."

"After all this bother," sputtered Carmer, barely managing to keep his voice down, "you don't want to go home after all?!"

"What I *want* is to find out where those metal beasts came from, and why a human magician has an army's worth of faerie magic. And I know something you want, as well." Grit hesitated, certain that she was about to break just about every rule that existed about humans and fae. "You want to win this competition. And I . . . I can help you do it."

"What do you mean," said Carmer slowly, "by 'help'?"

"If you take me around the city, if you use your knowledge of this world to help me find what's attacking the faeries . . . I'll use my magic to help you win this magic competition. I trust you'll be the only one with a faerie princess in your corner."

Carmer looked thoughtful for a moment. Grit knew he was remembering how she'd made the lamp explode in the alley. Hopefully, they would solve *her* mysteries before it was time for her to prove her magical prowess. The less Carmer knew about her abilities (or lack thereof) the better.

"I can't believe I'm saying this," Carmer said, "but you've got yourself a deal, Grit."

LATE THAT NIGHT, when the Amazifier and Kitty Delphine were asleep, Carmer crept up to his workstation in the attic laboratory. He held Grit in his hand like a living lantern. Her soft golden glow lit their way along the creaky staircase; he shut the door as quietly as he could behind them.

That such a small room could contain so much *stuff* seemed a miracle to Grit. Countless bottles and vials covered every surface. Bowing shelves with jars of mysterious herbs and powders were stacked haphazardly along the walls, as if they had been erected only when the Amazifier realized he was completely out of space on all the others. Thin, spidery handwriting labeled nearly every specimen, while other drawers full to bursting with wires and cogs were labeled in a fresher, more precise print. Something viscous and purple smoked on a gas burner despite an apparent lack of heat.

A scale model of the solar system—well, what the humans knew of it—hung from the ceiling. It took Grit a moment to notice that the planets were actually *moving* ever so slowly around the plaster sun. There were diagrams of engines and clocks and automata, and maps of faraway places Grit had never heard of. A model railroad circled the entire room on a track suspended from the wall, still and silent at the moment. Half-empty cups of tea perched precariously on various surfaces, long forgotten amidst all the other clutter.

Carmer's desk, however, was distinguishable by its neatness. A two-foot-tall automaton in full military regalia stood at attention on the smooth wood surface. It even had its own tiny bayonet. A few of the cylinders Carmer had thrown in the alley also sat on the desk; Grit gave *those* a wide birth.

"Did you make this?" Grit asked, taking in the soldier's shiny brass fingers and smart suit and cap.

"Kitty made the costume," said Carmer shyly. "She named him as well. 'Lieutenant Axel Hudspeth,' at your service." He noticed Grit eyeing the smoke bombs and carefully tucked them in the top drawer. "But yes, I mess about with things. A bit."

"I think it's marvelous," said Grit sincerely, gazing up at the spinning planets. If only she'd known Carmer when she was planning Dusten's harness!

"You'd be one of the first to think so," said Carmer. He reached for the toy soldier, cranked a handle on its back a few times, and set it down again. After a few shuddering motions, the soldier marched back and forth across the desk with only the slightest of creaks as his mechanical joints propelled him forward.

Grit leapt out of the way.

"Sorry," said Carmer, hurriedly stopping the soldier's progress with his hand. He pulled another lever in the automaton's back, and it was still. "I suppose I should've warned you about that."

"No, it's all right," said Grit rather shakily. "It's just . . . that cat."

"Oh. Right."

Carmer pushed the soldier to the far end of the desk.

"You said you'd never seen any auto-whatsits—

"Automata—"

"Like it before."

Carmer shook his head and grabbed the soldier again, displaying its back to Grit. "See this handle here? Most automata have something like it. It's a winding mechanism connected to the mainspring . . . like a metal ribbon. You'd see it if I opened him up. Well, when you wind him here, all the energy is stored in the mainspring. That energy gets released as the ribbon unwinds and powers the motion of the automaton. Until it runs out, of course."

Grit tried to look less like Carmer was speaking in tongues and nodded slowly. It was the most she'd ever heard him speak since she met him.

"But that cat was different. Its range of motion, its speed, its longevity . . . that is to say, it never seemed to wind down . . . it suggests a different sort of power altogether. Beyond pure mechanics!"

" . . . So?"

Carmer deflated slightly, looking embarrassed. "Sorry. I get a bit excited."

"Apparently," said Grit. "So, energy gets stored in these mainspring things. But what if instead of normal energy, someone found a way to store *fae* energy? To capture a faerie's magic and force it to power a machine?"

"Two days ago, I would've said it was impossible." Carmer ran a hand through his hair. "But I would've also said you were impossible. Therefore, I can only conclude that it's entirely probable."

"Entirely probable?" repeated Grit. "That's the best you can do, *entirely probable*?"

"Without knowing more about the cat that attacked us, I can't tell much else." Carmer shrugged. "If I could only examine it . . ." He stood up and paced around the room.

"Oh, right, we'll just put a bowl of cream on the stoop and hope it turns up," said Grit. "Maybe if we offer to scratch its belly it won't try to claw our eyes out."

"You said other faeries, the ones who live on the streets, have been attacked, too?"

Grit nodded.

"Maybe they can tell us what they've seen."

"I'm sure they could," Grit snorted, "if we could find them. Not all of us have bumbling human boys to come to our rescue."

Carmer stopped pacing, his ears flushing. "I'll take that as a compliment. You're *sure* you're the only one who escaped?"

"*Echo* . . ." mumbled the water fae. "*Name's . . . Echolaken.*"

Grit's wing fluttered involuntarily. She turned away from Carmer and pretended to study the diagram of the soldier on the wall.

"No," she said finally. "There's someone else."

Apparently, Grit's unfortunate visit to the Green Goddess wasn't to be her last.

TRACKING DOWN ECHOLAKEN proved to be a more difficult task than Grit had expected. The brewery near the Green Goddess's entrance was crawling with humans during the day. Carmer and Grit could hardly traipse around and start shouting questions at the ground without raising a few eyebrows. Carmer stood hovering in the entrance yard, trying and failing to look inconspicuous. Two men rolling great barrels of beer into a waiting cart were already watching him.

"I thought you said you had a plan," Carmer muttered to Grit, who was once again under his hat.

"There's never been this many people here when I've come!" she protested. "Plus, they probably won't let me in without faerie dust. Especially not when I'm with you."

"Excellent." Carmer sighed.

"Hey, you!" said one of the two men. "You have business here, boy?"

"Um, well, not exactly . . ."

"I haven't got all day. We've no work, if that's what you're after." Other men were starting to stare.

"But—"

"Scram," the man said flatly, going back to his work.

Carmer had no choice but to obey. He was about to turn back the way they'd come when a rustling sound and a shout stopped him.

Out of nowhere, a murder of crows dive-bombed the entrance yard, circling around the men's heads and cawing loudly. Carmer and the men all ducked for cover, clutching their hats.

To Carmer's surprise, Grit laughed as she peeked out of her hole.

"It's all right!" she said. "Look, follow them!"

Immediately, the crows took off away from the brewery, flying south. With only a moment's hesitation, Carmer darted past the confused workmen and followed suit. The birds led them away from the street traffic, dropping off in ones and twos, until only a solitary crow—actually, it looked rather *big* to be a crow—soared above the deserted alleys and industrial lots.

"Why are we following a crow?" asked Carmer.

"It's not a crow, it's a raven. And she's a friend."

"Good to know you're on friendly terms with *someone* in this city."

Grit scuffed her toe against his ear.

"Caw!" The raven landed on the back of a bench in a shabby little park that looked quite out of place at this edge of the city. There were only two benches and a handful of sad little trees that looked ready to keel over with the next strong wind.

Grit rapped on the inside of Carmer's hat, and he took it off. She stepped onto his shoulder.

"Thank you," Grit said, addressing the raven seriously.

Carmer laughed, and then blinked. One moment there was nothing there but their unlikely guide, and the next, the second faerie Carmer had ever seen stood right in front of him. She looked fierce for one so tiny, and her long black braid brushed the backs of her calves. She wore a belt of blades that looked dangerously sharp despite their size. Her wings were a dark purple and, unlike Grit's, fully functioning.

"Princess," said the faerie, bowing from the waist and flicking her wings back and forth. A shimmering golden powder rose from them and fell onto the bench. "I sensed you were near."

"Ravene," said Grit, "I'm not your princess."

"No, but you are *a* princess. You've no idea how many faeries are looking for you."

"They're not the only ones." Grit explained the attack from the automaton and how Carmer had intervened.

Carmer noticed she left out the part about him not *actually* being a Friend of the Fae. Ravene, however, still regarded him skeptically.

"Carmer's going to help us find the Wingsnatchers," said Grit, with more confidence than she felt. "And to do that, we need to talk to Echolaken."

Ravene looked around them and, apparently satisfied that they were alone, floated down to sit on the bench. She motioned for Carmer and Grit to join her, but shook her head. "I don't think it's a good idea."

"Haven't any of you talked to her about what happened?" asked Grit. "Abby Absinthe, or any of the Free Folk?"

"The water faerie won't speak to anyone. She wouldn't even stay in the Green Goddess, weak as she is."

"And you let her leave?" Grit sputtered. "She'll get snatched up by that cat by nightfall, if she hasn't already!"

"A Free Fae's business is her own," Ravene said tartly. ". . . But that doesn't mean we haven't been keeping an eye on her." She looked askance at Carmer. "Can I trust this human?"

"He hasn't put *me* in a jar yet." Grit shrugged.

Carmer felt a tad silly for being intimidated by a six-inch-tall faerie, but there was something about Ravene's pressing stare that made his hair stand on end.

"Still, he doesn't go," decided Ravene. "Not when Echolaken can't defend herself."

"Ravene—"

"That's the deal, or I don't tell you where she is."

Grit flushed, and despite only knowing her for a day and a half, Carmer was beginning to learn when she was about to go off in a temper.

"Fine by me," Carmer said lightly.

Grit glared at him, crossing her arms. "How am I going to get there?"

"You'll ride Sootlink, of course," said Ravene. She brought two fingers to her teeth and whistled at a pitch too high for Carmer to hear. A moment later, another very real raven landed on the bench. "He'll take you wherever you need to go."

"I don't suppose he's expandable, too?" Carmer joked, thinking of Madame Euphemia's vardo. Still, you never knew.

"You'll have to make your way on foot, I'm afraid. *Away* from here," said Ravene.

Carmer took the hint. "Meet me back at the Moto-Manse tonight," he told Grit. "I'm going back to the Orbicle to see what I can find out about the Mechanist."

"The Mechanist?" asked Ravene.

"I'll explain later," said Grit.

"Um, nice to meet you," said Carmer, awkwardly tipping his hat to Ravene, who regarded him as stonily as ever. "See you later, Grit." He started to make his way back to the city proper.

"Carmer?" Grit called.

He turned around.

"Be careful, right?"

"Right," he agreed with a somewhat surprised smile, and was off.

Ravene finished her whispered instructions to Sootlink and gave Grit a boost onto the raven's back.

"I hope you know what you're doing with that boy," warned Ravene.

Grit rolled her eyes and tried to squash the sudden and inexplicable desire for Carmer to come with them.

9.

BEHIND THE CURTAIN

THE ORBICLE DURING THE DAY WAS AN ENTIRELY different place from when the curtain rose at night. A cleaning crew dusted the chandeliers and swept the aisles—Carmer overheard one of them complaining about "all the darn *feathers*"—and the stage crew was going over a lighting cue with the slimy-looking announcer, Conan Mesmer. Mesmer's goatee was not quite as expertly waxed as it had been the night before, and he looked rather bored.

Carmer assumed, given Mesmer's comments about the Mechanist before the magician's entrance, that the Mechanist was no stranger to the Orbicle's stage. Most of the other competitors, like the Amazifier, had to make do with temporary arrangements in the chorus dressing rooms, everyone jammed together and jockeying over mirrors. But if the Mechanist was popular here in Skemantis, it seemed likely he'd weaseled into a private dressing room for the duration of the competition.

Carmer slipped unnoticed backstage and into a long corridor with doors labeled "Costumes," "Propsmaster's Office," "Woodworking," and such. A little way down, some of the doors had stars on them, with little slates hanging on each door bearing the names of performers. Carmer did not have to walk far before he found a door labeled "MECHANIST."

He knocked sharply three times and, after no answer, quietly pushed the door in. He was thankful but unsurprised to find the room had no lock; this was not unusual, as it deterred high-strung actors from locking themselves in their dressing rooms and refusing to go onstage. However, easy access to the room also meant that no self-respecting magician would ever leave anything of value in it— especially not during a competition, where every magician would be out to poach the others' secrets.

Carmer didn't expect to find anything incriminating, but a quick look around couldn't hurt. He closed the door behind him and prepared an excuse about delivering supplies and taking a wrong turn should any of the theater employees stumble upon him.

The dressing room was much like any other. The Mechanist had not put many personal touches into it.

There was a vanity circled by lights—electric, Carmer noticed—big enough to comfortably seat three, a faded pink velvet settee with a tea table next to it, an empty rolling rack for costumes in addition to a large black armoire in the corner of the room, and a slightly worn writing desk with a high-backed chair. But it was the item slung over the back of the chair that really caught Carmer's attention.

The Mechanist's cloak.

Carmer was drawn to it as if a magnetic pull were guiding him. He remembered the way it had shimmered so magically under the stage lights, and curiosity got the better of him. The multicolored, faceted fabric glittered like crystals, casting rainbow-tinted shadows on his hands. It felt impossibly delicate under his fingers, as if one wrong slip of his hands might tear the whole thing, but also strangely resilient. It could probably repel water, if anyone dared to test it. Carmer tried to remember where he'd seen such a peculiar texture before, and then it hit him.

The Mechanist's cloak was made of faerie wings. Hundreds of them, perhaps thousands, were woven together and sewn into the silk. If Carmer looked closely, he could see the thin strips of cartilage running through the gossamer membranes. Fascination immediately turning to revulsion, he dropped the cloak back onto the chair.

It was then that Carmer heard the sound of approaching footsteps. The doorknob turned and he had just enough time to dash into the armoire before the Mechanist himself strode into the room. Carmer recognized the magician's back through the slit in the wardrobe's doors. There was something about his commanding stance that gave him away.

Resisting the temptation to keep the door open and watch, Carmer ever so slowly pulled it fully closed. He didn't want to attract any attention to his hiding spot, and he prayed the Mechanist would not need to access his costumes just now.

"What do you have to say for yourself?" asked the Mechanist angrily, and for a moment, Carmer thought he was discovered. But a pair of answering footsteps told him someone else must be in the room as well.

"I apologize, Master," said the second voice, and Carmer recognized it as Gideon Sharpe, the Mechanist's haughty apprentice. He did not sound quite as confident now. "The bands aren't powerful enough to cut through chains that thick . . ."

SLAM. A hand banged against the armoire, making Carmer jump. He clapped a hand over his mouth to keep himself from shouting and rubbed his shoulder where it had bumped into something hard. The looming shape next to him became clearer as his eyes adjusted to the darkness, and he nearly jumped again.

An Autocat sat across from him in the wardrobe. Its ghastly face was illuminated only by a few rays of light leaking in through the doors, but Carmer was sure of what it was. Instead of glowing orange, this cat's eyes were pale blue, but they were also dull and lifeless, nothing more than faceted jewels cut into almond shapes. The cat showed no signs of animation at all.

"I grow tired of your excuses, Gideon," threatened the Mechanist.

"But, Master—"

"I will not tolerate another abysmal rehearsal. The second round of the competition is tomorrow. The tank will be ready by the third."

" . . . Yes, sir."

"Find me an amplifier, Gideon," the Mechanist growled. "Find me an amplifier, or I will find myself a new apprentice."

Convincing himself there was no imminent danger of being attacked by the lifeless automaton next to him, Carmer listened closely.

"I will, Master," said Gideon.

"Ready your beasts and meet me at the factory in an hour. Thanks to your incompetence, we shall have to make alternate preparations."

The Mechanist slammed the dressing room door behind him. Carmer chanced a peek through the armoire doors and saw Gideon sitting on the settee, head in his hands. Perhaps, like Carmer and the Amazifier, the Mechanist was the only mentor Gideon had left in the world. Carmer couldn't help but guess he'd gotten a much better deal than the young Mr. Sharpe.

And where was this factory? Would the source of the

Mechanist's faerie magic be there? Carmer wished he could follow Gideon, but he'd already promised to meet Grit back at the Moto-Manse. Tailing a nasty and powerful magician probably wouldn't fall within her definition of being careful. Gideon was a sharp boy—no pun intended—who would probably notice someone as clumsy as Carmer following him.

It seemed ages before Gideon finally left, gathering up a few things (including the Mechanist's gruesome cloak) and tidying the vanity on his way out. Carmer almost felt sorry for the other boy, then thought of his attitude at the stables. Clearly, the student was learning manners as well as magic from his teacher.

Carmer briefly studied the Autocat before he snuck out. Its aquamarine eyes were still motionless, as inanimate as the armoire it sat in. Yet the *potential* for life seemed to ooze out of every orifice. Carmer hurriedly closed the armoire door in its face. Though he knew it was impossible—well, at least improbable—he could almost feel the stare of the pale blue eyes boring through the polished wood, as if they knew an intruder was near.

At the very least, Carmer's visit had taught him one thing. The nickname *Wingsnatcher* was more accurate than any of the faeries knew.

"HELLO?"

Grit crept through the browning grass and weeds that

hung over her head and listed in the breeze like tall weeping women. The overgrown garden linked a pair of once grand but now abandoned town houses; they were nothing but empty shells now, long since looted in a neighborhood that had seen much better days. Side by side, they looked like two old eyes in a sunken face. The house on the right had been ravaged by fire some time ago, and now the face was half skeletal.

Sootlink would only go as far as the rusted front gate and cawed in protest when Grit tried to coax him onward. She'd made the rest of the way on foot through the narrow, overgrown path between the houses. The weeds were so thick she could barely see between them.

"Hello?" she called again. "Echolaken? It's Grit—ouch!" She stubbed her toe on a rusty old wheelbarrow that seemed to appear out of nowhere in the sea of tall grass. Grit hopped around, clutching her foot, until she quite suddenly found herself out in the open.

The grass was cut off by a stone walkway that spiraled inward until it reached an empty fountain in the center of the yard. A statue of a girl with birds resting along her shoulders and taking off from her fingertips festooned the top of the fountain, but no water ran from her extended hands.

Grit followed the pathway to the fountain warily, conscious of how out in the open it was despite the tall garden walls. This was not a wise place for a faerie with one wing to live, especially not with those awful cats prowling about.

Grit gripped the mossy stones on the side of the fountain carefully, finding purchase in the wedges between them, and climbed. Her fingertips had just reached the top when a weak voice called out.

"Go away," said Echolaken.

Grit hoisted herself up onto the fountain's lip and sat down, her feet dangling over the inside. "Sorry," said Grit, slightly out of breath. "I heard you could use some company."

Echolaken leaned against the base of the fountain. A cheerful, pastoral engraving of shepherdesses frolicking with their flocks stood in sharp contrast to the miserable-looking faerie in front of them. Someone had cropped Echolaken's mossy hair short, perhaps to better disguise the patches that were torn out, but it only made her look skinnier and more forlorn. Her right arm was braced to keep her from jostling her wing muscles, but it looked like she hadn't cleaned up from the accident much. There were still oily streaks on her pale face and legs.

"Do you remember me, Echolaken?"

"I told you to leave."

"My name is Grit. I'm the one—"

"Who told them to cut it off," said Echolaken. "I know." The water faerie curled her knees in and hugged them to herself with her good arm, shivering and glaring at Grit.

"Why did you leave Abby's?" asked Grit. "You're not well yet."

"And I'll never *be* well, will I?" snapped Echolaken, her eyes filling with tears. "So what's the point?"

Grit leapt down into the fountain in one expert jump, landing lightly on her feet. She didn't even slip in the wet leaves that lined the bottom.

"Do I look like an invalid to you?" Grit asked.

Echolaken sniffed. "It's different for you. You've always been that way. And . . . and you're a *princess*, for goodness' sake."

Grit had little to say to that. "Is someone at least coming to check on you?"

Echolaken nodded. "I just couldn't stay at the Goddess. Not with everyone looking at me like . . ."

"Like you're a two-headed toad from down the marsh?"

Echolaken chuckled weakly. "It's not the toads' fault!" she protested. "It's all the rubbish the humans dump in there."

"And this isn't your fault, either, Echo," said Grit, sitting down next to the water faerie. Grit put a tentative hand on her shoulder. "You fought off the Wingsnatcher. You were the only one who could."

"And my sister? What was she?" asked Echolaken, shrugging away from Grit's touch.

"Brave," said Grit simply. "Just like you." Grit looked up

at the stone birds taking flight, frozen forever. "Echolaken, I'm trying to find whoever's behind this, but I can't do it without your help."

"Oh, that's rich," said Echolaken, crying in earnest now. "We all know perfectly well you and the Seelie Court aren't going to lift a finger to help us."

"What? Why not?"

"Queen Ombrienne's called in all the faeries in her kingdom and closed off the Arboretum. None of our kind can get in *or* out — not since *her daughter's gone missing*." Echolaken narrowed her red-rimmed eyes.

Grit's mother had refused to help the Free Folk because of *her*. Queen Ombrienne thought the Wingsnatchers had captured Grit, and now she wouldn't risk any of her own subjects to help the street fae. It was exactly the kind of paranoid move Grit should have known she'd make.

"I'll get a message to her to let her know I'm safe," insisted Grit. How she would manage that without getting dragged back to the Arboretum, she didn't know, but she would try. "But I've got help on this, Echo, real help, and I think we might be onto something. But I need to know what happened the night you were taken. Anything you can remember."

"I . . . don't want to talk about it," sobbed Echolaken. "Why can't you just leave me alone like everyone else?"

"You may have noticed," Grit said with a wry smile, "I'm hardly like everyone else."

GRIT FLEW SOOTLINK to the nearest spot of running water she could find, a leaf-filled, mealy creek gamely fighting to make its way to the Bevel River to the west. She clutched a lock of Echo's mossy hair in her fist and swirled it under the murky water, whispering the words of encouragement the water faerie had taught her. It took a few tries, but the ripples soon danced at her touch, and she found herself looking at another reflection entirely—this one from one of the fountains in the Arboretum.

No one seemed to be around, but that didn't mean no one was listening.

"Tell my mother I'm safe," Grit said into the water, willing it to carry her words through the faerie kingdom. She heard a branch snap and flinched, but it was only Sootlink poking through the moist earth for worms. She wondered how long it would be before she stopped expecting mechanical beasts to leap out at her from every shadow.

"Or at least," Grit conceded, "I'm working on it."

10.

THE PHOENIX ENGINE

THOUGH CARMER KNEW IT WOULDN'T BE WISE TO follow Gideon all the way to this mysterious "factory" alone, he couldn't resist sneaking behind the other boy as Gideon made his way out of the Orbicle, the Mechanist's cloak tucked in a suitcase under one arm. Gideon showed no signs of the tongue-lashing he'd just received from his master, and in fact looked haughtier and more like he owned the Earth than ever.

Carmer tailed him through the crowded streets to the theater district's Relerail station. Gideon pulled out a ticket from his wallet and fed it into a slot at the gate; it swung open to the stairs going up to the platform. He strode to the other end and out of view. Carmer scurried after him, only to realize he didn't have a ticket.

"Please insert your ticket," said a curt, if rather fuzzy-sounding, female voice.

"Whoa," said Carmer.

"Please insert your ticket."

Carmer looked around until he spotted the row of phonograph horns peering down from the gate's archway overhead. Somehow, the contraption was registering his movement and playing prerecorded messages accordingly.

Fascinated, Carmer squatted down to examine the ticket machine. He felt something beneath his feet give way just slightly as he moved.

A second phonograph horn crackled on. "If you do not have a ticket, please move away from the gate."

"Brilliant," said Carmer. The foot or so directly in front of the gate was actually a separate platform, not part of the sidewalk at all. He bet that when it registered his weight, some sort of spring mechanism was triggered to let the machine know a passenger had approached.

"If you do not have a ticket, please move away from the gate."

"How do I even get a ticket?" Carmer muttered, but the churning sound of an incoming train interrupted him. Gideon Sharpe was going to board that train and get away, and here Carmer was wasting time poking around the gate!

Carmer edged past a few people rushing up to make the train, hoping to sneak in with the crowd, but a purple satin–gloved hand shot out of nowhere and grabbed him by the shoulder.

"And just where do you think *you're* going?" demanded Kitty Delphine. She was carrying a large carpetbag and looked about as stern as anyone in such a shocking shade of violet could manage.

"Kitty, not now—" Carmer protested lamely as she dragged him away by his ear.

"I hope you're going to the Orbicle to set up some awe-inspiring trick that's going to save our sorry backsides, Felix Carmer, because we're sure gonna need a miracle to make it past the second round of this thing."

Kitty swung them around to the underside of the platform. Carmer thought he had misheard her under the train's rumble.

"The second round?" repeated Carmer, amazed. "You mean we made it? We didn't get cut?"

"No thanks to you," Kitty sniffed, shifting the heavy bag slung across her shoulder. "We're just lucky Madame Mystique set her hair on fire."

"Ah."

"Thank goodness for small blessings!"

"Kitty, what are *you* doing here?" asked Carmer. He gestured to her bursting carpetbag. "What's all that stuff?"

"Never you mind. You're coming with me back to the camp."

"But—" Carmer glanced up to see the Relerail pulling out of the station. Gideon Sharpe was getting away!

"No 'buts.' The Amazifier says 'just because our fortunes are in the flighty hands of fate,' there's no excuse for you to neglect your schooling. Do you have a Relerail pass?"

Carmer shook his head.

"Honestly, Carmer, we've been here for *days*. For a boy who plays around with machines so much, you sure are slow to join us in this century."

Defeated, Carmer followed Kitty to the ticket kiosk attached to the nearest theater. Gideon Sharpe was long gone.

Carmer sighed, half with relief and half with worry. He wouldn't be able to rely on misfiring pyrotechnics to inch them over the line into the final round the next time. What they needed was a miracle, and he wasn't going to find it by chasing Gideon Sharpe into the underbelly of Skemantis. It was time to start holding Grit to her end of the bargain.

It was time for some *real* magic.

THE MOTO-MANSE WAS easy to spot even in the middle of a circus camp, the pointed turret of the attic laboratory sticking up as high as the biggest striped tent. Grit steered

Sootlink down to the window and found Carmer already there, his nose buried in a sketch pad. Sootlink tapped the glass with his beak to get the boy's attention, and the boy let them in.

"Thanks, Sootlink," said Grit, clambering down from the raven's silky back and onto the windowsill.

The raven looked expectantly at Carmer.

"Oh, yes. Thank you . . . sir," he muttered.

"Caw!" shrieked Sootlink, tossing his head dismissively. He flew away into the fading light.

Grit hopped down onto the shelf below the window, carefully avoiding landing in a jar of pickled somethings. "Sir?" She laughed.

"I don't think he likes me very much." Carmer tore the sketches he was working on out of the pad and stuffed them in a drawer.

"I wouldn't take it personally. Neither does Ravene!" Grit added cheerfully. She strolled around the jars on the shelf, squinting at the labels and occasionally making faces at the specimens inside.

"Well, they've got good reason to be suspicious of humans," said Carmer. He told Grit about his visit to the Orbicle and the Mechanist's gruesome cloak.

Grit shivered and paced along the shelf.

"All of those faeries . . ."

"And why?" asked Carmer. "I mean, winning the Symposium competition would be great and all, but . . . I think there's more to it than that. The Mechanist mentioned meeting Gideon 'back at the factory' today. I tried to follow him, but—"

"I think I know where that is," interrupted Grit. "Echolaken told me that she and her sister were investigating a chemical spill at an abandoned factory in the Vallows when they were ambushed."

"What are the Vallows?"

Grit shuddered again. "The Hollow Valleys. Even the humans call it that. It's not far from the circus camp, actually. The hills used to be a mining town—I think you humans call it 'pyrite'—but they sucked the place dry. Whole streets sank into the ground from all the blasting and digging they did. All the factories finally closed, and no one goes there anymore. The water and earth faeries are the only ones who'll go near the place, to help some of the animals still left. And the Free Folk, of course, but they go lots of places other faeries won't."

Carmer looked at her blankly.

"The street fae who live on their own, like Ravene," Grit clarified. "Keep up, will you?"

"We'll visit the factory, then," Carmer said, ignoring her, "but after the performance tomorrow."

"But what if there are more of those Autocats prowling around? We didn't do such a great job of handling that one last time, if you remember."

"That's because we didn't know what we were dealing

with last time," explained Carmer, a gleam of excitement in his eyes. He tore off another piece of paper from his notebook and beckoned Grit forward. "I was scared out of my wits by that thing in the closet, but I was able to get a closer look at it, if only for a second." He made the finishing touches on a surprisingly accurate sketch of an Autocat.

"The eyes are gleaming and creepy, yes, but they're just colored stones for all that. Some other power source is what really keeps them alive." He pointed to his sketch. "I noticed that the most heavily armored part on these things is the chest. It stands to reason that whatever powers them is probably located behind there—where the heart is, if you will. It makes sense you'd want to keep the heart protected."

Grit stared at the Autocat on the paper, then at Carmer's enthusiastic expression. "You're kind of crazy sometimes. You do know that, right?"

Carmer's shoulders sagged.

"Besides," Grit added, "how does this make them less scary, exactly?"

"Everything is less scary when you know how it works." Carmer shrugged. "The next time we meet the Autocats, we know there's a good chance of disabling them if we go for the heart. We'll be ready for them."

"Sure, I'll just stab them with my hatpin," deadpanned Grit. "I'm sure that'll do lots of damage."

"If you know where to stick it," countered Carmer. "And I've seen you do plenty of damage on your own."

Grit shook her head. Like it or not, it was time to admit she'd been less than honest about her capabilities. "I made a lamp explode," she said. "Your average poltergeist can do that."

"Wait, there are *poltergeists*?"

"Never mind. The point is, don't get your hopes up." Grit sighed. "The Mechanist might have dozens, even hundreds of faeries at his command."

"And?"

"*And* . . . I may have *slightly* exaggerated my powers when we made our deal."

Carmer frowned but didn't look terribly surprised. "How much exaggeration are we talking here?"

Grit gazed out of the open window, avoiding his eyes. "A lot of faerie magic comes from faerie dust, which I can't make with one wing. You need the friction they generate. I . . . I'm not as strong as other faeries," admitted Grit. "I'll never have enough power to make something like we saw the other night."

"Well . . . who said we have to be like the Mechanist?" asked Carmer. "There must be something you're good at that we can 'glitz up a bit,' like Kitty says."

Grit watched the flickering of the other campers' fires in the distance. "I *am* a fire fae," she said slowly. "Most faeries are more attuned to specific elements than others—earth, water, fire, air. We draw our power from their energy." Grit took a deep breath and rubbed her palms together. It had been a few days since she'd practiced, but when she turned to face him, it was with a handful of dancing flames.

"Spirits and zits," breathed Carmer. "That's incredible!"

"Not by fire faerie standards," disagreed Grit, extinguishing the flames. "I can't do much more than that."

Carmer looked thoughtful. "Did you use fire to blow up the lamp in the street?"

"Well, no," said Grit. "Not exactly. That move is sort of a cheat." Grit snapped her fingers and a gold spark flared to life with a crack, like flint struck against steel. "It's more like . . . the spark before a fire. At least, that's what it feels like. It's easier for me than making a whole flame." She sat down and hugged her knees to her chest. She wasn't entirely comfortable talking about the limitations of her powers with a human boy—or with anyone, for that matter. It only served to remind her how different she was from the other faeries. "I haven't found a good use for it, but I guess if you want something to explode, I'm your gal."

Much to her surprise, Carmer looked delighted. "Actually," he said, "I think we can work with that."

THE SECOND ROUND of the Seminal Symposium of Magickal Arts was an even grander and more ostentatious affair than the first. Gone were the amateur conjurers and half-baked mentalists, the inexperienced and the unlucky. (Madame Mystique, for her part, sat sulking in the audience, hair artfully arranged to cover a decidedly singed patch of scalp.) Ticket prices had gone up; even in the so-called nosebleed seats in the third tier, much fewer of the common folk were to be seen. For all of the well-to-do Skemantians' insistence that magic was a pastime of the poor and uneducated masses, this was quite the affair.

Conan Mesmer, outfitted this evening in a ghastly green sequined suit that sparkled from head to toe under the stage lights, was clearly enjoying himself.

"Welcome, ladies and gentlemen, to the second round of the greatest magical competition, the most impressive demonstration of the strange, the mystical, and the impossible in all the land! Many have dazzled us with fine feats already, but tonight we separate the kings and queens from the jokers, the maestros from the novices! Tonight, we take one step closer to finding the greatest magician in the world!"

Backstage, Carmer squeezed Kitty Delphine's hand.

"At least these folks don't have tomatoes," Kitty joked, taking a deep breath. She cast him a sideways glance. "Do I even want to know what's in that hat of yours?"

Carmer's trademark hat had in fact undergone a transformation. Unbeknownst to everyone else, the inside rim was now lined with a small wooden balcony on which stood a nervous faerie, waiting to whisper instructions to Carmer. It also had the added bonus of making the hat now fit quite comfortably on his head. Grit had insisted on an easy exit in case of emergency, and so the hat looked more odd than ever, with a tiny door that opened outward onto the brim.

"Probably not," was all Carmer answered.

Kitty sniffed. Her own costume was altered as well; her usual glitter, lace, and frills had been replaced with a simpler but striking bright red gown and smart leather bodice with feather trim. The open sides laced up with gold wire and gears as fasteners. Even Grit had eyed Kitty's workmanship approvingly.

"All ready below, boy?" the Amazifier whispered, coming up behind them. He placed a hand on each of their shoulders.

Carmer nodded. The trap room was prepped and ready to go, though the real source of their magic would be under Carmer's hat. It hadn't been easy convincing Kitty and the Amazifier to try out any of his new ideas, especially considering his abysmal performance in the first round. He'd dragged them to the theater at the crack of dawn to practice, having gotten only an hour or so of sleep himself, insisting that secrecy was paramount.

"Trust me, Master Antoine," pressed Carmer. "We don't want anyone to see this before we go onstage tonight."

"Or be witness to our untimely demises, should one of

your inventions malfunction?" asked the Amazifier with a wink. Kitty had only groaned.

Now Carmer could only hope Kitty and the Amazifier would still trust him after this round of the competition, though for completely different reasons from before. With enough tinkering, he and Grit had managed to spruce up the Amazifier's Cremation Illusion while keeping Grit's involvement a secret. Though Carmer knew better than to surprise a magician in the middle of his own act, he had to take his chances and hope he could pass it off as a last-minute addition. Grit refused to reveal herself to more humans, and so for better or for worse, her magical boost to their illusion would be making its premier in front of the live audience.

"Whatever happens tonight," said the Amazifier, "I will always be proud of the wonders, big and small, that we have accomplished together." He gave their shoulders a comforting squeeze.

"Spirits and zits, Master Antoine," mumbled Kitty, dabbing at her eyes. "You're gonna turn this mascara into runaway train tracks right down my face."

Antoine offered her his handkerchief, which Kitty blew into noisily.

"If all goes well, they won't be the only ones on the stage tonight," joked the Amazifier.

Kitty kissed him on his weathered cheek and even gave Carmer a quick peck that left bright red lipstick—and a substantial blush—on his face. "Break a leg, everyone!" she said.

"Let's make some magic," agreed the Amazifier, the familiar gleam of excitement in his eye.

With one last look at his mentor, Carmer slipped away and down the rickety staircase that lead under the Orbicle's stage. "I hope so," he whispered to himself, then winced as a spurred boot poked him in the scalp.

"Thanks for the vote of confidence, human," she hissed.

"Anytime, Grit. Anytime."

Out onstage, Conan Mesmer announced the Amazifier's entrance, and the show began.

GIDEON SHARPE WATCHED Antoine the Amazifier toddle out onto the Orbicle's stage with amused derision. He and his assistant had changed their look a bit, but there was nothing special about them—no grand entrance to grab the audience's attention, not even a trail of smoke to suggest an air of mystery. They'd barely made it into the second round after their first "performance," and Gideon was sure this one would be memorable only in its mediocrity.

" . . . and my lovely assistant, Miss Kitty Delphine!" the Amazifier was saying.

The dark young woman with the shockingly blonde hair appeared carrying an unlit candelabra and curtsied to polite applause. Her red outfit with feather trim made her look like an oversized exotic bird. She held the candelabra out to the Amazifier. He leaned over and blew on each candle; they lit up one by one as he did so.

The polite applause surfaced again — Gideon did not join in — and the assistant placed the candelabra on what Gideon knew to be a trapdoor on the stage floor. A rope swung down from the catwalk and something that looked like the top of a giant birdcage lowered from above. A curtain was strung up around its rim, ready to be lowered at a pull from the rope. Gideon recognized the trick at once: the Cremation Illusion. Shortly, either Miss Delphine or the Amazifier would appear to go up in flames underneath the curtain, only to reemerge without a scratch. Gideon stifled a yawn.

"The fine people of Skemantis are well accustomed to technology and innovation," said the Amazifier. "No doubt many of you have even come to view steam power as *old hat.*"

The magician shrugged and doffed his own hat, and a small tendril of steam poured out with a whistle like a teakettle. He clapped the hat down again, feigning a sheepish look, and the audience laughed. He was really buttering them up for this one.

"But what I am about to show you has never been attempted before, not even in Skemantis."

Kitty Delphine wheeled out the bottom part of the illusion, a tall three-legged stool with a winding track suspended all around it that climbed up in a widening spiral several feet high. At the bottom of the track rested a model railroad train, complete with a bright red caboose. Gideon began to doubt his earlier prediction. What *was* the old fool up to?

"You have all seen a steam engine powered by a boiler," said the Amazifier, "but have you ever seen a steam engine powered by a *girl*?"

A ripple of interest ran through the crowd. Miss Delphine centered the stool over the candelabra, but the handful of gasps this earned from the audience was unwarranted; the tiny candle flames were at least half a foot away from it. The Amazifier helped the girl up onto the stool, and the model railroad tracks wound around her lower body like metal snakes. She really did look like an exotic bird in a cage.

"Please note that this train is no mere windup toy," explained the Amazifier. "Neither myself nor my assistant have touched it, as you have seen." He stood back with arms wide.

The Amazifier snapped his fingers and a hush fell over the crowd.

"Ladies and gentlemen, prepare to be amazed."

In a fluid motion, the Amazifier yanked on the rope and the velvet curtain dropped over Kitty Delphine. The candelabra's flames shot skyward, engulfing the curtain in flames on all sides. Only the model train remained untouched. The flames licking the curtain and the edges of the tracks shifted in all shades of red, orange, yellow, and even pink and purple. No one could have survived a real inferno like it.

A long whistle cut through the air, impossibly loud to come from such a small train (and a fake one at that). The flames retreated. Another yank of the rope and the curtain ascended.

Kitty Delphine was gone. All that remained on the stool was a pile of glittering ash—but that wasn't what made everyone gasp.

"May I present to you . . . the Phoenix Engine!" cried the Amazifier.

The model train was climbing up the spiral train tracks, gaining speed with every blow of its whistle. Real smoke billowed from the chimney as it moved up and around. Gold sparks flared around its wheels with each chug forward.

The train sped faster and faster until it was a metal blur spinning up and down and around the loops of tiny tracks, much faster than any real model could ever move.

Another yank on the curtain, another shower of rainbow sparks and flame, and, just when it seemed the train would sail right off its tracks—BAM! Golden sparks rained outward in a blinding cloud. The train disappeared, tracks and all. The echo of its last whistle reverberated throughout the theater.

The flames receded, the curtain lifted, and Kitty Delphine emerged whole and unharmed, not a single blonde hair singed on her pretty little head. The Amazifier escorted her down off the stool to take their bows amidst enthusiastic cheers. Shouts of "Amazing!" and "Bravo!" rent the air, and quite a few sections of the audience stood up. Gideon Sharpe, however, stayed firmly in his seat, and told himself that what he was seeing was impossible.

Gideon had only ever seen lights like those golden sparks once before. It was impossible that the *Amazifier*, the blundering old fool, could have access to the same kind of power as Gideon's master! It was preposterous! And yet . . .

He knew, though he dreaded the conversation, that he had no choice but to tell the Mechanist. How would they keep their edge over the competition—their edge over the entire city—if someone else had access to their secret weapon?

Somehow, some way, the Amazifier and his fool of an apprentice were using faerie magic. And now it was Gideon Sharpe's job to stop them.

11.

THE HOLLOW VALLEYS

THE CELEBRATION IN HONOR OF THE MOTO-Manse's occupants seemed likely to last well into the night. The top five finalists who would go on to the last round of the Seminal Symposium of Magickal Arts were throwing their own parties all over the city, but the Amazifier was the only one from the circus camp to achieve such an honor. The alchemists, animal tamers, acrobats, and all manner of entertainers A through Z were delighted that one of their own had gotten so far, and they all jumped on the chance to eat, drink, be merry, and, of course, show off.

Chili, stews, and fried dough of every kind from every region of the world simmered and bubbled over dozens of crackling fires. Music, laughter, and the ringing of bells on dancing feet filled the air. It was almost hard to see through all the smoke, but here and there one could catch glimpses of the unusual and amazing—a fire-eater spitting blue flame, a contortionist doing back flips with her ankles under her armpits, step dancers with feet moving so fast they seemed to blur.

Carmer leaned back against a log, comfortable in his seat by the fire and feeling pleased for the first time in days. He watched Kitty, a few yards away, being entertained by the identical acrobats from next door. That someone had managed to find four sets of identical twins who could *all* stand on their heads was quite a feat. A fiddler was playing a merry tune, and Kitty clapped along with the music, laughing as the men tumbled and flipped over one another.

"Of course, there were still dragons in the west, then, you know . . ."

The Amazifier was surrounded by admirers, regaling them with stories of his adventures all over the world. Each telling of a tale grew progressively more outlandish as he was supplied with "just one more" cup of wine. Carmer shook his head but couldn't help smiling. He'd gotten the chewing out of his lifetime on the way back to the camp for his unauthorized changes to the Phoenix Engine—"You could have roasted me alive!" Kitty had shrieked—and the Amazifier had just started to press him for more details about the model train when the party engulfed them all. Carmer was grateful for the stalling time, and besides, everyone deserved a night off.

"You did it, Grit," he said quietly. Though she was several feet away, Carmer knew she could hear him. He looked around to make sure no one was watching him, but their attentions were elsewhere.

Grit sat cross-legged *in* the fire, just near the edge. It was like the fire never touched her; her hair, skin, and clothes all remained intact, none singed in the slightest.

She looked tired, but less so than before. The fire seemed to be energizing her. Every once in a while she would sink her fingers into the embers beneath her, reigniting them as she took a deep breath and closed her eyes. She looked more beautiful and more inhuman than Carmer had ever seen her. It was true he'd just witnessed magic—*real* magic—but this was different. There was much more to the fae than parlor tricks and flying around on ravens. He wondered how much, if anything, he would learn about them in the future.

"Yes, I did," said Grit with satisfaction, opening her eyes. "You helped a bit, too, I suppose."

Carmer smiled.

"But we need to find those faeries," she added seriously.

While their own performance had gone better than they'd hoped, the other magicians were nothing to sneeze at, and the Mechanist blew the audience away yet again.

He had turned half the stage into an ice rink from a single spilled glass of water.

Carmer shivered, despite the heat of the fire, and nodded. "I made a promise, Grit," he said. "I mean to keep it."

Grit raised an eyebrow. "Want to start now?"

"Now?" asked Carmer. "As in tonight?"

"It seems to me that *your* 'magical' community is more than a little distracted this evening," she said with an amused look at the Amazifier. "What better time to do some poking around?"

Carmer had to admit that Grit was probably right. The Mechanist was probably at a party in one of the fine hotels in downtown Skemantis, surrounded by wealthy patrons. He was unlikely to be keeping too close of an eye out for his competitors tonight. "And where should we start poking, exactly?"

"I think we should go to the factory in the Vallows where Echolaken and her sister were taken. There might be some traces there that can tell us something about the Autocats' attack. It might even be the Mechanist's secret base! That's where *I* would put it, if I were an evil human mastermind," said Grit.

Tramping across the city in the dark of night to snoop around an abandoned factory while under constant threat of ambush from ferocious metal beasts did not sound like a particularly enjoyable evening, nor one that boded well for their chances of survival before the third and final round of the competition. And yet, Grit had a point.

"Let's get on with it, then," said Carmer, relinquishing his seat by the fire. He pretended to be warming his hands while surreptitiously lifting Grit onto her now habitual seat on the brim of his hat. Carmer straightened up and looked at the merriment around them. He hoped Kitty would remember to make the Amazifier drink plenty of water before bed. His own misgivings aside, it was easy for Carmer to slip unnoticed away from the crowd.

Carmer untied Eduardo from the other side of the Moto-Manse, where the horse was munching on the grass, utterly indifferent to the revelry around him. Grit scurried down Carmer's arm and sat between Eduardo's ears.

"Make haste, great steed!" teased Grit, affectionately scratching his head. She'd taken an inexplicable liking to the old horse since their first meeting. "Well, a decent trot would be nice."

"Going somewhere?"

Eduardo whinnied, rearing up, and Grit had to cling on to his mane for dear life. Carmer calmed the horse as best he could, looking around wildly until his eyes fell on two figures making their way from behind the tree line.

Two of Madame Euphemia's wooden puppets soon stood before them. Nearly identical, they were outfitted like butlers of fine estates.

"My bones had a feeling you two whippersnappers might try something foolish soon enough." The old crone's gravelly voice echoed strangely out of one of the puppet's mouths.

"You mean you've been spying on us again," corrected Grit.

"This is Manymostly and Merelymuchly," added Madame Euphemia. "They are at your service for as long as needed." The puppets bowed.

"Th-thank you," stammered Carmer, still caught off guard. "But I don't think—"

"Oh, I know they don't look like much, especially Merelymuchly here," interrupted the one on the right.

Carmer assumed this was Manymostly.

"But they can look after themselves, and you, too." Manymostly and Merelymuchly grinned in unison, exposing rows of frighteningly sharp wooden teeth whittled down to points. Their mouths clapped shut once more with a *clack.*

Grit gulped, and Eduardo shied away.

"We can use all the help we can get," Carmer agreed before Grit could protest. "We don't know what will be waiting for us in the Vallows. Thank you, Madame Euphemia."

And so with much coaxing and bribery with apples, Eduardo was convinced to let the puppets ride on his back with Carmer. The boy imagined they must be quite a sight:

a magician's apprentice, two puppets, and a faerie princess riding a horse that was about a decade past due for the glue factory.

Their strange party ventured out into the night, leaving the comfort of the warmth and merriment of the circus camp behind. The Vallows beckoned, cold and uncertain, a dark blight on the glittering skyline of Skemantis.

DANGER!
RESTRICTED AREA
KEEP OUT
Trespassers Subject to Arrest on Sight

A RUSTY, LOPSIDED SIGN hung from the barbed wire fence blocking the entrance to the Vallows. It swayed in the crisp autumn wind, creaking back and forth. Carmer reached for it with one hand, held it up straight, and let it fall back down again with a forlorn *clank*.

Looks like they've rolled out the welcome mat, he mused. Just behind the gate, he could see the ghostly outlines of abandoned buildings and giant slag heaps. They'd left Eduardo tied up a few minutes down the road so as not to attract undue attention.

"The fence has iron in it," Grit muttered from her perch on his hat.

Carmer brushed his fingers across one of the wires,

careful not to cut himself. A liberal dusting of rust flaked off on his hand. "How could you tell?" he teased.

"I just know," Grit said flatly. "Iron repels all things fae. Honestly, even *humans* know that. Didn't your mother ever read you bedtime stories? Nail a horseshoe to your house's front door?"

"Wouldn't know," Carmer mumbled. "Never had either of those."

"Oh," said Grit.

Carmer shuffled his feet in the dirt. "Well," he ventured over the awkward silence, "how are we going to get in now?"

"I think our bodyguards have an idea," Grit said, pointing farther down the fence.

Sure enough, Manymostly (or was it Merelymuchly?) stood at attention, one wooden arm extended toward the Vallows.

"I can't decide if it's creepier when they talk, or when they don't," Grit said as Carmer walked over to the puppet.

They leaned close to examine the area of fence the puppet indicated. Sure enough, two posts in the fence looked slightly newer than the others, and they were metal instead of wood.

"A little light, Grit?" requested Carmer.

"Are you sure that's a good idea?"

"I think we'll have to chance it."

Grit turned her light on just enough to see by, and

Carmer examined the swath of fence. He brushed his fingers along the wire between the posts; no rust.

"There!" he exclaimed in a whisper, pointing at a knot in the wire near the bottom of one of the posts. But it wasn't a knot at all — it was a small handle. Carmer turned it counterclockwise, and the new section of fence swung open without the slightest creak. Carmer bent down to screw the gate shut behind them, but Grit stopped him.

"If the Free Folk taught me anything," she warned, "It's to always have an easy exit. Especially if you're surrounded by a giant iron trap."

They made their way through the slag heaps and abandoned alleyways, careful to send at least one of Madame Euphemia's puppets ahead to check the integrity of the ground. Of course, Carmer thought, whether the hollowed out earth could support *his* weight as opposed to that of a wooden puppet was largely a matter of chance.

"Do you even know where we're going?" Carmer asked. "All of these buildings look the same to me."

"I'll know it when I see it, Carmer," Grit snapped. All the iron was making her edgy. "Echolaken described it to me. Just because *your* shabby human eyes can't see more than two feet in front of — "

Grit stopped. Quite suddenly the alley had opened up onto a main road very different from the others. This one was clearly meant to be residential. Small cabins lined either side of the street, identical shabby tin boxes with copper-plated shingled roofs long since turned crusty and green. Though the Vallows had been abandoned for many years, nature hadn't reclaimed the space. It was as if even the moss didn't dare encroach on such a cold and hopeless place. Carmer felt suddenly exposed, like a deer caught in the headlights of a speeding steam carriage.

At the end of the street stood a massive building that dwarfed all the others around it. It was far more decorated than any of the houses, with a crumbling marble façade of tall pillars. Perhaps this had once made the building look classic and formidable, but now it only emphasized the state of disrepair. The gray speckled archway surrounding the main doors barely stood up. A great, gaping hole sank into the ground beneath it.

The smell of smoke wafted over the breeze from the direction of the building, but the cloudy night made it hard to see exactly where it came from.

"I think we found it," said Carmer.

"Maybe it was the main entrance to the mines," Grit guessed.

Carmer shrugged.

"Scared, Felix Carmer III?" she teased.

"Definitely."

Carmer crept down the center of the deserted road, slowly placing one foot in front of the other. He didn't like the look of the empty houses on too-straight streets surrounding them on either side, even flanked by Many-mostly and Merelymuchly.

When Carmer reached the archway of the main building, he breathed a sigh of relief and put a hand on the marble to steady himself. A chunk crumbled off in his grasp, sending him reeling over the edge of the great hole until the puppets grabbed him under the arms and set him upright.

"Thanks," said Carmer breathlessly.

"Okay, I'm kind of glad they came," admitted Grit.

They edged more carefully under the archway and around the edge of the hole. Carmer tried to keep from looking down into it, but he couldn't help himself. It was all blackness as far down as his eyes (and probably Grit's) could see. They skirted along the entryway, feet scraping on loose pebbles and remnants of concrete, for about twenty feet, until the puppets suddenly leapt forward into the darkness.

"Wait!" Carmer shouted, but his alarm was unwarranted. They'd reached the end of the hole safely; plain but solid-looking floor extended to the back wall. Gently sloping hallways continued on either side. "Which way should we go?" Carmer asked.

"The right one," said Grit.

After a closer look, Carmer saw she was right. Small, slick splashes of oil dotted the corridor on their right, glittering and fresh.

Too fresh, Carmer realized at the same time as Many-mostly and Merelymuchly, who bared their pointy wooden teeth and held glinting carving knives at the ready.

Carmer heard their metallic growling before he saw them. Two Autocats slunk out of the darkness of the right tunnel, orange and blue jeweled eyes flashing.

"The left one! The left one!" Grit shrilled.

Carmer didn't need to be told twice. He took off running.

The hallway continued its downward slope as the Autocats gained on Carmer and Grit, their metal paws clacking against the concrete floor. When the cats were close enough to start nipping at Carmer's heels, Merely-muchly and Manymostly launched themselves at the attackers, knives swinging wildly. The clanging sounds of their fight followed Carmer down the corridor. He tried locked doorway after locked doorway until he was forced to turn at the end of the hall. The puppets could only buy him so much time.

And it wouldn't be enough. Carmer stopped dead in his tracks, nearly toppling over and sending Grit flying. There was no escape. Somehow, he'd led them into a hoist room — a true entrance to the mines below, where workers could be lowered down in groups. A giant mine cage blocked their path, large enough to fit fifteen men. It hung crookedly, suspended by rusted chains over a cavernous drop.

A yowl, a sickening crunch, and the sounds of splintering wood let Carmer know that at least one of Madame

Euphemia's puppets had performed its last show. He yanked open the door of the elevator, ran inside, and slammed it shut behind him. The whole contraption swung from side to side.

"What are you doing?" yelled Grit.

"Improvising!"

Carmer looked around wildly and picked up one of the loose chains on the floor of the cage. He wound it around the door handle several times and knotted it as best he could from the inside. Hopefully, it would be enough to keep the Autocats out, but it also locked him and Grit *in*.

Seconds later, the cage rattled ominously as the two Autocats slammed themselves against it, silver teeth bared and claws extended. Carmer noted with a small amount of satisfaction that the blue-eyed one had a knife stuck in its eye.

"What do we do now?" Grit said worriedly, hatpin sword in hand.

Carmer hadn't thought that far in advance. The blue-eyed cat pawed at the chains wrapped around the door handle, trying to loosen them, but the other one slunk back and paced in front of the elevator, orange eyes flashing. Carmer got the feeling this one was the brains of the operation.

Suddenly, the orange-eyed Autocat leapt against the cage again, sending it swinging. But instead of swiping at Carmer and Grit, the cat started climbing up the side, flakes of rust raining down like snow as its claws raked against the aged metal.

Carmer looked up and realized what it was about to do a second before it happened. "This is not good," he said.

The cat clamped its jaws on the cord that wound around the device keeping the elevator suspended from the ceiling. It used its mouth like a saw, sliding up and down the thick wire cable.

Carmer guessed they had seconds before the cat cut through it and sent them plummeting into the infinite blackness below. He stared up at it, horrified but fixated. They had two options—stay in the cage and fall to their deaths, or leave it and be mauled to death by giant automaton cats. Neither seemed an attractive option.

"Carmer!" snapped Grit, yanking him from his fear-induced stupor.

"What?"

"Smoke bombs. Do you have any left?"

Carmer fumbled in his pockets, coming up with a single, tiny cylinder that smelled faintly of violets.

"Give it here!" ordered Grit.

Carmer held it up to her, and the faerie placed her hands on it, whispering in a language he couldn't understand.

Carmer lost his balance as the cage lurched to one side, sending him careening against the edge. The orange-eyed Autocat had nearly cut the cord through. Carmer darted forward and untied the chains around the door, avoiding the blue-eyed Autocat's swiping claws as best he could. Grit rolled the now-glowing smoke bomb over the brim of his hat; he caught it in shaking fingers.

Carmer kicked open the door with all of his might, sending the Autocat flying. He jumped onto solid ground just as the elevator cable snapped. The orange-eyed Autocat leapt off it with a yowl, and the cage plummeted into the unknown depths below. If it ever hit the bottom, Carmer never heard the crash.

He threw the faerie-enhanced smoke bomb directly at the Autocats and hit the blue-eyed one square in the chest. Whatever happened to the Autocat, Carmer didn't have a chance to see. A cloud of purple smoke as thick as pea soup immediately consumed the automaton, blocking it from view. The purple smoke spread outward in clumpy tendrils, filling the whole hallway. Carmer ran straight at what he hoped was the space between the two cats, dashing back down the hall as fast as his legs could carry him. The cats yowled behind him, bumping into each other and crashing into the walls in their blindness.

Back in the main entryway, Carmer stopped for a moment to catch his breath, hands on his knees. "Let's just hope they don't have nine lives," he gasped.

"What?" asked Grit.

"Never mind. Where are the puppets?"

"Probably in splinters somewhere down a giant hole," Grit guessed darkly. "Let's get out of here!"

She turned her light on brighter to get a better view of the crater in the middle of the floor, now that Manymostly and Merelymuchly weren't there to guide them. Besides, there was little point in secrecy now.

They edged slowly, step by step, toward the main entrance. Carmer thought for a brief moment of the unexplored hallway on the other side, but Grit was right. They needed to get out of the Vallows as soon as possible.

As careful as they were, Carmer's foot caught on something hard jutting out of the rubble, and he nearly tripped.

"I couldn't have run into someone a *little* more coordinated?" Grit said. She hopped down to his shoulder and sat there instead, thrusting her hatpin through the collar of his shirt for extra support. For all of her complaining, though, she was careful not to pinch him with it.

"Sorry," Carmer muttered, distracted. He looked down at the object he'd tripped over; it was an old padlock wedged between two crumbling pieces of what remained of the concrete floor. There was an insignia of some sort engraved on it. He bent down to take a closer look.

The logo was long since worn away, but the engraved text above it was still very much readable in Grit's light:

PROPERTY OF
TITAN INDUSTRIES

12.

AN OFFER YOU CAN'T REFUSE

IT HAD TO BE A COINCIDENCE. IT HAD TO, BUT IT wasn't.

Carmer remembered Titus Archer addressing the crowd around the Hyperion, the captive audience hanging on his every word.

"What if I told you that Titan Industries has recently patented a previously untapped energy source, one that is both clean and unlimited? That we have refined a method of producing electric light that cuts down on nearly half the machinery required and all of the waste?"

Suddenly, the reason for the Mechanist's mask became quite clear.

"Carmer, whatever it is," urged Grit, "it can wait!"

"I don't think it can," Carmer said, standing up slowly. They were halfway across the great chasm, but a glance in either direction told him they had nowhere to go. The orange-eyed Autocat had caught up with them; it stalked back and forth across the back of the hall. Two more Autocats emerged out of the shadows in front of them to block the exit, their jeweled eyes and shiny metal hides glinting in the moonlight. Carmer and Grit were surrounded.

The grating growls of the Autocats echoed in the cavernous dark, increasing in pitch until Carmer was forced to cover his ears. He was just beginning to entertain the notion of jumping into the abyss below when a man's voice cut through the din.

"Stop!"

Titus Archer stepped out from under the crumbling archway. He held a pulsing silver lantern that spilled light into the room, making Carmer see spots in front of his eyes. The Autocats ceased their caterwauling immediately and slunk back into the shadows, their glowing eyes still fixated on Carmer. They looked disappointed to see their prey snatched right out from under their paws.

"Walk toward the light, my boy," said Archer from the doorway. He was dressed in the same unassuming business attire Carmer had seen him in at the technology expo. It made him look even more out of place in their derelict and mysterious surroundings. His expression was inscrutable; he didn't look pleased, but neither did he look inclined to order his Autocats to rip out Carmer's throat.

"What should I—" Carmer started, looking down at his shoulder for Grit. But she wasn't there, and he stopped himself immediately.

Carmer blinked, slowly and deliberately, and glanced down again. Grit was still there. She brought a single finger to her lips and shook her head. Hopefully, her magic was enough to fool Archer.

"I mean, where should I go?" Carmer corrected hastily.

"Just keep to the wall and walk straight ahead," said Archer. "I'm not going to eat you, boy."

But your cats might, thought Carmer grimly, pressing on. Grit climbed up the back of his neck and through the door in his hat. At the end of the vast hole, Titus Archer extended a hand and helped Carmer over the last few piles of crumbling stone. Carmer let go as quick as he could and stared at his shoes, shamefaced and terrified.

Titus Archer and the Mechanist were one and the same. The strange feeling Carmer had gotten during the Hyperion demonstration finally made sense. Archer hadn't invented his own power at all—he'd found a way to force the fae to make it for him.

"I see you've discovered my security system," Archer noted, slightly amused. Two Autocats crept forward again, and Carmer backed away warily, but they simply sat down on their haunches on either side of their master. Archer stroked one of them affectionately behind the ears. "They can be a little overzealous," he admitted. "But . . . effective." He looked stern again.

Carmer gulped.

"Walk with me," said Archer. "Mr. . . .?"

Archer started off before Carmer had a chance to respond. Carmer didn't think he was in a position to refuse to follow.

"Carmer, sir." He followed Archer to the deserted main street, the silver lantern casting a strange half light around them. Something was different about the still, silent houses on either side, as if both their stillness and their silence came less easily now. Carmer couldn't shake the feeling of being watched from just beyond the reach of the lantern's glow.

"Now, Mr. Carmer," said Archer, "would you like to tell me what an upstanding-looking young fellow such as yourself is doing lurking about in the Vallows after dark?"

Carmer glanced down at his muddy boots and tattered patchwork coat. He was far from an expert in such matters, but he was fairly certain he looked the exact opposite of upstanding.

"I was, um . . ." Carmer trailed off. "Well, you see . . ."

Grit was pacing back and forth along her perch inside his hat; Carmer had to reach up and grab the brim to keep it steady.

"Because you know," said Archer, "if you wanted to explore Titan Industries further, all you had to do was ask."

Carmer stopped short.

"Oh yes," Archer said with a chuckle. "I remember you from the Hyperion demonstration. Inquisitive minds can always spot a kindred spirit."

A kindred spirit? Carmer thought. Archer had nearly bitten Carmer's head off for getting too close to the machine.

"I do wonder what you thought you would find all the way out here," said Archer, continuing his stroll through the darkened streets. The gritty slopes of the slag heaps glittered in the lantern's silver light. "Surely, Theian Foundry and the rest of the International Exhibition would have more to hold your interest than an abandoned mine? Few people even remember that Titan Industries was involved in the goings-on here at all."

Carmer's heart hammered in his chest. Archer was trying to figure out how much Carmer knew. Carmer had to say *something*, and say it soon, but his mind was blank. As the moon came out from behind a cloud, a gleam of metal caught Carmer's eye; an Autocat loped from shadow to shadow, following their every step. More were surely close at hand.

"Carmer," a voice hissed into his ear. Carmer nearly jumped out of his skin before he realized it was Grit. "The *birds*."

And then he saw what was different about the houses. The burst of moonlight cast their silhouettes into relief, and the jagged edges lining each rooftop were impossible to miss. But they weren't jagged edges. The mechanical birds from the Mechanist's magic show were perched in silent, watchful rows on every house on the street—hundreds upon hundreds of beady silver eyes trained squarely on Carmer.

Titus Archer saw Carmer notice them and paused, lantern held aloft. His own eyes blazed. Carmer didn't even think to look surprised.

"Ah," Archer said quietly. "It seems the cat's out of the bag, as they say."

The Autocats were suddenly right beside them, one crouched in each doorway on either side of the street.

This is how I die, thought Carmer. All he could do was stare back at the rows of metal doves and picture their sharp, pointy beaks pecking out his eyes. He blurted out the first and only thing that popped into his head: "How do they fly?"

Titus Archer tilted his head, eyes narrowed like one of his cats. "What's that, Mr. Carmer?"

"The birds," Carmer clarified. "I . . . I'd like to know how they fly."

Archer looked at him then—*really* looked at him, the way Madame Euphemia looked at people, like she could see right through their skin and their bones and all the way into the deepest, darkest, locked-up parts of their hearts.

Fortunately, whatever Archer saw there seemed to satisfy him.

"I'm sure you would." With a wave of his hand, Archer shooed away the Autocats, spun on his heel, and kept walking as if nothing at all had happened. "As you can imagine, Mr. Carmer, I am not overeager to have my identity as the Mechanist revealed to the general public. It may be a passing dalliance, but my performances as the Mechanist give me an opportunity to test my new inventions and their various capabilities . . . in the field, if you will. So much of what was once illusion can now be reality, Carmer. It has *been* reality for thousands of years, unbeknownst to most of us." Archer winked.

Under Carmer's hat, Grit shivered. Somehow, Archer knew she was there.

"In return for your silence in the matter, I will compensate you twofold," explained the inventor. "Firstly, I shall let you and any of your . . . associates who may be nearby walk out of here unmolested and without prosecution. This is private property, you know, and a breaking and entering charge would most certainly be a strain on both your finances and your freedom."

Carmer paled. He'd been so concerned about being eaten by the Autocats, he hadn't really thought about what would happen if he were caught by the police.

"Secondly," Archer continued, as if he didn't notice Carmer's distress, "I would like to invite you to my factory tomorrow. My *real* factory."

Carmer stopped walking. "You . . . you want me to what, sir?"

"This little hole in the wall—if you'll pardon the expression—is merely the Mechanist's hideaway; a place to store my magical artifacts, practice my act, and train my assistant without attracting undue attention," explained Archer, continuing on his way toward the barbed wire fence. "Which reminds me, I'll have to have a talk with him about those birds of his."

Carmer scurried to keep up with the man's confident stride.

"As a fellow man of vision, I'd like you to see the real Titus Industries at our research and development head-quarters in downtown Skemantis. I assume you are famil-iar with Theian Foundry."

A small part of Carmer—the part that built his own automaton soldiers and studied combustion engines and wanted to forget faeries existed—would have jumped at the chance to see the laboratory of the legendary Titus Archer.

But Carmer's heart told him that Archer's achieve-ments were suspect, at the very least, and downright evil at most. This latest invention—the electricity-generating Hyperion—was almost certainly powered by dozens, if not hundreds, of enslaved faeries. On the other hand, if Carmer said no—if he walked away from an invitation to observe the Mechanist in his own workshop—he knew he would never have another chance to find the missing fa-eries, repay his debt to Grit, or win the magic competition for the Amazifier.

Carmer wasn't even sure he was at liberty to refuse. The Autocats flanked them on either side, silver claws barely retracted. All it would take was one word from Titus Archer, and he and Grit would be cat food, pecked to death, or tossed down a mineshaft to rot—or possibly a combination of all three.

They reached the edge of the Vallows. The Mechanist stood with one gloved hand on the disguised entrance and looked at Carmer expectantly.

"What do you say, Mr. Carmer?" he asked. "How would you like to learn even more secrets than those of a handful of toy doves?"

"Thank you, sir," was all Carmer could manage, but it was apparently enough for Titus Archer. He extended his lantern in front of them at the gate, lighting up the road back to Eduardo.

"You will come to my home at noon," said Archer. "My apprentice will send you the address." He tipped his own gray bowler hat, and Carmer was forced to do the same, knocking Grit about inside of it.

Carmer winced and looked down to see his fingers smeared with red. Both of his hands were bleeding, covered in small but deep gashes where the blue-eyed Autocat had clawed at them in the cage.

"Don't worry," the Mechanist assured him. "My cats have had all their shots."

Carmer took a deep breath, fighting the wooziness that

suddenly washed over him like a wave. He set his jaw and walked past Archer as steadily as he could manage.

"Oh, and Mr. Carmer?" Archer called to Carmer's back.

Carmer stopped, but didn't turn around.

"Don't be late."

"ABSOLUTELY NOT." GRIT stomped her foot in defiance, then grumbled as her spur pierced the fluffy cushion under her boots. Her foot sank into the plush like quicksand. She yanked it out, a few down feathers coming with it, and scowled. "There is no way you're going into that madman's secret laboratory alone," she insisted. "Look at what he's done to you already!"

Carmer hunched over Madame Euphemia's card table while the old woman cleaned his wounded hands as best she could, dabbing at the cuts with some sort of stinging and smoking mixture that she'd ground together herself with an ancient mortar and pestle. A puppet in an old witch doctor's costume, complete with beaked mask, cut strips of long white linen bandages with a small, sharp scythe.

"The princess has a point," said Madame Euphemia.

Carmer hissed in pain as her homemade remedy hit a particularly deep cut.

"Hold still. If even my boys were no match for these cats of his," the old woman continued, "I fear this man is a more powerful foe than we could have imagined."

"I'm sorry about Manymostly and Merelymuchly, Madame Euphemia," Carmer apologized. It was strange how easy it was to remember their names now that they were gone. "Grit, it's too risky for you," Carmer continued. They'd been having the same argument all the way back to the camp. "Who knows what would happen if Archer caught you and found a way to control your magic?"

"So his stupid lamp would glow a little brighter," Grit scoffed. "I'm willing to risk it—"

"You shouldn't be," Madame Euphemia interrupted, surprising them both. "You're a royal fire faerie, Princess, whether you like it or not. If the Mechanist were to gain control of your power, he would be nearly impossible to stop."

"See?" said Carmer.

Grit sat on her cushion with a huff. She didn't understand why everyone seemed to think she was so powerful. Certainly, Queen Ombrienne had never told her as much. Until a few days ago, Grit wasn't sure that her own magic could be half as good as an average faerie's. And now, even so . . .

"What if he can give you what I can't?" she asked. She had to. "What if he promises a guaranteed future for you and Kitty and the Amazifier? What will your answer be then?"

Carmer tried not to be hurt by her suggestion, and mostly succeeded. After all, the only reason he'd started helping Grit in the first place was in exchange for her magic. She had no reason to believe he had altruistic motives where the fae were concerned.

"Girl, you've got some nerve," scolded Madame Euphemia, now wrapping Carmer's hands in the bandages helpfully supplied by the wooden witch doctor. "This boy got himself diced up like minced meat for you, and you think he's going to hand you over for a few pieces of silver?" Madame Euphemia shook her head, the beads on the ends of her rainbow braids jingling.

Grit looked abashed, a blush creeping across her cheeks. "I only meant that—"

"It's all right, Grit," said Carmer. "But we need to know what the Mechanist is up to. And if other faeries are there, I promise, I'll do everything I can to get them out. But you need to stay here in the camp with Madame Euphemia. It's probably the only place in the whole city you'll be safe."

Grit wasn't pleased. She bounced up from the cushion and drew her hatpin from its sheath. "Oh, what I wouldn't give to poke one of those stupid cats right in the whiskers!" she said. "You know, Carmer, you should really think about getting a sword yourself."

Carmer laughed. The idea that he would ever be coordinated enough not to stab *himself*, never mind a swiftly moving automaton, was certainly amusing. "As hard as it may be to believe," Carmer said, wincing again as Madame Euphemia tied up the ends of his bandages, "my life was a lot less full of danger before I met you. I don't think I'll be making a habit out of it."

Madame Euphemia made a sound that might have been a snort, and the witch doctor puppet brandished his scythe with a cheerful swish.

13.

IN THE LION'S DEN

AS HE STOOD ON THE DOORSTEP OF TITUS ARCHER'S town house, Carmer couldn't shake the feeling that he was about to be turned away or tapped on the shoulder and told to scram by a passing city watchman. Every inch of him felt shabby compared to the pristine whitewashed mansions and meticulously trimmed flower beds around him.

A silver-faced humanoid automaton opened the door and silently ushered him inside, gliding along subtle grooves inlaid in complicated patterns all over the white marble floor.

The place was hardly what Carmer imagined an evil lair looked like. It was actually a surprisingly light and open space. Contrary to the style of the time, the first floor was sparsely furnished, with polished silver and chrome accents the only nod to the industrialist's immense wealth. The one brightly colored feature of the room was a very real, fully grown tiger lounging on a zebra-striped rug in the middle of the floor. It barely lifted its massive head to glance at Carmer as he entered. Perhaps it decided he wouldn't make much more than a snack.

Titus Archer's fascination with cats of every kind was apparent in his home; they were everywhere. No Autocats—Carmer hoped *they* were safely back in the Vallows—but cats, all the same. There were cats carved in shiny black onyx standing guard on the mantelpiece, a complete lion's skull in a glass case, electrical lamp bases with cats sculpted in twisting silver wire, the bulbs held in their upturned paws, and twin bookcases with howling spotted leopards carved in the corners—each and every detail intricately rendered. It was a *lot* of cats.

The door shut behind Carmer with a click.

The butler automaton gestured to Carmer's hat with its bladelike fingers. Carmer almost handed it over until he remembered the faerie-friendly alterations inside. Though the Mechanist probably knew about Grit, there was no reason to add fuel to the fire.

"I, uh . . . I'll hold on to it, thanks," said Carmer. He could've sworn an eyebrow-shaped ripple raised itself in the automaton's smooth metal face, but it didn't reach for the hat again. It motioned for him to sit down and bowed, gliding backward up a ramp that ran alongside the stair-case and out of sight.

Carmer lowered himself onto a high-backed white sofa as far from the tiger as he could get—which, due to the arrangement of the room, was not very far.

Directly in front of him, a display of ornate masks hung over the fireplace, like the kind performers wore at the opera or during Carnivale. All were in metallic shades of gold, silver, copper, and bronze, and while many were feline-inspired, some were not; Carmer spotted a sun and moon, a wolf, and a knight's helm. Off to one side, blend-ing inconspicuously with the others in the display, was the Mechanist's silver clockwork mask.

"It's a bit cheeky of me, I know," admitted the Mechanist. He stood behind the white sofa, his hands resting inches from Carmer's head. His silver wristbands peeked out from the cuffs of his sleeves. Carmer had no idea how long he'd been standing there.

"But I can't resist tempting fate every now and again." Archer crossed to the fireplace and took down the silver mask. He held it up to his face and dropped his hands, but instead of falling to the floor, the mask hovered in the air before him. It floated toward his face, impossibly small gears clicking and spinning. The whirring noise continued as it adhered to his face, the metal bending and twisting to accommodate every facial feature. When the Mechanist turned to face Carmer, his face was half silver, and even without his gruesome cloak, he looked more terrifying than he ever had on stage.

"And as usually happens when you tempt fate," said the Mechanist, "you get caught."

The Mechanist seemed amused, like he was congratulating Carmer on finding him out, but it was hard to tell his expression behind the mask. All Carmer saw was white teeth and flashing eyes.

"Shall we go to my laboratory?"

"EAT SOMETHING, GIRL."

Grit stood in the windowsill of Madame Euphemia's vardo, watching a tentative rain sprinkling down outside. Dark clouds were circling over the camp; soon, it would be raining in Skemantis, too, if it wasn't already. Grit hoped that a few showers would be the most of Carmer's problems this afternoon.

Madame Euphemia had set out tea for them with the help of one of her puppet maids. (The wooden girl looked rather dejected in the absence of her butler comrades.) There was a thimble full of honey for Grit, along with roasted pumpkin seeds and baked cinnamon apples. The autumn feast was clearly meant to cheer her up, but it just made her homesick. As much as Grit hated the suffocating confinement of the Great Willow, she missed Bressel and Dusten and even—though she would never admit it out loud—Queen Ombrienne. Her kingdom was in real trouble, and for all she knew, they thought she had abandoned them to run off with the Free Folk and left them to face the Wingsnatchers alone.

"I'm not hungry, thank you," said Grit stiffly. No old human woman, Friend of the Fae or not, was going to tell her what to do.

"As you like," said Madame Euphemia, "but these cards tell me you'll be needing your strength, soon enough." The old woman was smoking a long purple pipe and knitting a lumpy shawl. Occasionally, she set down her needles to idly flip through her faded set of tarot cards.

"Your cards told you Carmer and I would be part of the 'great change' coming to Skemantis, and we haven't solved anything. It would be nice of them to tell you something useful for once."

"When your mother looks into the stars, when she takes a cut of the root of the Great Willow and studies its rings, does she always know what the signs are trying to tell her?" asked Madame Euphemia.

Grit blushed.

"I didn't think so. And I'm far from being a faerie queen. So you'll pardon my lack of an instruction manual."

"I wanted to ask you about that," said Grit. "I've heard of Friends of the Fae, but I've never heard of one commanding the kind of power you do. This wagon, the puppets, your Sight? How do I know for sure you're different from the Mechanist?" Grit felt badly for suggesting it as soon as the words were out of her mouth. It was obvious that Madame Euphemia was anything but evil.

"I was born with the Sight, Grettifrida," said Madame Euphemia, taking a long draw from her pipe. She blew out bright purple smoke rings that danced around the room. "Is a human with a touch of the Second Sight such an impossible thing? A bit like a faerie with one wing, no?" She winked, and then sighed. "That was a long, long time ago. Before I met the Thorn with Wings."

"The Thorn is my grandfather," said Grit. "Queen Willowright chose him to continue her line. But he disappeared . . ."

"Ah, so that's what they're telling the young folks these days," said Madame Euphemia with a chuckle. "Funny how all creatures can be a bit selective about their stickier bits of history."

"Selective?" asked Grit, raising her eyebrows.

"The Thorn was Willowright's partner, this is true, but he was also mine," explained Madame Euphemia. Her flashing knitting needles paused in their work as she smiled.

"*You* were the Thorn's . . . partner?" Grit asked, a blush creeping up her neck. "But how?"

"He made the ultimate sacrifice," said Madame Euphemia. "After I was named a Friend, he took human form to be with me, and left the fae behind forever."

Grit gasped. The idea of faeries giving up their power

to live among humans was something only talked about in whispers, and many thought it wasn't even possible. It was a myth among the mythical.

"He used up all of his magic for the change," said Madame Euphemia sadly. She sniffed, eyes suddenly misty, and the puppet maid handed her an embroidered handkerchief. She blew her nose with gusto. "Thank you, dear," she said to the puppet, then turned to Grit again. "Or so we thought. He lived as a human for the rest of his life. It wasn't always easy, but we were happy as clams."

Grit hadn't met many clams, but she assumed this was pretty happy. "And now?"

Madame Euphemia took another puff of her pipe and blew out more purple smoke rings; this time they were shaped like hearts. One crept over Grit's head, and she batted at it until it dissipated.

"When a faerie dies," said Madame Euphemia more seriously, "their heart's magic goes back into the earth. It goes into the dirt that makes the grass grow, the first spark that lights a fire, a little baby's first laugh. And most of all, it goes back to the fae themselves; the power circles onto the next generation. This is the natural progression of things."

Grit nodded; she had never seen a faerie die, but that much she knew.

Madame Euphemia turned over three cards. "But it doesn't have to be," she continued. "When the Thorn died, the magic keeping him human was freed again, and he left it to me instead. His gift is what makes my little home bigger on the inside, what gives my puppets life and lets me speak through them. Queen Willowright made me a Friend, but the Thorn's legacy made me much more than that."

"Is that what your cards told you would happen, back when you were young?" asked Grit. A faerie not only giving up his magic to live as a human and die a mortal death, but bequeathing his powers to a human as well? It was unthinkable, and up until now, Grit had thought it impossible. She imagined herself giving up her magic to a dolt like Felix Carmer III and nearly laughed aloud. She jumped onto the table and surveyed the three cards beneath her: the Magician, the Queen of Wands, and the Wheel of Fortune.

"Well, they weren't as specific as all that," said Madame Euphemia.

"What about these? What do they say?"

The paper Magician seemed to look up at her with a knowing smirk. She resisted the urge stomp on his face with her spurs.

"Oh, these aren't my cards, Grettifrida." The old woman grinned. "They're yours."

THE MECHANIST'S SECRET laboratory was hardly secret at all, a fact Carmer tried to not find too disappointing. Theian Foundry was only a few blocks away from Archer's town house, but the inventor insisted on taking a circuitous route via the Relerail, which was, according to him, the best way to see the "true scope" of the city. He even explained how the platforms worked. (Carmer had been right about the springs under the plates.)

Like many things in Skemantis, Theian Foundry was a hodgepodge of old and new, a cluster of multipurpose and repurposed buildings nestled between the loose borders of the theater and financial districts—some bustling with activity, others ominously silent except for the regular puffing of their smokestacks. The brand-new streetlamps scattered every few yards were dim now, and though Carmer could see no power lines aboveground, he was willing to bet they were electric.

Solemn white marble columns framed the entryway of the main laboratory, a stark contrast against the gleaming black front door. Carmer remembered the similar columns at the crumbling entrance to the Vallows and suppressed a shiver.

This was the innovation hub of Titan Industries. Inside, orderly rows of lab tables extended from one wall all the way to the back of the building. They were covered with bits and pieces of automata in various stages of completion, dissected lightbulbs in all shapes and sizes, miniature dynamos spinning idly, flames floating in glass mantles filled with multicolored oils, machines with no immediately obvious use churning and clicking away. The walls were lined with shelves upon shelves of glass vials, bottles, measuring equipment, ropes of cables, wires of copper and silver and gold, spare gears and hammers and nails, and even a few jars of pickled things Carmer suspected had once been alive. Serious-looking men, both young and old, worked in clusters at each station. The entire ceiling was one large mirror that made the lab seem to go on indefinitely.

Carmer thought of the shabby room in the Moto-Manse he shared with the Amazifier and felt suddenly self-conscious. All of this equipment was top of the line, the glassware so clean it shined, every gear and cog turning smoothly. This was how a proper inventor should work.

A plain black door near the back marked AUTHO-RIZED PERSONNEL ONLY with a curious hole in the door-knob caught Carmer's attention, but Archer shook his head.

"I'm afraid that door is for a time when we are a little better acquainted," was all Archer said, and ushered Carmer up a grand staircase to the second floor. Another black door with an odd, concave doorknob met them at the top of the stairs. Archer rolled up the cuff of his sleeve, exposing the wristwatch-like band Carmer had glimpsed during the Mechanist's performance. The small bright orb mounted on the inside of it was a swirling jewel of silver and white with a faint bluish hue. Archer pressed the stone into the door handle; it pulsed with the silvery glow that usually accompanied the Mechanist's magic, and the door sprang open.

"Welcome to my personal study, Mr. Carmer."

The first thing Carmer noticed about Archer's office, other than its extraordinary size, was the books. Every wall was lined from floor to ceiling with shelves upon shelves of leather-bound volumes. Each section was impeccably organized, labeled with brass tags on every imaginable subject matter from anatomy to history, physics to zoology, even poetry. It was a scholar's paradise.

The second thing he noticed was that the room had no floor. There *was* a floor, of course, but it was made entirely of glass, offering a complete view of the laboratory below. The workers there seemed unaware they were being watched — or perhaps they were just used to it.

"A two-way mirror?" Carmer asked. He took a few tentative steps and was relieved to find he did not plummet onto the men below. It was an odd sensation, like walking on air.

Archer smiled. "One of my better ideas, if I do say so myself."

Carmer glanced up at the black ceiling; there was no mirror there, but Carmer could tell it was made of glass. Perhaps Archer could spy on whatever was above as well as below.

Carmer turned his gaze back to the study. Like Archer's home, it was sparsely furnished, except for Archer's desk and a few showpieces — mostly complex automata, some humanoid and some not, that made Carmer's windup soldier look like a nutcracker. They were polished to a shine, but their stillness was unnerving. Carmer was careful not to get too close as he walked among them.

"Well, what do you think of my little operation, Mr. Carmer?" asked Archer.

"It's . . . it's very impressive, sir," said Carmer truthfully. He noticed the black door was shut behind him, though he hadn't heard it close.

"Theian Foundry is the leading research and development center in the country," said Archer. "The first of its kind, really. Here, the brightest minds converge every day, at my personal invitation, to invent and improve the kind of technology people couldn't even dream of ten years ago."

"Electricity, you mean, sir?"

"Electricity," agreed Archer. "And other things."

Carmer reached a display case filled with butterfly wings, each labeled by species in a delicate hand. He could only hope they all came from butterflies. "Other things?"

"There are untapped resources this earth has provided us with, Mr. Carmer," said Archer. "Resources a select few, including myself, have only started to unlock the wonders of."

Now they were getting to the point.

"You mean the telluric currents, sir?" prodded Carmer, harkening back to the Hyperion display at the exposition. But playing dumb wasn't his strong suit, and Archer knew it.

The older man pressed his lips together in a thin smile. "I believe the currents are an important part of it, yes. Many of them fall along what some of your magically inclined associates might call 'ley lines.' Did you know, for example, that the old arboretum right here in Skemantis is a cross section of not two, but *three* ley lines?"

Carmer shook his head.

"Some superstitious folk here think the ley lines are what power the lights there, that the energy in those currents is what makes our machines go haywire in the vicinity. They would have inquiring minds keep our noses out, as it were. But at Theian Foundry, we aim to separate fact from fiction, and all old wives' tales have a grain of truth, if one looks hard enough."

Carmer made himself meet Archer's gaze. "Did you find what you were looking for, then?"

"That," said Archer, "and more."

They had nearly reached Archer's desk. Behind it, a picture window offered a spectacular view of the city beyond. The silhouettes of towers, spires, train tracks, and smokestacks pierced the bright afternoon skyline like pieces of a shadow play.

"Have you ever seen what a coal miner's lungs look like, Mr. Carmer?" Archer asked abruptly.

Carmer stared at him. "No, sir."

"They look like this." Archer swung a standing display case covered in maps around—did *everything* this man owned run on wheels?—and Carmer was faced with specimens much more sensational than butterfly wings.

Two shriveled gray lumps were pinned beneath the glass, pockmarked and eaten through with black. "They say Skemantis is the city of the future, and I believe it can be. But these are just some of the consequences of our so-called revolution so far."

The skeleton of a clubbed foot, a rubbery enlarged heart, and a few other gruesome souvenirs completed the board. Carmer couldn't help it; he looked away.

"Every man who dies with an invisible weight crushing his chest from the inside," said Archer, "every child who loses a finger working long hours with merciless machines, every street that remains dark in order for another to be lit thousands of miles away. They are left behind."

Much to Carmer's surprise, Titus Archer actually sounded . . . sincere. It was certainly the last thing he'd expected to hear from him.

"I admit to being a crusader for the tide of progress, Mr. Carmer. I cannot pretend otherwise. It is what made me the man I am today."Archer sighed and settled himself in the throne-like chair behind the desk.

Carmer stood, but it didn't keep him from feeling small all the same.

"But I was once a boy like you, Mr. Carmer, with nothing to my name except a burning desire to understand how the world works. And because I was that boy, I know it can work better. It *must* work better, if any age of progress is to be a real one."

For just one moment, Carmer was almost caught up in Archer's spell. The man really seemed to *believe* in what he was saying. And if it was true, if he really had come from nothing and gotten this far, become this successful, then maybe someone like Carmer stood a chance, too. Archer honestly seemed to *care* about the people he was inventing things for, which is not something Carmer could say about a lot of the men of science he'd studied, or even (if he was being truthful) about himself.

Then Carmer remembered that Archer's idea of the world as a better place most likely involved the enslavement of an entire species.

"How would you like to help me?" asked Archer.

Carmer nearly jumped. "What?"

Archer steepled his long fingers together.

"I, um, sorry. Sir."

"I see a lot of promise in you, Mr. Carmer," continued Archer, as if Carmer had not spoken. "I see a lot of myself. With a proper education, you could do very well on my team. We even have a boarding house for the young men here. Imagine working each day with peers who actually shared your interests?" Archer raised his eyebrows knowingly. "We both know you're no magician, Mr. Carmer. Leave that nonsense behind you, and leave the Magickal Symposium to me. When the dust settles, you'll have the apprenticeship of a lifetime waiting for you."

"I already have an apprenticeship, Mr. Archer," said

Carmer quietly. He remembered how Archer had yelled at Gideon Sharpe in the dressing room when he thought no one was listening. Whatever face Titus Archer showed to the world when he thought it counted, it was as much of an act as his performance as the Mechanist.

"Do you?" The teasing malice in his eyes was unmistakable now. Archer would find a way to stop the truth getting out, whether Carmer joined him or not.

"I do. And I should be getting back. But thank you for the offer, sir."

Archer's eyes darkened, and for a moment, Carmer had a horrible vision of all of the automatons springing to life and dragging him away to whatever grisly fate usually awaited those who discovered the inventor's secrets. But they stayed still and quiet as the grave.

Carmer bowed with more respect than he felt.

"I encourage you to think carefully about the side you have chosen, Mr. Carmer," said Archer, voice cold. "I will not ask again."

Carmer nodded, and turned to leave.

It was over twenty minutes later, while Carmer was on the Relerail back to the edge of the city, when he thought of the perfect reply.

Sorry, Mr. Archer, but I'm afraid I'm allergic to cats.

14.

MEN IN BLACK

GRIT FINALLY MANAGED TO BARGAIN HER WAY out of Madame Euphemia's claustrophobic sitting room with the promise that she would go straight to the Moto-Manse, but there wasn't much to do there besides wait for Carmer to return. She entertained herself by making the model train zoom around the room until sparks flew out from the tracks, shooting the little bolts of energy that flowed, almost naturally now, from her fingertips through its insides. She tried coming up with ideas for the third and final round of the Symposium, but it was impossible to settle on anything; she didn't know enough about Carmer's kind of magic to put together something magical *and* plausible on her own.

She finally lay down on top of Carmer's desk, watching the planets in his model solar system make their slow journey around the plaster sun, and just for a moment, she let herself feel homesick. Staring at the colored spheres until they blurred in front of her eyes, she could almost imagine they were the colors of the Arboretum—the lush green of the grass in spring, the blue roses in full bloom, the fiery leaves at their autumn peak just before the real cold of winter set in. Everything would be nearly brown and sleeping by now, though. (Humans might even say "dead," but the fae knew better.)

There were things Grit didn't miss about living in the castle, of course. Like her mother's constant scolding, or worse—the times when Ombrienne ignored Grit, retreating into cold silence and disappointment. Grit would climb to the very top of the Great Willow, where not even the armored crickets or Bressel would follow her, and look out into the kingdom—*her* kingdom—wishing for nothing more than to be able to fly away from it all.

Grit had thought her outings with Ravene and Remus were exciting adventures, but now she was in the middle of a real one, and it was far more dangerous than she'd ever imagined. The fate of her kingdom was in her hands and the hands of a strange human boy, and her people had no idea.

But she'd faced the Wingsnatchers—poor, "defenseless" little Grit—and survived. She and Carmer could best the beasts yet, she was sure of it now. She'd discovered a power she didn't even know she possessed, all because an oddball human boy thought she could work miracles.

Felix Cassius Tiberius Carmer III. His social ineptitude and frequent thickheadedness baffled her, but she had to admit that if she couldn't have run into a Friend of the Fae in the alley that day, she was glad to have run into him. He'd come in pretty handy against the Autocats, after all. Now he was walking into the dragon's lair . . . but Grit refused to admit that she was worried about him. Wallowing in homesickness was quite enough wasted feeling for one day, thank you very much.

Grit blinked, bringing the spinning planets once more into focus. She heard a footfall on the stair and scrambled off Carmer's desk. She didn't want to be spotted, and she needed to conserve her energy for magic in the final round of the Symposium. She ducked into a slightly open drawer in Carmer's filing cabinet just as Antoine the Amazifier shuffled in. She peeked out and watched him fiddle with a few fizzing mixtures and scribble notes in his untidy scrawl, all while humming absently to himself. She hoped he wouldn't decide that tonight was a fine night to spend hours in his study.

A great chime suddenly rang out, like someone striking a gong. The entire Moto-Manse shook from the sound. Startled, Grit let go of the edge of the drawer and fell inside the cabinet, crushing papers beneath her. She cringed, but the Amazifier was more preoccupied with the thunderous chiming.

"Kitty!" he called down the stairs. "Would you get the door, my dear?" He mumbled something about guests running away before he could answer the door, and how he should *really* get around to adjusting those acoustics, before he toddled off, shutting the door behind him.

Grit exhaled. She extricated herself from the crumpled papers, swearing. She'd torn one sheet with the spurs of her boots. *Great*, thought Grit. As if Carmer needed something *else* to complain about. Grit clambered out of the drawer, pulling the file with her. She smoothed it out on top of the cabinet as best she could—and then stopped, hands frozen in mid-motion.

The drawing on the paper was a diagram of a wing, and not just any wing: a faerie wing. And yet it wasn't. Instead of joints and tissue, there were gears and plates and wires. Notes in Carmer's handwriting were scribbled in the margins—"Weight of glass?" and "Aerodynamic functionality?" and "How to control—manually? Depends on muscle strength." He'd even designed a pulley system attached to the wrist that would (in theory) allow the wing to open and close.

Grit backed away from the paper, a flush rising in her cheeks and bile in her throat. Her heels left scorch marks as they skidded across the drawing.

So this was what Carmer had planned for her. When it came down to it, she was no more than a science experiment to him, another creature to stick in a jar and prod at, another pet project, like his stupid soldier. Another machine to *fix*. He'd told her she was powerful, that her magic could be different, that he had faith in her. But just like her mother, just like the street fae, he didn't really accept her. People just couldn't accept an impossible thing, however much they pretended to try.

She imagined Carmer staring at her, studying her wing without her permission. Leave it to humans to think that their feeble inventions could achieve what ancient faerie healing magic could not! The arrogance was infuriating.

Grit unsheathed her sword and hacked savagely at the parchment, hot tears stinging her eyes. It was only the sound of raised voices outside the Moto-Manse that brought her back to herself.

"This is an outrage!" protested the Amazifier.

Grit leapt to the window and saw the old man hastening out the front door behind a tall, imposing stranger in a black robe.

"You have no proof!"

The stranger turned to face him so suddenly that the Amazifier nearly walked into his chest.

"Nevertheless," said the other man calmly, "the accusation has been made, and an inquiry must follow." He swept away with a swish of his well-made cloak.

Kitty and Carmer hovered nervously nearby. They looked as surprised to see the man in black as Grit was.

"Master Antoine?" Kitty asked. "What in heavens is going on?"

Carmer's face fell as he watched the retreating figure. "I think I have an idea."

"DO YOU KNOW what I was doin'? The other afternoon at the theater?"

Kitty spooned a liberal amount of sugar into her tea and took a fortifying gulp. She and Carmer huddled at the Moto-Manse's tiny kitchen table with their feet resting on the stove. It was a chilly autumn night, and neither of them felt like socializing with the other campers around a fire that evening.

Carmer shook his head. As preoccupied then as he was now, he vaguely remembered something about Kitty's bag being bigger than usual.

"I was showin' samples of my work to the costume designer at the opera house," admitted Kitty. "One of the girls who cuts and drapes there complimented me on my costume after our show. She said they'll need more hands on deck when the holiday season gets in swing."

"Were you always going to leave, Kitty?" asked Carmer. He tried to keep his voice even.

"You and I both know this trip was the last hurrah, honey," said Kitty, crossing her arms. "Did you really think we were gonna win that competition and keep runnin' the circuit like old times? Or maybe, we'd book our own steady gig at the Orbicle?" Kitty laughed. "I knew you were dumb, Carmer, but I never took you for stupid. And you know what I mean."

Carmer shut his mouth and sipped his tea. The Amazifi-er's cup sat on the table next to him, cold and untouched. The old man had retreated to the sleeping berths and hardly said a word after he told Kitty and Carmer about the man in black. The man was one of the judges of the com-petition, and he'd come to inform them that the Amazifier was suspended from the Seminal Symposium of Magickal Arts on suspicion of cheating. An "anonymous source" had placed a formal complaint with the judges, and now a full-scale inquiry would be made into the Amazifier's act.

The magical world was rife with theft—this was noth-ing new—but it would be bad press to ignore an official and public complaint during the Symposium, when the public eye was trained directly on the Orbicle. Until the in-ternal investigation was over, the Amazifier was forbidden to compete, and since the final round of the competition was less than two days away, he was effectively blocked from the competition for good.

Carmer couldn't blame Kitty for making contingency plans. Not really. They all needed to survive in this world, and Kitty was a talented girl. What skills did Carmer have to fall back on? He didn't think tinkering with toy soldiers would count for much on his application to any of the sci-ence academies in Skemantis.

All at once, the futility of entering the Symposium seemed to crash down on him. Had he really thought they had a chance? Their little band of misfits barely scraped by on tips from small-town crowds who wouldn't know a hat trick from a handkerchief. Even if they won the competition with Grit's magic on their side, what happened after she went back to the Arboretum? People would start asking questions—questions Carmer couldn't answer—and it wouldn't be long before the public figured out that Antoine the Amazifier wasn't so amazing after all.

"I hope you get the job, Kitty," Carmer said, and he meant it. It had been foolish of him to expect things to stay this way forever.

Kitty ruffled Carmer's hair. "But then, I think," she said in mock horror, "'Who's gonna make those poor boys their tea?'"

AS SOON AS Carmer smelled burning paper, he knew something was wrong. He vaulted across the attic to the smoldering sheet on his desk and grabbed the nearest pair of safety gloves. He patted the embers out and looked around for other signs of fire, but there were none.

Grit sat in the open window, still as a statue, her face turned away.

"Grit?" Carmer asked. She didn't acknowledge him. Carmer looked down at the ruined papers in his hands and recognized them instantly: the rough plans he'd sketched for a mechanical wing. *Her* mechanical wing, eventually. "Grit, I didn't—"

"Didn't what, Carmer?" Grit interrupted, still facing the window. "Didn't want me to see those until they were finished? Didn't think I'd mind? Or didn't know, because you never *asked* me?" She whipped around then, and Carmer could almost see the fire in her eyes.

"I thought you'd be pleased!" he said, suddenly annoyed. As if his day could get any worse. "I thought maybe I could help you. You could fly on your own, you wouldn't have to hide in my hat all the time . . ."

"Oh, there it is," said Grit, standing up. The lamps in the room started to flicker of their own accord. "There's the real reason you thought of this—for your own convenience! Getting tired of carting your defective faerie around? Did you think I'd *stay* with you after all this was over? That I'd flutter behind you like your old horse in his reins, your own personal pet?"

Carmer stood in stunned silence. He wasn't good at confrontation—he never had been—and all the words he wanted to say in his own defense jumbled up in his head, ricocheting around in inarticulate streams of thoughts and feelings. Like when he was cornered by the bullies in the alley, or the other children in the orphanage so long ago, or by the adults who took his oddness and curiosity for insolence. Somewhere inside of him, a wall went up, and anything he might have said stopped right at the great lump in his throat.

Grit saw the tears well up in Carmer's eyes and let loose the breath she hadn't realized she'd been holding.

"You didn't even ask me," she repeated quietly. "You didn't ask me what *I* wanted."

"I'm sorry, Grit," Carmer managed.

"I'm used to it," she scoffed. "Most people don't." *I don't know why I thought you'd be any different.*

Carmer crumpled the ruined plans in his hand and threw them in the overflowing wastebasket. He sank down onto the floor and tossed aside his gloves. "We've been suspended from the competition," Carmer said, lowering his head into his hands.

"What?!"

"*Someone* lodged an official complaint with the judging committee accusing us of cheating."

"But that's ridiculous!" exclaimed Grit.

Carmer just looked at her.

"Oh. Well . . ."

They both smiled grimly.

"Do they have any proof?" she asked.

"Not yet, but that doesn't mean they won't find any. It's not safe for you here, Grit."

"It's not safe for me anywhere," Grit countered.

Carmer sighed. "It's all the Mechanist," he said. "Titus Archer. He offered me a deal. Let him win the Symposium, keep quiet about his identity, and I get to work with him in his lab. I said no."

So an accusation of cheating was the Mechanist's response to Carmer's refusal. Grit couldn't help feeling proud of the boy. "Oh, Carmer."

"I should never have used your magic in the first

place," he said. "If I hadn't, maybe things wouldn't be so messed up."

Grit's sympathy vanished. "Wait a minute, so this is *my* fault?"

"Grit, I didn't say that. Why do you always have to—"

"No one forced you to help me, Felix Carmer," said Grit, indignant once more. "We had a deal, and I held up my end of the bargain."

"Well, so did I!" Carmer said. "And look where it got both of us."

They turned away from each other, sulking in silence.

"If that's the way you feel about it, fine," said Grit primly. "I know who the Mechanist is now. I can handle things on my own from here."

"Grit, wait a second!" protested Carmer, but the faerie jumped from the window ledge and shimmied down the ivy growing down the Moto-Manse's side. She'd already climbed down from the wheel spokes and fled into the tall grass before Carmer even made it to the window. She was *fast* when she wanted to be.

"Grit!" Carmer called, looking desperately for her small form in the thick, reedy grass. It was too dark outside to see much more than a few feet from the Moto-Manse.

"Carmer, what on Earth are you yelling at?" came Kitty's voice from downstairs.

Carmer gave a frustrated sigh. "Nothing, Kitty!"

Grit ran away from the Moto-Manse as fast as her short

legs could carry her, the light of the moon peeking through the tall blades of grass her only guide. She didn't look back. It was better this way, she told herself. For both of them.

From her post in the shadows of the Moto-Manse, a little wooden maid watched the faerie princess dart away and shrunk back into the darkness.

IT WAS VERY, very late.

Probably too late for respectable young ladies to be out on the town by themselves, Kitty Delphine knew, but then again, respectable young ladies didn't run away from home to join the circus, either. She'd never been a conventional girl.

Kitty tugged her faux rabbit fur shrug around her shoulders and took a fortifying sip of her drink. She sat at the bar in the lounge of the Legerdemain, one of the fancier hotels in Skemantis. It was a favorite of wealthy thespians, visiting businessmen, and all sorts of new money types looking to show off their wealth in the lap of luxury. She'd only managed to sneak in with her best gown and a promise to show one of the kitchen boys how to breathe fire.

The gaslights were turned low — to add to the mysterious ambiance, Kitty supposed — and she had to squint to make out the faces of the group of men smoking at the billiard table on the other side of the hall.

Not for the first time, she questioned what she was doing here, but then she remembered the look on poor little

Carmer's face when she'd mentioned looking for another job, and she steeled herself. She stole another glance at the men across the way from underneath her eyelashes. Sure enough, she recognized at least two of them as judges from the Symposium. The judging committee members were supposed to be a secret, but it was one of the worst kept in the city. But how to approach them?

A man sat down next to her at the bar, blocking the group from view. Kitty dropped her gaze back down to her glass.

"A rum swizzle, if you'd be so kind," the man told the bartender. His smooth voice sounded awfully familiar.

The bartender nodded and busied himself preparing the man's drink.

"And another glass of champagne for the lovely lady here," added the man.

Kitty nearly jumped.

Conan Mesmer, the charismatic—if slightly slimy—emcee of the Symposium smiled wolfishly at her. "What brings you to this fine establishment, Miss Delphine? I would have thought the Amazifier's retinue would be packing up by now."

Kitty wondered how he remembered her name.

"I'm surprised you recognized me, Mr. Mesmer," she said with a tinkling laugh. "Most people don't pay us assistants any mind."

The bartender placed their drinks in front of them.

"I make it a point to know all of the talent that graces my stage." Mesmer slid a crisp bank note across the counter and told the bartender to keep the change. He was so slick it was almost comical; Kitty was surprised his hands didn't leave a grease stain behind.

"Word on the street is that your employer's been suspended from the competition," he stage-whispered. He, too, looked over at the table of smoking men, and even waved to one of them in greeting.

"Which makes me wonder," Mesmer continued, "what you could possibly be doing here at the very hotel where the majority of the Symposium's judges are staying?" He raised his eyebrows suggestively, but his tone wasn't accusatory. In fact, he looked almost amused.

Kitty flashed a smile right back at him. "You caught me," she whispered, leaning in closer to Mesmer. "I'm here to poison all the old coots' drinks and blackmail them into giving us first place."

She'd taken a chance, but it paid off; Mesmer nearly snorted into his drink with laughter. He coughed and dabbed at his mouth with his handkerchief, carefully smoothing his silly goatee.

"The Amazifier should let you write his bits," Mesmer said, chuckling. "He has quite the comedienne on his hands."

"There won't be any more laughs for us if we can't make

it into the last round," Kitty said, pouting into her drink. "I *was* hoping I could run into one of the committee members here and persuade them to speed the inquiry along."

"And how exactly were you planning to persuade them, Miss Delphine?"

Kitty took another sip of her champagne and shrugged, feeling foolish and out of place. It had been a mistake to come here. "Do you have a better idea?" she asked archly. She was tired, her feet hurt, and the sequins on her dress were chafing in uncomfortable places.

"Fortunately for you," said Mesmer frankly, swinging back his drink, "I have a soft spot for the underdogs in life, and I'm loathe to see the 'marvelously modern' Mechanist strut home with the grand prize three years in a row. It's bad for business when the show gets predictable." He shrugged.

"You mean you'll help us?" Kitty asked incredulously.

Mesmer held up a hand. "I'll see what I can do, but I wouldn't get your hopes up. Your little act has ruffled quite a few important feathers around here, Miss Delphine."

"I know," said Kitty heavily. "No one's more surprised than me."

Mesmer gave her a questioning look, but didn't press the issue. "You should be getting back to the camp. Have the front desk call you a cab."

Kitty's heart sank down into her knees. She hadn't

given much thought to getting back, and she certainly couldn't afford a carriage ride all the way to the city gates.

"I'll tell them to put it on my tab," added Mesmer casually.

"Oh, sir, I couldn't—"

"Nonsense. You can and you will," interrupted Mesmer. "Call it superstition, but everyone in this town knows it, and so should you. Skemantis is not a safe place after dark."

A chill ran up Kitty's spine despite the warmth of the room. "Thank you, sir." She turned to leave, but Mesmer's voice stopped her.

"And Miss Delphine?"

"Yes, Mr. Mesmer?"

"I do hope you're not actually cheating. It would be very disappointing indeed."

Yes, it would, thought Kitty on her way out of the lounge. She'd swallowed Carmer's muddled explanations about the Phoenix Engine trick—there hadn't been time to do much of anything but learn how not to roast herself alive—and she'd believed that all the improvements were his own inventions, a concerted effort to make up for the first poor performance. But now that they were serious contenders, someone *really* wanted them out of this competition, and accusations like this just didn't come out of thin air. Felix Cassius Tiberius Carmer III had some serious explaining to do.

15.

UNDER INVESTIGATION

ANTOINE THE AMAZIFIER, KITTY DELPHINE, AND Felix Carmer looked out into the nearly empty house of the Orbicle and shielded their eyes against the bright stage lights. They stood in a row, unintentionally ordered shortest to tallest, like criminals in a lineup—which is exactly what they felt like, Carmer most of all.

A messenger had come from the Orbicle that morning instructing all members of the Amazifier's act to present themselves at the theater for questioning that very afternoon. They had just enough time to wrangle all of their supplies together; Carmer hastily rewrote his notes for the Phoenix Engine, editing out everything to do with Grit and trying to string together a plausible explanation for the trick that did not involve a faerie princess driving a train.

The Amazifier had clucked about the injustice of it all, but his relief was plain. He clearly thought Carmer would be able to explain that everything was just a big misunderstanding.

Kitty Delphine, however, made her suspicions clear. "Carmer, I wanna win this thing just as badly as you do," she murmured on the way to the theater, out of earshot of the Amazifier. "But you haven't been honest with us. You can babble all you want about new 'propulsion mechanisms' or the latest 'naphtha derivative,' but we've been doing things I can't explain, and neither can Master Antoine."

Carmer couldn't make himself meet her eyes. "I told you, Kitty, I've been learning lots at the Titan Industries workshops at the exposition. I . . . it'll be fine."

Kitty shook her head, blonde curls bouncing around her ears. "I hope you can do a better job of convincing the judges than you just did with me, Carmer. I really do."

Now, Carmer could only stand and watch as one of the committee members—a stern man named Tellaferror with iron gray hair and the customary black cloak— ascended the stage stairs and made the one simple request Carmer had been dreading the most.

"Antonin Tataziak and associates, welcome. We apologize for the inconvenience," said Tellaferror, not sounding sorry at all. The Amazifier ignored the slight of being called by his given name. "But the formalities must be observed. We will begin with a demonstration. Please perform, to the best of your ability, your modified cremation illusion known as the 'Phoenix Engine.'"

"Certainly," said the Amazifier, at the same time Carmer blurted out, "We can't."

The silence that followed was only a brief pause, but to Carmer, it felt like an eternity.

"You may make any preparations necessary," clarified Tellaferror, thick and wiry eyebrows raised in mild surprise. "We will wait."

The second silence was, if possible, worse than the first.

"Carmer?" asked the Amazifier. "Is there a reason why we cannot oblige Mr. Tellaferror in his request?"

"I . . . I forgot the curtains," said Carmer, thinking of the velvet drapes currently folded in the black trunk of supplies right at his feet. "Back at the camp."

"No, we didn't," blurted Kitty. "They're right—oh." She snapped her mouth shut, eyes wide.

Tellaferror turned his steely gaze on all three of them in turn. A murmur swept through the seated judges. "It appears a demonstration will not be necessary." He spun on his heel, graceful for such a large man, and began descending the steps into the house.

"Wait—" stalled Carmer, but Tellaferror kept walking, his cloak billowing like the wings of a large bat.

"I do not see that there is more to discuss," said the judge. "You can provide no evidence that you are capable of the feats that so dazzled our audience a few nights ago. Unless you would care to enlighten us?"

"Perhaps you could enlighten *me*, sir," the Amazifier spoke up. "Is there anything to suggest that we aren't capable?"

Even in the dark, Tellaferror looked taken aback. Carmer could tell he was a man who wasn't used to having his authority questioned; he had the air of a federal alchemist about him.

"I don't take your meaning," said the judge flatly.

"You say my illusions are inexplicable. I have done my job well then, I expect. But we are not here to prove my capabilities as a magician or the plausibility of my accomplishments. We are here to address the accusation of cheating. So tell me, sir, is there any indication that I have directly pilfered any of my accuser's illusions?"

The judges seated in the house tutted and whispered amongst themselves.

"The absence of any glaring wrongdoing does not an innocent man make," bristled Tellaferror.

"This is true," said the Amazifier, shrugging. "Though it seems the *actual* glaring wrongdoing that plagues this community is much easier to ignore."

The murmurs from the committee grew louder; a few of the men stood up.

"Now listen here, Antonin—"

"Antoine, if you please, *Gerald*," corrected the Amazifier. "My reputation as an artist and a man of honor precedes me. I have been pulling rabbits out of hats since before some of you were born. I have nothing to hide."

"You may not," retorted Tellaferror. "But *he* does." The judge pointed an accusatory finger at Carmer.

Silence fell at once.

"We have several stagehands who will testify to seeing this young man enter the private dressing room area a few days ago. What business could he have there, during off hours, when your base of operations is clearly in the camp outside the city?"

Dread pooled in the pit of Carmer's stomach. He had thought no one had noticed him sneak into the Mechanist's dressing room, but clearly he had been wrong. "I . . . I thought Master Antoine had left his hat back at the theater," said Carmer lamely.

Tellaferror continued as if Carmer had not spoken, striding back and forth across the stage. "We have also received a complaint from another competitor who witnessed you lurking about outside his home yesterday afternoon."

"I wasn't lurking!"

"Then tell us, boy, what *were* you doing there?"

Carmer said nothing. How could he explain why he'd been visiting the Mechanist? The judges would either think him a cheater, as they did now, or just plain crazy, if he told them the truth.

"Carmer, can you explain this?" asked the Amazifier patiently. His calm request was somehow even harder to bear than Tellaferror's blatant accusations. Yet the only way Kitty and the Amazifier might be allowed to compete was if Carmer was out of the picture.

"I was visiting another magician yesterday," said Carmer, "but it wasn't to steal from him. I was asking for a job." He heard Kitty inhale sharply, but couldn't bring himself to look at the Amazifier's face. "I felt I was outgrowing my apprenticeship with Master Antoine," lied Carmer, staring straight ahead. "So I've been looking for another magician to study under. I didn't want Master Antoine to win the competition. I wanted him to know what a mistake he was making by . . . by giving me so little to do. So I tampered with his illusions to draw suspicion. It was all me."

"Spirits and zits, Carmer!" exclaimed Kitty, her eyes filling with tears. "How could you?"

The color drained from the Amazifier's wrinkled face.

Tellaferror regarded Carmer shrewdly. "So you confess to sabotage, Felix Carmer?"

Carmer gulped and nodded. What else did he have to lose?

"I suggest you remove this ungrateful youth from your employ immediately, Antoine," suggested Tellaferror. "He is no longer welcome at the Orbicle or in any other theater in Skemantis. Of that, we will make sure." The judge made no effort to disguise his disgust.

"Now listen to me, Tellaferror," said the Amazifier, "the decision to sack my employees still rests with me, not you, and—"

"No," Carmer interrupted. "I resign. I don't deserve to be your apprentice, sir." Carmer could barely keep his voice steady, but he made himself look Tellaferror in the eye. "Master Antoine was ignorant of any wrongdoing, sir. That's why you haven't found anything. He's innocent."

Carmer hoped he hadn't just destroyed his entire future for nothing. Surely, if he distanced himself from the Amazifier, the committee couldn't find the magician guilty? They didn't have Grit's magic anymore, but the Amazifier still might have a shot at second or third place if he and Kitty gave the show everything they had. It was a small chance, but it was all he could give them.

Smack. Kitty's hand slapped across his face and left a smarting red blotch behind. "You bet your patootie he's innocent!" she cried. "You selfish, lying little—"

"Enough." The Amazifier held Kitty's hand back as she raised it again. She stormed off the stage in tears.

"Well, that was quite the spectacle," said Tellaferror. "If you are all quite finished?" Carmer and the Amazifier both glared at him. "I will confer with my associates and we shall determine if your testimony is sufficient evidence to allow you to remain in the competition."

The judge glided back down the stairs to meet with his fellows in the audience. They had come so close to having a real chance, and now it was all ruined. Carmer had hurt the one person in the world who cared about him when no one else did, who'd cobbled together a life for him and Kitty from a few magic tricks and a house on wheels.

The Amazifier leaned over stiffly, looking ten years older, to pick up their trunk full of props. Carmer moved forward to help, but the Amazifier stopped him.

"No, Carmer," he said, "I think you've helped enough for one day."

It seemed ages before Tellaferror appeared again, this time flanked by two other black-robed judges. "The committee has decided to allow you, Antoine the Amazifier, and your assistant, Miss Kitty Delphine, to remain in the Symposium," he announced. "As for you, Mr. Carmer, you will find yourself most unwelcome here. Your name will be blacklisted in every theater and music hall in Skemantis and beyond, and you would be wise not to test our reach. No magician will employ a known saboteur, Mr. Carmer. Good day, gentlemen."

Tellaferror and the other judges filed out of the theater, talking amongst themselves.

Carmer turned to the Amazifier. "Master . . ."

"I am not your master anymore, Carmer," said the Amazifier sharply. "I am sorry that I proved to be a disappointing one."

The Amazifier wandered off the stage to find Kitty

Delphine. Carmer stood alone, blinking into the spotlight until it finally winked out, plunging him into darkness.

GRIT SHOULD HAVE known better than to trust a human. What had she been thinking, letting Carmer use her magic like that? Letting him use *her* like that? In the end, all he cared about was winning his stupid fake magic competition—and he wouldn't even admit that the only reason he had a *chance* at winning was because of her! Grit had thought nothing could be more frustrating than being cooped up with her mother in the Arboretum, but Felix Cassius Tiberius Carmer III (and honestly, who had *that* many names?) had a nearly supernatural ability to infuriate her.

Her anger at Carmer fueled her on the long and muddy journey through the circus camp and back to the city gates. It was easier going at night, though riskier, too—it would be much simpler for any prowling Autocats to snatch her up under the cover of darkness. She drew energy from the campfires she skirted around, slipping silently past snoring old magicians, stretching acrobats, and meat turning on spits. Occasionally, she caught puppet-shaped shadows out of the corner of her eye, but they didn't try to stop her, so she kept on her way.

It was nearly sunrise by the time she made it to the edge of the camp and scurried through a mouse burrow that ran under the city gate, pausing briefly to thank the surprised inhabitants for their hospitality. Their alarmed squeaks as she surfaced offered the only warning that she was no longer alone.

Using nearly all of her energy to deflect attention away from herself, Grit scrambled out of the burrow and under the looming shadow of the city gate. No sooner had she crossed a foot of browning grass than an Autocat leapt after her, teeth bared. It barely missed her, but Grit was fairly certain it couldn't see her while she used her magic to stay unnoticeable, even if it could sense her general presence.

Grit darted and weaved through the cat's paws, but the effort to keep herself invisible was taking its toll. She would tire of this dance long before the Autocat would. Did they even *get* tired? Grit wasn't sure. She tried to remember what Carmer had said about going for their hearts, but she barely had time to dodge its deadly claws and gnashing teeth, never mind look for a weak spot.

Grit wasn't fast enough. A silver paw swiped at her from the side, pinning her down like a mouse any real cat would make a meal out of. The paw pressed her into the dirt, knocking the air out of her.

All she could do was gasp and wriggle ineffectually as the cat peered down at her, perhaps deciding whether to play with its food before it ate her. A rose gold tongue slid out from the cat's jaws; it licked its nonexistent lips with the chilling scraping sound Grit was becoming all too familiar with. Her vision started to go black around the edges, the claw pressing into her throat.

Just when she thought all was lost, tiny figures launched out of the grass on all sides, pinging against the cat's metal frame. The cat released its hold on her to swat at one of its new assailants. Grit rolled out of its reach as fast as she could, still fighting for breath.

The Royal Guard was here! Grit guessed Madame Euphemia must have tipped them off somehow. The armored crickets worried at the cat, crawling into its mouth and out through its eyes, pushing out the glowing purple amethysts with sickening pops. Their magically strengthened legs slashed at the cat's wiring anywhere they could, swarming over the beast inside and out.

A particularly well-outfitted cave cricket in silver and moonstone armor broke off from the others and hopped in front of Grit.

Chirp! It gestured wildly in the general direction of the Arboretum, where Grit hoped reinforcements would be waiting.

Chirp! Chirp!

Flanked by crickets on all sides, Grit was forced to abandon any notion of avoiding the faerie kingdom. The Autocat ground to a halt behind her, its wires shorting out as it hacked up sparks and grease like hair balls. Even as she ran for her life, Grit couldn't help but think a worse fate surely awaited her at home: the unchecked wrath of a very, *very* angry faerie queen.

A small part of her had to admit she'd rather take her chances with the cat.

16.

LIGHT 'EM UP

THERE IS A HUMAN SAYING THAT GOES, "NEVER put all of your eggs in one basket." Humans are wrong about a great many things—this is especially true if you ask a faerie—but even the Fair Folk are inclined to agree with this piece of advice. It is important to keep this in mind when discussing the Great Willow, because if it is a risky business to put all of your eggs in one basket, it is an even riskier business to put all of your faeries in one tree.

The Great Willow was the biggest and most ancient tree in the Arboretum, as wide as it was tall, roots stretching out halfway across the kingdom, a veritable humming beehive of magic. Even the dullest human could recognize the power in such a tree; surely it would be simple for the Mechanist or his ilk to simply stride into Oldtown Arboretum, chop down the Great Willow, and enslave or destroy all the faeries in the kingdom? This might be so, if the Great Willow were always a willow, and if it always stayed in one place.

The Great Willow, however, is much smarter than your average willow (and this is saying something, as willows don't have a reputation for wisdom for nothing). Years of faeries moving in and out of you, singing parts of you up and parts of you down, and making their homes in your deepest of deep, deep hearts will make a tree a Tree, and an ordinary willow a Great Willow, in no time. The Great Willow was clever and loved its faeries dearly, and so just often enough to confuse any humans who might be watching too closely, the Great Willow changed.

One day it might be a majestic white oak or a sycamore, reaching out far and wide, right in the center of the kingdom. The next, if it is a particularly fine fall day, it might be a yellow birch with plumes of golden leaves reaching up toward the sun and planted right at the North Gate, saying, "Come in, come in! Aren't my colors lovely today?" It might be an American elm, if it's feeling rather rebellious, or a hemlock with dainty needles and perfect faerie-sized pinecones, trading secrets with the shadows of the Whispering Wall. A faerie or Friend true of heart can always find the Great Willow by walking toward the heart of the Arboretum and knowing where they want to go; either they'll find the faerie castle, or it will find them.

Today, the Great Willow was a wide American beech tree with a smooth silver trunk that discouraged anything with creepy crawling claws from finding purchase in its bark. Beech bark is not usually very tough, but the Great Willow was fortified with faerie magic that made it nearly as strong as steel. Beechnut husks made good armor—mostly helmets and shoulder pads—but the wood was brittle. The leaves should have been a lime yellow this time of year, but Queen Ombrienne's mood had turned them brown with purple shadows, like a photograph's negative.

The queen herself stood in her throne room in a gown of autumn leaves with a bee bristle collar and a headdress of gold-tipped pine needles. The teeth of small animals were strung along intricately woven braids around her head. Two thick auburn plaits fell on either side of her neck and trailed down nearly to her ankles. Grit had always thought it highly unfair that *she* was expected to wear frilly petal dresses when her mother walked around like a warrior goddess.

"You have put us all in grave jeopardy. Do you realize this, Grettifrida?"

A small army of faeries-in-waiting fluttered around Grit, stripping her out of her worn and filthy clothes, attempting to comb out the fuzzy bird's nest that was her hair, and dabbing at her various scrapes and bruises. Only a few strategically placed butterflies provided her with any semblance of privacy. She was lifted from behind and unceremoniously plunked into a birch bark bowl filled with healing rainwater. She came up sputtering and glaring, enchanted steam pouring out of her ears.

"And how do you figure that, Mother?" Grit asked acidly. She tried not to sigh with relief as the hot water worked out all her knots and kinks and soothed her scratches from the Autocat's claws. She was determined not to show weakness in front of her mother, but it's a bit difficult to look tough and determined when one is in the bath.

"Leave us," said Ombrienne to the other faeries.

They scattered without comment, though one or two shot Grit sympathetic looks. Now Grit would be at the mercy of her mother's sharp tongue without any witnesses to defend her (although on the grand scale of punishments, this was preferable to a chewing out *with* an audience).

"Not only did you put the legacy of this kingdom in jeopardy with your ill-timed escapist antics—"

"But Mother—"

"Do *not* interrupt me," said Ombrienne with such force that the whole castle shook, sending errant pinecones crashing to the throne room floor.

Grit sank up to her chin in the water.

"Not only did you put the legacy of this kingdom in jeopardy, you divulged our deepest magical secrets to a *human*—a human who is not even a Friend of the Fae!"

"I hardly think shooting sparks counts as divulging our deepest magical secrets."

"Our magic is not a parlor trick, Grettifrida! It is an

ancient art, not a passing amusement for entertaining humans. You risked our exposure in front of hundreds of people. You abused the power bestowed upon you by your ancestors, the power whose sole purpose is to keep this kingdom alive."

"That's what I was *trying* to do, Mother!" protested Grit as the butterflies flew under her armpits and lifted her out of the tub.

Ombrienne waved a hand and a warm wind blew in from the west, carrying a handful of pink flower petals with it. Where her mother could find pink flower petals even in the middle of autumn, Grit would never know. She grimaced but stood still as the petals molded themselves to her body to form a frothy dress trimmed with soft green moss from the Arboretum floor. Her mother's only concession to Grit's natural style was a crown made of pinecone scales that she placed over Grit's unruly hair herself.

"There now. That's much better," said Ombrienne. She reached down to stroke Grit's cheek, but Grit turned away.

"You're not listening to me," Grit said, backing away and nearly tripping over her silly dress. "I only helped Carmer because he agreed to help *us*! We found out who controls the Autocats—I mean, the Wingsnatchers—and that he's stealing faerie magic to make something called *electricity* for the humans, but the captured faeries are still alive somewhere! And the Hyperion—"

"I have neither the time nor the desire to listen to the

details of your wanton bargains with humans," Ombrienne said dismissively. The birch bark bowl sprouted legs and scuttled away, as if it, too, were afraid of the queen's temper.

"What about this magic you keep talking about?" asked Grit. "You've spent my entire life telling me my power is too weak, I need to be protected, I shouldn't strain myself . . . and now you're terrified of me being out of your control! I *do* have power, I *can* handle myself—"

"Because you were doing *so well* when the Royal Guard rescued you from the clutches of that metal monster."

Grit flushed.

"Now listen to me, child," continued the queen. "You have a responsibility to your people. The royal magic that flows through your veins is the only thing that will keep the Arboretum a safe haven for our kind after I am gone." Ombrienne circled Grit as she spoke, the ends of her auburn hair curling and uncurling in an unnatural breeze. "You will not jeopardize this community again with your selfishness."

Splinters of wood began ripping themselves apart from the tree trunk floor and spinning around her, tearing countless little gouges beneath their feet.

"You will not experiment with your magic until I have given *express permission* for you to do so."

The splinters circled closer around Grit, weaving in and out, latching on to one another in an intricate lacework.

"And until you are queen, you will never. Leave. This castle. Again."

The pieces of interwoven wood spun closer and closer, fitting together like puzzle pieces to form a circle around Grit. The sides built up and up, a basketlike prison, until Grit could no longer see her mother's face in front of her.

"NO."

The word came from deep inside of Grit, forcing its way out of her lips and into the world, a sharp, tangible thing. The cage stopped spinning and started to smoke, little red embers lighting up the ends of the splinters, and with a great *poof*, it vaporized in a cloud of ash.

Grit stood in the center of the ring of ashes, breathing hard. Ombrienne stared at her daughter as if she had never seen her before.

Suddenly, a great buzzing filled the air, like a hundred hornets taking flight at once. The Great Willow's branches filled with flickering faerie light. The noise *was* hornets, summoned into attack formation by some threat to the Arboretum. They buzzed around the Great Willow, dodging nervous faeries. Grit panicked for a moment, thinking she had somehow caused more destruction than she'd intended, but then the chatter of the other faeries surrounded her.

"Queen Ombrienne!"

"Your Highness, we're sorry to interrupt, but—"

"Humans! At the North Gate!"

"They've got saws!"

"And shovels!"

"There're so many of them!"

"What do we do?"

Queen Ombrienne collected herself in an instant, her face slipping back into its usual smooth mask.

"The Royal Guard and I will go," she said. "Coniferus, gather the lamplighters. Sprout Mother Rutabella, take your charges underground and stay close to the castle; the Willow is bound to move again shortly. The rest of you, to your posts!"

Queen Ombrienne rose up into the air with the hornets. The crickets skittered down the Great Willow's branches to follow her along the ground.

"Grettifrida?" Ombrienne paused as her beechnut armor attached itself to her chest. "Stay here . . . please." She sped off without waiting for an answer.

The ashy remains of Grit's wooden prison drifted away in the crisp autumn breeze, but she was still trapped up there in the Willow.

Just then a bristly green head poked out from behind a thick silver branch. "Psst, Grit!"

"Bressel?!" Grit raced to her friend and embraced her in a bone-crushing hug. "I am so glad to see you!"

"Oh, me, too!" said Bressel, her bushy green eyebrows scrunching together. "But I'm still mad at you for leaving me like you did!"

"Can you be mad at me later?" implored Grit. "What's going on at the North Gate?"

"Do you want me to tell you, or do you want me to show you?" asked Bressel.

Grit took a step back. "Who are you and what have you done with my old friend Bressel?"

"Replaced her with a browbeaten faerie who has realized that you always do what you want anyway. Now hop on before someone notices us!"

Grit clambered onto Bressel's back and sneezed as faerie dust flew in her face when Bressel took flight.

"Did you get heavier in the human world?" Bressel grunted under Grit's weight.

"Did I mention you're my favorite faerie in Skemantis?" Grit nuzzled Bressel's shoulder affectionately and grinned. They were off.

"LADIES AND GENTLEMEN, today you are witnessing history in the making!" Titus Archer's voice echoed over the sounds of digging as a handful of men completed a two-foot-deep trench that ran right up against the North Gate. He addressed a small crowd of important-looking businessmen and a few scribbling journalists. One of them set up a cumbersome-looking camera. "With the trial installation of Titus Industries' new Hyperiopower in Skemantis's legendary theater district, we are ushering in a new age of modern technology and convenience! My competitors know very well that we must rely on the use of limited resources to produce electricity. How much coal must be burned to power a fine city such as this? But the Hyperion is a generator with infinite capabilities. Hyperiopower can produce electricity for the public without reliance on coal, gas, or even water—"

"No, just the lives of innocent faeries," snarled Grit under her breath. She and Bressel watched from the middling branches of a nearby holly tree, well hidden from hornets or faeries patrolling the skies high above.

Archer droned on about the development of the modern age and the tide of progress, but Grit and Bressel were hardly listening. They were transfixed by the digging men, who had hit the roots of a linden tree that had dared creep beyond the Arboretum gate. Two of them hacked at the roots in their path, iron weapons swinging, while the others laid down cables in the ground. Grit assumed they connected to the streetlamp outside the gate, but she wasn't sure. She wished Carmer were there to explain it to her.

Grit couldn't blame Queen Ombrienne and the faerie warriors for not going on the offensive against Archer, especially with their power so much weaker outside the kingdom's boundaries. The humans of Skemantis and the faeries of Oldtown Arboretum had left each other alone for over a century. No matter what expansion went on outside its gates, the Arboretum itself was a sacred place for humans to enjoy and faeries to live in peace. But now, the magic under Archer's control *outside* the Arboretum rivaled that on the inside. The old peace was being broken, and the humans were practically cheering it on.

"There's something strange about that man, Grit." Bressel shivered. Even a garden faerie, unaccustomed to thinking much about the magic outside her own vegetable patch, could sense Titus Archer's terrifying power.

"You don't know the half of it," Grit agreed.

More men were filling in the trench now, the mounds of churned earth like fresh scars covering a wound.

"It's dying," Bressel whispered, her eyes filling with amber tears as she looked at the linden.

Grit didn't question her friend's prognosis; she too could almost hear the tree's plaintive cries. "I can't believe this."

Someone finished screwing a shiny new bulb into the nearest streetlamp and carefully placed the original glass globe over it.

"It is time!" said Archer, consulting his watch. He clapped his hands together and all the men stepped back. A zipping, crackling sound filled the air for a few seconds, and then there was a burst of light. The entire theater district was now officially electric. Dark back alleyways were illuminated, bright signs broadcasting each theater and hotel's name attached to the tops of every building. The crowd applauded, and people in the streets jumped back in surprise as the city came to life around them.

"There you have it, my friends! Hyperiopower in action!" crowed Titus Archer.

The scribbling journalists peppered him with questions.

"But how does it work?"

"When will the whole city be wired?"

"How soon before we see this technology in the homes of the average Skemantian?"

Grit climbed as high as she dared in the holly tree, Bressel flying branch to branch behind her. She looked out into the newfangled theater district. How hadn't she realized Archer's plans were this far along?

The Symposium had only been a place to show off, just like Archer had told Carmer. It seemed the *real* testing ground was expanding by the day, and Grit had no idea how to stop it.

DESPITE HIS INCREDIBLY fae-filled existence the last few days, Felix Carmer had never actually been to Old-town Arboretum, the very center of faerie life in Skemantis. He made his way to the South Gate now for no other reason than he had nowhere else to go. He'd wandered around the city all afternoon, from the gleaming towers of the financial district to the smelly stalls of the leather workers, to the Penny Market and back again, like any tourist taking in the sights, all the while carefully skirting the place he knew was Grit's home. Whether or not she was there, he doubted the rest of the faeries would be pleased with him.

Few people milled about the Arboretum tonight. The lamps along the paths, which Grit had told him were usually illuminated by faerie light, were dark and empty, leaving only the moon to guide the way. Looking to the north, he thought of the newly electrified theater district humming with its artificial glow. Carmer and Grit hadn't guessed the Mechanist had developed his dynamo to such an extent. Where once he would have watched the new display of lights with gleeful curiosity, now Carmer felt only sadness and a nagging sense of regret. He could only hope Grit had made it back to her people in one piece. After giving up life as he knew it, a little hope was all he had.

Carmer arrived at the South Gate, where the stone gargoyles perched on either side seemed to judge him. Carmer figured they'd found him lacking, but the double gates swung open at his touch. He looked around but saw no one.

Carmer wasn't sure where he was going, or even why he was there, but as he walked along an oak-lined path, he noticed the ground start to slope upward. He'd chanced upon a map of the Arboretum earlier at the visitor's center in the old brick City Hall building, so he recognized the area as the beginnings of Widdershinner's Hill, one of the highest points in the city. Perhaps from there he could see how far Titus Archer's electrical system actually extended.

The wind picked up as Carmer walked. He drew his threadbare coat more tightly around his shoulders and clamped a hand on his top hat when a particularly stiff breeze tried to make away with it. He felt a surprising pang of loneliness when his hand brushed the little door built into its side. There was no need for that anymore.

Was it just his imagination, or was the hill getting steeper? With each step, the ground seemed to shift from under him, throwing him off balance and making his thighs burn with the effort. The gnarled, winding limbs of the oaks snaked in and out of one another in an arch overhead, letting only the barest hints of moonlight leak through. It cast trickster shadows along the oak's trunks; one moment, the silhouette of a little girl flickered against it. The next, a knobby, ancient face peered at him, mouth open wide in a scream echoed in the whistling, whirling wind. The Oldtown Arboretum was on the defensive.

Still Carmer pressed on. He could not say why it was so important now that he reach the top of the hill, but it was. No matter how fiercely the wind blew, how much the slick leaves and damp soil squelched underfoot and tried to pull the shoes from his feet, how the mean old trees threw acorns at him and whacked their branches in his face, he couldn't stop now. Maybe Carmer couldn't win the magic competition. He couldn't keep his family together. He couldn't make his first real friend without ruining everything the first chance he got. He couldn't save the faeries and he couldn't stop Titus Archer. But Carmer could keep walking.

The Great Willow is very clever, as you know, and

more than capable of making her own decisions. Even if Queen Ombrienne, in all her wisdom of many years, had ordered the Arboretum to close itself to outsiders until further notice, the Great Willow was older and wiser still. And we can suppose that even if the statues guarding the Arboretum found Carmer's gumption lacking, the Great Willow did not, for she chose that moment to knock Felix Carmer's prized top hat right off his head.

"No!" cried Carmer as the hat spun away. He jumped up to grab it, caught his toe on a tree root, and fell flat on his face.

The howling wind quieted. The rogue roots shrunk back, a little embarrassed at their behavior. The oaken limbs retracted to their normal size, and the gnarled faces in their trunks had the decency to look sheepish. The moon burst through the clouds, flooding the path with light.

Carmer slowly got to his knees. His brain felt a little scrambled, but other than a few scrapes, he was unhurt. He was also at the top of the hill.

His hat was waiting for him, thoroughly enjoying its ride atop a little dust devil still swirling in harmless, lazy circles. Carmer spared a quick moment to glance at the city sprawled below him, a sizeable portion of it glowing and blinking against the night sky, but his victory was short-lived. He spotted his hat and made a grab for it, but it danced just out of reach, whirling down the other side of the hill.

"Hey, wait!" Carmer yelled, realizing a little too late that he was yelling at a hat. As arduous as his ascent of the hill had been, his descent was over in a matter of seconds. The path was so clear and steep he couldn't have stopped running even if he'd wanted to. He careened down it, arms and legs flailing, his errant hat bobbing just out of reach. He had just a few seconds to dig in his heels before he crashed into a crumbling stone wall with a sound somewhere between a thump and a crunch.

"Unfhgmuh," or something like it, was the only sound Carmer could make. His hands had borne the brunt of the impact, and some of the scabs from the Autocat's claws had opened again. They left faint red smears on the gray stone in front of him. He pushed himself back and sank to the ground against the wall.

The top hat floated down and gently placed itself around Carmer's ears. He almost laughed.

Carmer took a few moments to catch his breath, leaning against the cool stone. Here and there, little rolls of paper, parchment, and even old newsprint stuck out from between the holes in the wall. Carmer traced the edges of one with his fingers, but didn't pull it out. It wasn't his place.

"I read about these today," Carmer said softly to the cool night air. "Some people believe that if you come to the Whispering Wall and whisper your deepest secret, the faeries will grant you a wish in return. This wall would have fallen down ages ago if not for all the wishes written down and slipped in the cracks." He pushed one of the notes in more snugly and looked up at the stars. "I don't know any secrets worth the kind of wishes I have," he said. "But . . . I do have an apology. To one of you in particular, but to all of you, really. I'm sorry I didn't do more. I'm sorry if what I tried to do was too much."

The wind whistling through the cracks in the wall was his only answer. Carmer hadn't really been expecting one, but he couldn't help feeling disappointed. A little hope was all he had, but it was getting smaller all the time.

"HOOT!"

A tiny gray mass of feathers came flying out of nowhere, sweeping so close over Carmer's head it nearly yanked out some of his hair with its talons.

"DUSTEN, THIS IS NOT WHAT WE PRACTICED."

Carmer would recognize that voice anywhere. He ducked just in time as the owl dove again, this time making an unsteady landing on top of the Whispering Wall, dislodging a few pebbles in the process.

"HOOT," it declared proudly, seemingly ignorant of the two disheveled-looking faeries clinging to its back. Grit clutched the owl's reins while a green-skinned faerie with hair like broccoli florets clutched at her.

"Bressel, you're squeezing the light out of me," complained Grit. She extricated herself from her terrified companion's grip and hopped down from the owl's back.

Bressel made a far less graceful descent and quickly ducked behind the creature, her bulbous green eyes peering at Carmer curiously.

"You're okay," said Carmer, relieved.

"You look terrible," said Grit, the corners of her mouth pulling up in a reluctant smile.

"I had a fight with your Arboretum. I think I lost."

Grit shook her head. "If you did, you'd know."

An awkward silence fell between them.

"Grit, we need to go right now!" Bressel piped up. "The Arboretum is on lockdown—"

"And it let Carmer in anyway. I'd say that's a good sign. Felix Cassius Tiberius Carmer III, meet Bressel, Junior Sprout Mother in Training and Professional Worrywart. Bressel, Carmer."

"Pleased to meet you," said Carmer, tipping his hat.

Bressel blushed dark green, and a small white flower blossomed in her hair of its own accord; she hid even farther behind the owl. Carmer couldn't help but feel like his first meetings with faeries were never destined to go well.

Bressel hissed warnings at Grit with her face in Dusten's feathers. "I never signed up for revealing myself to this boy, Grettifrida—"

"BRESSEL."

"Grettifrida?" Carmer asked with a smirk.

"It's Grit." Grit brandished her hatpin. "And I will use this."

Carmer nodded quickly and Grit sheathed her sword. She sat down on the wall and scooted closer to him.

"Now. About what you said."

"I *am* sorry," said Carmer. "It wasn't your fault we got kicked out of the Symposium. Your help was the only reason we got so far in the first place."

"You know it," agreed Grit, crossing her arms. She sighed. "And I suppose I'm sorry, too. I shouldn't have jumped down your throat about . . . you trying to help me. You're the only human who knows or cares what the Mechanist is really up to, Carmer. I could . . . *we* could really use your help." Grit looked down at her feet.

"Of course, Grit," said Carmer. "But I don't know how much use I'll be."

"Oh, I think you'll be quite useful," insisted Grit, looking impish. "But we're all going to have to work together on this one."

"All? You mean with the other faeries?"

Grit nodded and vaulted onto the brim of Carmer's hat. She looked nervous and a little green, even compared to Bressel.

"Carmer, I think it's time you met my mother."

17.

MEET THE PARENTS

THE WALK TO THE GREAT WILLOW WAS MUCH LESS eventful than the journey up Widdershinner's Hill, for which Carmer was grateful. The path seemed to know where they wanted to go and adjusted itself accordingly every few yards or so. Grit sat with her feet dangling off the brim of Carmer's hat and filled him in on the details of all she'd observed at the Hyperiopower installation. Bressel trailed nervously behind them, darting this way and that.

The spruces and pines around them soon gave way to a grove of beeches, silvery trunks shining in the moonlight.

"We're here," said Grit, and Carmer stopped. Aside from a few leaves rustling in the breeze, Carmer could neither see nor hear any evidence of faeries.

"Are you sure?" he asked.

Grit thumped her fist against his hat.

"Ow, okay!"

"Look," she said. "Bressel, a little help?"

"I still don't think this is a good idea," complained the green faerie, but flew closer all the same. She hovered inches from Carmer's nose, beating her wings faster and faster, until a golden, shimmering powder fell from them and was carried on the breeze right into Carmer's face.

"What the—" He sneezed, and Bressel flew out of reach with a little shriek. Carmer rubbed his eyes and blinked.

Standing quite incongruously in the middle of the grove was a sprawling weeping willow that most certainly had not been there moments before—or, at least, not to Carmer's human eyes. He still didn't see any faeries, but it seemed to him that the rustling of the leaves had gotten louder, and if he listened hard enough, he could hear a chorus of whispers traveling back and forth all around them.

"It's all right, everyone!" Grit called. She stood up on his hat. "You can come out now! This is Carmer, and I promise, you have nothing to fear from him. He saved my life—more than once—and he's going to try and save all of us. The Mecha— the Wingsnatchers took his family from him, just like they've taken ours. Please at least listen to what he has to say."

"What have I got to say?" whispered Carmer nervously.

"Relax, we'll think of something," Grit hissed. She raised her voice again. "Just . . . tell them about the Mechanist."

And so Carmer did. He told his invisible audience about his first time seeing the Hyperion in action, his meeting with Grit and the Autocats, their disastrous trip to the mine, and Carmer's refusal to join the Mechanist. As his story went on, little pockets of light sprang to life in the Great Willow branches and all around the clearing. He saw flashes of pointed ears; bony limbs the exact texture of tree bark unfurled as they listened to his tale, and pale iris-colored faces blinked at him with great pools of inky black eyes. Though he stuttered and stumbled through bits of the story, their attention never wavered, and by the time he caught up to the present, the beech grove was full of golden, glowing faerie lights.

"And so . . . and so I told the judges I'd sabotaged my mentor's magic, so he could still compete. I'm all alone now, and I'm not sure what I'm going to do about it. But if I can help save your friends and expose Titus Archer for what he is, then . . . well, at least something good might come out of this mess."

Carmer had tried to keep a stiff upper lip, but he couldn't help the small crack that crept into his voice at the word "alone." To his surprise, a portly faerie with curly gray hair who looked like a flying plum alighted right on his shoulder.

"Oh, my poor dear," she fussed, patting his ear affectionately.

This broke the other faeries' silence entirely. Soon

more of them were flying up to him, circling him and Grit and peppering them with questions and condolences.

"Could you really stop the . . . the dyno-whatsit?"

"The dynamo. And I think so, if I knew where it was."

"The other faeries are still alive!"

"Princess, are the Wingsnatchers really *cats*?"

"Thank you for saving Princess Grettifrida!"

Grit hopped down to Carmer's shoulder. "Hey! I hardly needed saving."

"What a fascinating story," said a cool, deliberate voice that echoed throughout the clearing. All chatter ceased at once, and the faeries flew back to the Great Willow, which had undergone yet another transformation. The head and torso of a beautiful woman was carved into the trunk, like the figurehead of a ship. The bark making up her hair and eyes was a rusty red that reminded Carmer uncomfortably of blood. "Yes, yes. Such bravery from ones so small." The bark moved and rippled as the figure spoke.

Carmer didn't miss the plural in that sentence, and by the angry noise she made, neither did Grit.

"Come closer, Felix Cassius Tiberius Carmer III," crooned the face in the Willow. "Let me look into the eyes of the boy who would manipulate my fragile daughter and expose us all for his own ends."

And things had been going so well. Every ounce of common sense Carmer had told him to cut and run, but he put one foot in front of the other all the same, until he was standing right in front of the likeness of Ombrienne Lightbringer, a queen of the faeries.

Her red eyes bore into him with such intensity that Carmer was sure they could see every selfish thing he'd ever done, every invention gone awry, every accidental minor explosion in the Manse's lab, every time he'd said the wrong thing to the wrong person. Memories of incompetence and guilt settled in his gut like a slimy creature determined to make a home there. But whatever those red eyes saw in him, they kept it to themselves.

"My daughter believes I should name you a Friend of the Fae," said Ombrienne. "Do you understand what that means?"

Carmer thought of Madame Euphemia and hoped it would not necessitate the purchase of puppets. "N-not exactly, no."

"To name you Friend is to lay ourselves bare before you. To give you a glimpse into the realm of Faerie and let you keep it in your pocket for the rest of your life. To allow you to call upon us in times of need. To share a small part of our magic to do with as you will. This is not a gift given lightly, and certainly not to little boys who hold faerie princesses hostage."

"He wasn't holding me hostage!" protested Grit. "I stayed with Carmer because we agreed to help each other. I keep my promises, and so does he. We need human eyes on the inside of the Mechanist's operation. And with a little faerie help, I think Carmer's the man for the job."

A few of the faeries nodded and flickered their lights in assent.

"How do you propose to infiltrate this man's headquarters, free our people, and make it out unnoticed? What is to stop him from coming after you and doing it all again?"

Carmer and Grit exchanged looks. They hadn't really thought that far in advance.

"The final round of the Seminal Symposium of Magickal Arts is tomorrow tonight," Carmer said. "That would be our best chance to sneak into his lab at Theian Foundry. The Mechanist will be at the Orbicle all evening—his assistant, too—and he'll be so focused on the competition, he won't be paying close attention to anything else."

"How can you be sure?" asked Ombrienne, a bark eyebrow raised skeptically.

"Trust me, Mother," assured Grit. "The Mechanist is a guy who likes to win."

"If we could use faerie magic to distract the Autocats—"

"And put my people in danger?" interrupted the queen.

"—we might be able to get into the lab unnoticed. I can't promise I can free the faeries then, but at least we'll be able to see what we're up against."

"Absolutely not," said Ombrienne. "The Seelie fae have already been dwindling in numbers for many years. I will not have you putting my few remaining subjects in harm's way for a sightseeing trip. If you're so determined to help, you can prove yourself by figuring it out on your own."

"Carmer's *already* proven himself, Mother," said Grit. "And who knows how long before the Mechanist starts to install Hyperiopower in the rest of the city? Before he can stroll right into the Arboretum with all of his stolen magic and capture us all? This isn't the time to hide in our trees or burrow into the ground like mice in winter. We can't hole up in here forever, Mother. The world outside is changing, and it won't be long before it reaches our gates. It already has."

Ombrienne turned her rust-colored eyes on Grit. "I suppose I'll never hear the end of this if I refuse," she said, sounding for a moment more like a normal put-upon mother than a ruler of realms.

A few cheers went up from the assembled faeries. Grit beamed, but Carmer was still wary. He was not in the habit of being judged by women wearing trees for faces.

The trunk of the Great Willow shuddered, and the faeries started to hum. Their harmonies, so close and effortless, blended into an eerie, ethereal tune that made Carmer sway on his feet where he stood. Grit squeezed his shoulder and he snapped to attention.

"What?"

"Just . . . try to keep your wits about you," warned Grit in a whisper.

Her advice was timely; the next moment, Queen Ombrienne's larger-than-life likeness popped *out* of the tree with a twisting, crunching sound that echoed like thunder. Her waist was still anchored to the tree trunk, but her upper body stretched toward Carmer and Grit, a wooden statue come to life. A shining staff appeared in her right hand. It was an apple branch cast in silver, topped by three perfect, golden blossoms ringing like bells. The sound was even sweeter than the faerie singing, and Carmer had to fight to keep his eyes from drifting shut.

Ombrienne extended the apple branch toward Carmer. White light spilled out of the cracks in the bark of the Great Willow, between the queen's wooden joints and out of the curls of her mossy russet hair. Carmer shielded his eyes from the brightness.

"Felix Cassius Tiberius Carmer III." Ombrienne's voice was no longer smooth and cool. It sounded like thunder and lightning and the roaring of the wind all at once. "Do you pledge your allegiance to the court of the Seelie Fae? To protect it, and all the fae, in times of danger? To guard the secrets of our magic with your life, and to use the power given to you wisely and justly?"

There was a small part of Carmer's mind that was still very much tethered to reality, and it sent off little warning bells pinging in alarm at the exact wording of such an oath—surely he should consult a lawyer before entering a binding agreement? What *exactly* was the difference between this "Seelie" and "Unseelie" business Grit talked about?—but much bigger parts urged him to say yes, to agree to anything the faeries wanted. The white light grew even brighter, but he didn't want to look away anymore. He wasn't sure he could.

"I do," Carmer said. "I swear it."

He grasped the end of the apple branch and the world exploded in gold and white. A jolt of energy rushed through him, from deep beneath the ground under his feet all the way up to the top of his head, and probably into the stars above. A pointy offshoot of the branch pricked his finger, drawing a drop of blood to the surface, but he felt no pain. He dimly wondered what any humans nearby must think of the light show suddenly emanating from the middle of a public park, but then realized they probably couldn't see it at all. *He* could now see what most people could only dream of.

Golden sparks illuminated everything in the grove. Where previously Carmer had only been able to see a thorny foot here, a shimmering wing there, or an indiscernible flicker of bobbing light, he now saw *everything*.

Carmer saw water sprites making the ripples of the pond at the foot of the Great Willow dance in glittering, swirling waves. Knobby-kneed hobgoblins danced a jig around the trunk, jumping higher than cave crickets over and under the giant roots. Hundreds of flowers went in and out of bloom in quick succession along the weeping boughs to the beat set by mushroom-eared salamanders banging drums of petrified wood.

There was music everywhere. A nightingale choir perched on one of the branches reminded Carmer so forcefully of a barbershop quartet that he laughed. Crickets in rainbow armor—armor!—played on their wings like violins. And above all, the faeries, every one of them in the grove, sang their haunting song.

Still on his shoulder, Grit turned her light on. She looked pleased but alert. "Carmer," she called over the music.

He grunted, distracted by the wonders around him.

"Carmer!" she yelled in his ear.

"What?!"

"Promise me you won't eat anything!"

Carmer's hand was fused to the apple branch, and it pulled him forward to Ombrienne—but he could no longer see her face in the tree. The Great Willow was bathed in bright light and splitting in two, right down the middle, and the voices that called to Carmer from within it could not be ignored. Wind rushed around them like a hurricane; Grit dug her heels into the wool of Carmer's coat and held with all her might.

"What? Why?"

"Just promise me!" yelled Grit. They were silhouettes against a doorway of white light.

"All right, all right!" agreed Carmer, but he wasn't really listening. He could barely hear her above the roaring wind.

Carmer stepped across the invisible threshold that led *into* the Great Willow. The faeries streamed in after him, all of them rushing toward the light. With a last great *whoosh*, the tree swallowed them whole.

Only the falling leaves and the skittering squirrels bore witness to the disappearance, and they weren't telling anyone.

TIME PASSED DIFFERENTLY in the Faerie realm; ten seconds could have easily been ten hours, for all Carmer knew. He was both inside the Great Willow and outside it, standing in the Arboretum he recognized *and* the Arboretum that was sharper and brighter and more magical than any human could comprehend. He was fairly confident he was in not another world, per se, but a diverted reality. It was a sideways-world, he decided — the place where Madame Euphemia's vardo existed, just outside the everyday here and now, where the shadows you noticed out of the corner of your eye or that sent shivers up the back of your neck were suddenly right in front of you, asking if you'd like to dance.

And dance Carmer did, with faerie lights and will-o'-the-wisps twinkling from every branch of the Great Willow. The tree had widened around them to the size of a grand ballroom, and though Carmer knew he and Grit were most definitely *not* the same size, it didn't shock him when her head suddenly came up to his shoulders and her hand fit snugly inside his as they twirled round and round.

240

"How are we doing this?" Carmer laughed, ducking and weaving through the other dancing bodies. Everything seemed so much funnier than usual, really. "Can you always change your size like that? All this time running around inside my hat . . ."

Grit shook her head and led him under an arch of branch-like arms that sprouted green shoots as they passed. The dryads responsible for this show burst into fits of giggles and ran off into the crowd.

"It takes far too much magic in the regular world," said Grit. "Even royal faeries can't sustain it for long, not without—"

"Wait, wait," Carmer said, stumbling a little. "Are we really not, er, *in* the regular world?"

Grit gripped him by the elbow and steered them toward the edge of the dance floor. "It's hard to explain," she sighed. She reached up and wiped a lock of sweaty hair out of Carmer's face and straightened his hat; the little door in its side had swung open. She, of course, wasn't subject to such human afflictions as sweat. "I'd say it's more like what the world was before it decided on what's real and what's not."

Carmer got it. Sort of. He nodded, but his head felt so heavy he almost fell forward. Grit grabbed him by the shoulders. She may have been human-*sized* to him then, but she most certainly wasn't human; her yellow eyes were still impossibly big, her ears still pointed beneath her pine-cone crown.

"I don't know why I'm even talking to you," she laughed. "All the magic in the air makes humans' brains fuzzy."

Carmer was about to protest that his brain was most certainly *not* fuzzy in any way, but then some of the faeries started shooting off fireworks (or whatever the faerie equivalent was) and his gaze was glued to the night sky.

"I *have* to find out the composition of those!" he crowed, craning his neck for a better view. "Do you know if the stars in them are pumped or rolled?"

Grit just stared at him. "You are unbelievable," she muttered, smiling all the same.

"Do you want to get closer?" asked a group of dashing-looking young men who danced into view, a graceful tangle of green armor and silver hair.

"Elf-knights," whispered Grit in Carmer's ear.

The elf-knights didn't have wings; they stood on shining leaves the size of tabletops that hovered over the ground. Their leader held out a hand to Carmer and cocked his head toward the fireworks above.

"Um . . ." Carmer looked to Grit. He had enough presence of mind to remember that her feelings about flying aids were conflicted at best.

"My feet burn holes in them if I get too excited," she said, shrugging at the floating leaves, "but you should go!"

Carmer thought her face fell a little, just for a moment, but the next second she was smiling again and pushing him toward the elf-knights. Their silver-haired leader took Carmer's hand and hauled him up as the others cheered and clapped him on the back. Their touch felt like dipping his toes in a cool, bubbling spring.

Before he knew it, they were ascending through the branches of the Great Willow toward the bursting colors in the sky.

But even with all the light around them, there were shadows here, too. Carmer glimpsed them through the spaces in between the Willow's branches and the hovering lights as they flew—a snarling mouth here, a pair of beady black eyes there, a grasping, gnarled black hand. He held onto his elf-knight a little more tightly than necessary.

"What . . . what are those things?" asked Carmer, slightly concerned that even in this realm of the impossible, he was seeing things other people couldn't.

"Oh, they're just the nosy ones from the Unseelie Court," said the elf-knight, his pretty mouth twisting with distaste. "They're attracted to the revel, like anything fae nearby. But not to worry, Friend! They can't enter a Seelie domain without permission."

Carmer was about to ask exactly what the difference was between Seelie and Unseelie faeries—the grimacing faces in the shadows certainly didn't look friendly—but then the flying leaves slowed their ascent and came to rest in the highest branches of the Great Willow. The tree had changed around them as they flew. Instead of the bowing branches of a willow, they were surrounded by the fresh scent and tickling needles of a pine tree that felt as tall as any tower in Skemantis. The sounds of the party below were fainter here, the flashes of the fireworks the only lights in the sky.

The elf-knight at Carmer's side suddenly leapt off their leaf with a wink and joined another; thankfully, his presence didn't seem to be necessary to keep it in the air. Carmer sat down and leaned back on his elbows, letting the crisp autumn wind wash over him. His leaf positioned itself between two branches, which helpfully grasped either end, suspending him in a slippery green hammock.

The faeries casting the fireworks flew even higher still, their tiny silhouettes just visible as they darted across the sky making shapes Carmer never thought possible. Flowers, flying birds, snowflakes, suns and moons and stars, even the outlines of mermaids swishing their tails, lit up the night sky, all moving in tandem with the faeries' hypnotic song. Carmer wished Grit were there to enjoy it with him.

"Magnificent, isn't it?"

Carmer sat up, sending his leaf swinging side to side, and clutched at the branch for support. A figure walked toward him from the other side of the tree, stepping from branch to branch as easily as a normal human might take a stroll down the road. The pale form was indistinct, obscured by furry swaths of pine needles blocking Carmer's view, but it grew clearer with each step.

It was a woman, her skin as pale as moonlight. Sheets of shining auburn hair fell to her ankles. With each step she took, leaves from the bottom of the real Arboretum floor rushed up the tree's bark to meet her, every autumn color of the rainbow. They fused together, one on top of the other, swirling up and around her body until she was clad in an entire gown made of leaves. To say that Queen Ombrienne was beautiful would have been quite the understatement.

She stopped at the base of one of Carmer's branches. It didn't even dip with her weight.

"Y-yes," he agreed. "Thank you. You didn't have to do all of this for me."

"The revel is a traditional part of the Friendship ceremony," demurred Ombrienne. She sat down with her back against the trunk, her flowing leafy skirts spilling out on either side of her. "It is a cause for celebration, yes, but also a chance for all of the fae to get acquainted with a new Friend." Ombrienne smiled at him. "Won't you join me for a toast?" she asked. "To our new Friendship together?"

Two birch bark cups appeared in her outstretched arms.

Carmer's leaf detached itself from the branches of its own accord and sidled right next to her. The prickly edges of the leaves on her dress brushed his skin and sent shivers down his arms.

"Grit told me something . . ." Carmer started, but it was terribly hard to concentrate just then, when suddenly all he wanted to do was look at the shining auburn waterfall of Queen Ombrienne's hair. It was funny how different it was from Grit's messy tresses shooting out in all directions . . .

The thought of Grit reminded Carmer of her warning.

"She told me not to eat anything here," he said, a little more sure of himself.

A few drops of golden liquid flowed over the tops of the cups and trailed down Queen Ombrienne's delicate white hands. "Well, *drinking* isn't exactly eating, is it?" she said with a small wink. It was like watching a very convincing ice sculpture try to pass for a human being, but Carmer blushed anyway. "Come now, just a taste. It is a party, after all." Her green eyes twinkled as she held out the cup.

"If you're sure it's all right?" Carmer said. Vague memories of an old story the Amazifier had told him long ago swam to the surface of his mind; something about a princess being trapped in the Underworld because she'd eaten of their fruit . . . or was it the story that passed around the orphanage once, about a magical floating market whose young customers were whisked away in the night, never to be seen again? Carmer had never had much time for stories—most of them just didn't seem *practical* for everyday life.

He was starting to wish he'd paid a little more attention.

"Don't worry, dear boy." The queen laughed. "I've no plans to keep you here forever. As a Friend of the Fae, you may come and go as you please."

Carmer nodded. It did seem rather rude to refuse a toast in his own honor . . .

He took one of the cups.

"To new Friends," Ombrienne said, holding up her own, "new alliances, and a brighter future for us all."

"Um. *L'chaim*," said Carmer. He had no idea what it meant, but the Amazifier always said it during a toast.

"And," the queen began.

Carmer paused with the cup to his lips.

"To my daughter."

That was something Carmer didn't mind toasting to. He smiled. "To Grit," he agreed, looking straight into Ombrienne's emerald green eyes, and drank.

18.

DOWN MEMORY LANE

FELIX CARMER'S EARLIEST MEMORY WAS OF SOME-
one playing with his hair. He couldn't have had very
much of it at the time, but he remembered the feeling of
someone's fingers brushing through it, drawing little swirls
around his ears, making funny shapes with the ends that
stuck up in all directions, smoothing stray locks away from
his face with gentle hands. Sometimes, mostly when he
was still at the orphanage, he let himself think it might've
been his mother. But only sometimes.

Now was one of those times. He was fairly certain
he was dreaming, because someone was running their
hands through his hair, and it felt exactly as it did deep
within those memories—places his mind explored only

in the space between dreaming and waking. No one he knew in real life would ever treat him like this, cradling his head in their lap like a child. He wasn't sure he would let them.

Yet he was only *fairly* certain it was a dream, because he couldn't remember falling asleep, and because the person stroking his hair was talking to him. He never remembered his mother talking to him.

"Felix Cassius Tiberius Carmer III," said the smooth voice from somewhere above him. "Such a big name for such a small boy."

He tried to wake himself up, but just turning his head felt like running a mile. He forced his eyes open, but all he could make out was a pale, blurry face above him.

Something crackled under his ear; he was lying on a pile of leaves.

"Being a Friend of the Fae is a great honor, Felix Carmer," said Queen Ombrienne, smoothing out the skirts he'd mussed up tossing and turning. Her fingers went straight back into his untidy dark hair, twirling locks of it into intertwining knots with deft hands. "But once you open that door, it's very, very hard to close again. And all kinds of things can slip through the cracks."

She paused and leaned over to cup his face.

"You wanted to be closer to faerie magic," she whispered. "And you are. But it's closer to you, too. I have to protect my daughter."

Queen Ombrienne bent down and placed a gentle kiss on Carmer's forehead. He could barely keep his eyes open.

"And that means keeping her away from you."

The waves of her hair fell down around him like a curtain, and the world went dark. If he hadn't been dreaming before, he certainly was now.

THE SUN WAS just beginning to peek over the horizon when Grit woke in her hollow in the Great Willow. Strictly speaking, faeries didn't *need* to sleep, but a refreshing nap after an all-night revel was nothing to scoff at. Mostly, faeries slept to dream. A vivid dream could warn the dreamer of trials ahead, or help them solve a nagging or overlooked problem too thorny to be tackled in the waking hours. A good dream could make an entertaining story the next morning, and stories were prime currency among the fae.

Grit did not have good dreams that night. Despite the frivolity of the revel, her dreams were filled with grasping shadows, shivering wingless faeries, and metal monsters that bit and slashed at her heels no matter how fast she ran. She'd called out for her mother, for Bressel or Carmer or anyone, but no one came. Carmer's face floated out of the darkness, but only for a moment, before he, too, was swallowed up into oblivion.

Grit woke calling his name and very much alone.

"Carmer?" she tried again, more quietly this time. Judging by the stillness around her, most of the castle was still asleep. Not a leaf stirred. The Willow was just a willow again—as much as a faerie castle can be "just" anything.

She rolled out of her hollow, rubbing sleep from her eyes, and padded out onto the nearest branch. The thinnest layer of frost crunched between her toes; autumn was nearly over.

Grit peered over the edge of the branch, expecting to see Carmer slumped against the thick trunk and snoring away—faerie revels were much more tiring for humans than for the fae—but she didn't see or hear anything remotely human. Now that she thought of it, she hadn't seen Carmer much at all the night before—not after he left to go watch the fireworks with the elf-knights. He was probably just on the other side of the Willow, abandoned by his playful new acquaintances when the magic of the evening began to wear off.

But when half an hour's climb around the entire Willow yielded no results, and none of the sleepy faeries she clambered over could give her a satisfactory answer, Grit was forced to accept that Carmer just wasn't there. He was probably waking up in some damp corner of the Arboretum, soon to be discovered by pointing, laughing humans or shooed off by a policeman rousting up vagrants. She needed to find him before he got himself into trouble.

A whistle and a few worm offerings later, Grit was soaring over the Arboretum on Dusten's back. Carmer should have been easy to spot; there were hardly ever any humans in the park at this hour. She flew to the West Gate and the

Whispering Wall first—no Carmer there. With much prodding, she steered the owl in a loop over the entire Arboretum, over the steep Widdershinner's Hill, through the hemlock grove and the birdhouse village and the wildflower meadow, dried and brown and reedy in the cold autumn sunrise.

Dusten hooted in protest when they finally made it to the North Gate; he knew the bounds of the kingdom, and would not go beyond. The city outside was waking up; merchants rolled their carts along the cobblestones, knots of bleary-eyed boys stumbled to their first shifts at the factories, and window-ticklers rapped on foggy windows to rouse those still sleeping in. And still, no Carmer.

Grit glared at the streetlamp just outside the gate. It was still shining merrily, though the sun was almost totally up.

"It's not even dark out," she groused, though she wasn't surprised. The Mechanist seemed determined to outdo everyone, including the sun. "Where *is* he?" Grit wondered aloud for the first time. She wasn't talking about the Mechanist. Carmer, Grit, and the queen were supposed to discuss today's plan, but the new Friend of the Fae was nowhere to be found.

"Are you waiting for someone?" Grit's mother touched down beside her on the gate. At one glance from the queen, Dusten flew off back into the Arboretum with what sounded like an apologetic hoot. Maybe the owl was smarter than he looked.

"Carmer's late," said Grit through her teeth. Her mother

was going to *love* this. "I'm worried something's happened to him."

"You cannot wait much longer out in the open like this, my dear," said the queen. "It's not safe."

Even Grit knew it wouldn't be wise to stand out on the gate in broad daylight, but she couldn't disguise her sigh of frustration as her mother lifted Grit under the knees like a little seedling of a faerie and descended to the Arboretum floor. She *hated* being lifted by her mother.

"He promised to help us," insisted Grit as they ducked under the cover of a bunch of sweet ferns. "He said he'd be here, so he'll be here."

"So you've said," said Ombrienne. "Perhaps he's merely been waylaid slightly, or gone back to his camp and overslept. Our revels can be quite the ordeal for humans."

"Maybe if we went back to the Whispering Wall," suggested Grit. "It *is* where we met before . . ."

"Don't worry, Grettifrida. Even in our absence, will not his Friendship with us guide him to the Great Willow?" asked Ombrienne. "We will all be safer in the shadows of its branches."

"I'm tired of hiding in the shadows, Mother," said Grit with a sigh. "I thought you were, too. I thought you agreed Carmer could help us."

"I did," agreed Ombrienne, "but I confess I'm starting to wonder if his help will come after all." Ombrienne weaved through the fern leaves, caressing each of them in turn. As her hand passed over each blade, it grew noticeably sharper and pointier—the better for snapping at the ankles of trespassing humans.

"It will."

"Are you so sure?" asked Ombrienne. "You have borne witness to this boy's selfishness before. You know he is capable of it. Perhaps now that he has obtained easier access to the magic he desired, he has left you behind?"

Grit shook her head. "Carmer's not like that. He wouldn't just abandon us."

"Then where was he last night, dear one? When he let himself be swept away by a few dashing elf-knights singing his name, and spent nary ten minutes with you?"

Grit had no rebuttal. It was true, Carmer had gotten rather caught up in the festivities, but it wasn't every day one was named Friend of the Fae. And Grit knew faerie revels were notoriously intoxicating for humans. She could hardly have expected Carmer to sit through it all being his usual inhibited, bashful self.

"I know he'll be here," Grit repeated stubbornly, crossing her arms and setting her jaw.

Ombrienne finished her stroll through the ferns and placed an arm around her daughter's shoulders. "I do hope so," the queen agreed. "If you insist on continuing your search . . . consider the Royal Guard at your disposal. They'll be more than happy to keep an eye out for your new Friend."

And the other eye on me, Grit thought.

"I've asked your friend Bressel to come and keep you company as well," said Ombrienne. "I know how you two get on."

Bressel, a dozen armored crickets and a battalion of hornets trailing behind her, appeared almost instantly on the path. Grit had the feeling they'd been lying in wait this whole time.

"Keep me company?" scoffed Grit. "You mean *sproutsit* me."

Bressel had the decency to look embarrassed.

"I'm not holing up inside the Great Willow and pretending this isn't happening," insisted Grit. "We need to wait. Just a little longer. Just until—"

"Until Carmer arrives. As you wish," said Ombrienne, with a nod to Bressel and the crickets.

Bressel curtsied low as the queen flew away.

"But do not let pride add fuel to the fire of your misplaced faith, my dear," warned Ombrienne from above. She and her hornets were gone before Grit could reply.

"I suppose you're here to wrestle me into submission and drag me back to the Great Willow?" Grit asked Bressel. "Gently, of course."

"Well," admitted the garden faerie, "we're supposed to wait a little while first."

CARMER WOKE TO the sound of water sloshing around his ankles. He was lying in a marshy wetland, surrounded by browning cattails, and unpleasantly damp down to his bones. The entire back of his body was sticky with mud. Worst of all, he had no idea how or why on earth he'd found himself in such a situation.

He sat up slowly, head throbbing with a dull ache and ringing ears. He took a few deep breaths and took stock of himself, but other than a few deep scratches on his palms—how had he ever gotten *those?*—he seemed to be all right. He got unsteadily to his feet, mud sucking at his ankles, and looked around. He heard the sound of rushing water and surmised it was the Bevel River, which meant he shouldn't be far from the circus camp outside the city. A glance to the west confirmed his guess; he could see the smoke rising from a few cook fires from where he stood.

But how did he get to be there, lying in the mud and feeling like he'd been both run over by a steam engine *and* out dancing all night? Neither of those seemed highly likely, but he couldn't seem to remember anything about the night before. He wondered if Kitty and the Amazifier knew where he was, then felt a surge of panic. If he was out here in the middle of nowhere with no memory of how he got there, where were they? He needed to get back to the camp as soon as possible and make sure they were all right.

You'll be lucky if they let you in the door, he thought, and then paused. Why would he think something like that?

A rush of hazy memories came back to him.

"I was visiting another magician yesterday," said Carmer, *"but it wasn't to steal from him. I was asking for a job."*

"I've been looking for another magician to study under. I didn't want Master Antoine to win the competition."

"I tampered with his illusions to draw suspicion. It was all me."

What had he done? Carmer remembered realizing the Mechanist was *actually* industrial tycoon Titus Archer after overhearing a conversation between him and his apprentice, but after that, things were less clear. He remembered visiting Archer's lab, Theian Foundry, and . . . being offered an apprenticeship of his own? It seemed impossible, but so did waking up in four inches of mud without knowing how he'd gotten there. But had he really accepted the Mechanist's offer? Had he really left Kitty and the Amazifier in the lurch right at the moment when they needed him most? None of it made any sense, but trying to remember exactly what had happened was like running his mind into a brick wall. He just . . . didn't remember.

Carmer needed to find Kitty and the Amazifier. He needed to make sure they were all right and apologize for his behavior. He didn't know who or what could have persuaded him to actively sabotage the Amazifier's act, but there was something *very* off about Titus Archer, and Carmer knew the rival magician was somehow involved in all this. With any luck, the Mechanist would be at the Orbicle preparing for the show as well, and they could clear up any misunderstandings.

He trudged through the marsh toward the circus camp, and it was nearly afternoon before he reached the Moto-Manse. People gave him odd looks as he walked through the camp, some of them openly hostile. He must look a fright, covered in mud, hands wrapped in filthy bandages, and generally looking like he'd spent the night in the swamp. Many of them had undoubtedly heard of his betrayal and weren't bothering to disguise what they thought about it. He couldn't blame them.

Carmer tramped up to the door of the Moto-Manse and knocked. There was no answer. He knocked again. Even if they were home, he couldn't expect a warm welcome.

"It's me," Carmer called into the door. "Please let me in. Something's happened. I . . . I need to talk to you."

Still no response. Hopefully, Kitty and the Amazifier had already gone on to the Orbicle to prepare for the night's performance, far away from whatever sorry business had led Carmer into the middle of a swamp in the dead of night. First, though, he needed a change of clothes. The doormen at the Orbicle wouldn't let him within ten feet of the building looking like a vagabond and smelling like a bog.

Carmer reached up to check the cleanliness of his hat, for which he did not have high hopes, and was surprised when his hand met empty air. Somehow, he'd lost his favorite top hat during the night. He felt curiously sad at its absence. He'd had that hat since the Amazifier first made him an apprentice.

But he wasn't the Amazifier's apprentice anymore, thanks to circumstances he still couldn't fully wrap his head around. Perhaps after a shower and a quick cup of tea, more of it might come back to him. He reached out to open the Moto-Manse's door and turned the knob.

It wouldn't open. They'd locked him out.

Carmer rested his head against the door. He'd never had a key to the Moto-Manse, because he'd never needed one. He was usually safely inside whenever the old magician locked it for the night. Now, he was an unwelcome outsider.

Unwelcome outsider or not, he needed clean pants. He scooted around to the back of the Moto-Manse and slipped under it—it hardly mattered whether he got dirt on himself now—and felt around just behind the boiler compartment until he found a latch. It squeaked as he pulled but eventually opened with a hole just big enough for a boy of his size. He slithered into the bowels of his former home and pushed up through a trapdoor into the engine room.

He tried very hard not to feel like everyone he knew had abandoned him, or like he had abandoned *them*, and didn't quite succeed. A cup of tea was definitely in order.

IN THE COLD stone shelter of Oldtown Arboretum's famous Whispering Wall, a flame was born. It came to life with a breath and a wish and the rubbing together of two tiny palms. It was no bigger than a candle flame, despite its maker's best efforts. This was no mere exercise, and today, a forest fire was exactly what she needed.

Well, perhaps not a whole forest fire—what had the poor trees ever done to her?—but a sizeable conflagration all the same. The hundreds of pieces of paper shoved into the cracks of the Whispering Wall would do just the trick.

"I don't see anything from up here!" called Bressel from the top of the wall. "What are you doing down there, Grit?"

"The crickets are searching the ground!" Grit shouted back. "Maybe he left something behind."

Grit said the words, but she didn't believe them. After hours of combing over every inch of Oldtown Arboretum, two things had become abundantly clear. The first was that Felix Cassius Tiberius Carmer III was no longer there, hadn't been for some time, and, from his lack of any sort of message, had no plans to come back. The second was that the Royal Guard was never going to let her out of their sight ever again.

The hope that flared so brightly within the kingdom the night before was but a dim memory now. With Ombrienne's encouragement, the faeries who usually inhabited the edges of the Arboretum retreated inward. Dryads wept thick, dark tears of sap as they abandoned their trees that skirted too close to the edge of the city outside. Lions, giraffes, and other animal-shaped topiaries inched away from the areas most populated by humans, penned in by earth faeries too frightened to let them amble freely as usual. The frog ponds froze over, and a thick frost spread outward from the Great Willow even in the afternoon sunshine.

Nothing was going to change after all. They were still running scared, the Mechanist's power was still growing, and Grit felt like she was the only one who was mad about it. She was certainly mad enough to keep fighting—Carmer or no Carmer.

Grit was done waiting for him, and if a few traitorous tears leaked out of her eyes at the thought, the cold wind whipped them away fast enough. If Carmer had truly abandoned her, it didn't change the fact that the Mechanist still had to be stopped. Perhaps she could convince the Free Folk to fight instead of flee, or even approach the Unseelie, though the thought of *that* meeting sent shivers up her spine. And if Carmer *hadn't* run, if the Mechanist really had found a way to keep him away from the faeries, then she needed to find him. At any rate, she had to get back in Skemantis, and being stuck in the Great Willow under the beady, watchful eyes of the armored crickets was *not* going to get her there. She needed a diversion.

Grit knew she didn't have much time before the crickets she'd sent searching around the Whispering Wall came back. She held her flame aloft, circling her hands around its dancing edges to make it as large as she could.

"I'm sorry," she whispered to a hundred years of wishes, and launched the flame at the stones.

Only a few of the notes shoved in the cracks truly caught on fire, but even the smoke would be enough to draw the crickets' attention, and her magically enhanced flames would spread soon enough. When the smoke started creeping up the wall, Grit ran in the other direction as fast as she could. The West Gate was the closest exit she could hope for; she barely managed to stay out of view of the panicked crickets swarming toward the fire.

"Oh, her mother is *actually* going to kill me!" whined Bressel from the wall, dithering between patting at the spreading flames and flying after Grit. "I'll be demoted to leek duty forever!"

"Maybe," Grit said to herself as she vaulted between the iron bars of the West Gate, "but at least there'll be leeks to look after at all."

19.

THE BELLY OF THE BEAST

CARMER RACED UP THE STEPS OF THE ORBICLE, only to be stopped by the doorman already stationed outside for the evening's performance.

"Sorry, performers only, kid," said the red-suited young man.

"I am a performer, sir," insisted Carmer.

"Hey, wait a minute," said the doorman's colleague on the other side. "That's the kid! The little snitch the boss told us about. Black-haired little munchkin in shabby clothes, he says."

"Are you the kid?" asked the first doorman, holding Carmer by the collar.

"Probably," admitted Carmer. He wasn't too sure of anything these days.

"Well, scram," said the doorman. "We've orders not to let you in." He steered Carmer around and gave him a shove.

"Please, it's important!"

"Ain't it always?" teased the other doorman.

"No, you've got to understand—"

"Listen, kid, do we have a problem here?"

They were starting to attract attention from passersby. Carmer would have to find another way in.

"No, sir. No problem."

"He's with me," piped up a familiar voice behind him. Gideon Sharpe stood on the steps, already changed into his full costume, looking every inch the proper magician. His long plait of blond hair fell over his shoulder and shone in the sunlight under a brand-new top hat.

Of all the people he wanted to come to his rescue at this precise moment, Gideon Sharpe was pretty near the bottom of the list.

"He has a meeting with my—*our*—employer. It won't take long. I promise you, no one will even know he's here," Gideon assured them smoothly. He clearly got his lessons in charm from his master.

"You're the Mechanist's boy?" asked the second doorman.

Carmer was sure he saw Gideon visibly chafe at being called someone's "boy," but he didn't think the doormen noticed.

"I'm his apprentice, yes," corrected Gideon. "And as we are regular performers in this establishment, I'm sure you know he doesn't like to be kept waiting."

"That he doesn't," admitted the first doorman.

The second nodded. "Make it quick."

"Oh, it will be," Gideon assured him.

Before Carmer could protest, the blond-haired boy was guiding him forcefully by the elbow into the theater. Carmer saw a flash of silver and felt something cold and sharp press into his back.

"What the—"

"Not a word," Gideon hissed, leading them through the bustling lobby, the flat of a knife pressed against Carmer's ribs. Around them, stagehands and producers and performers were in a flurry of activity getting ready for the night's final show; there was to be an opening spectacle in addition to the magicians' performances. No one noticed the terrified boy being herded at knifepoint by the Mechanist's assistant.

They walked down a red-carpeted corridor and into a nearly deserted tile hallway. At the end of it, Gideon kicked open a door, revealing nothing but a staircase going down into darkness.

"In," he ordered.

"But—"

"Now." Gideon poked Carmer with the tip of the knife, nearly breaking the skin.

Carmer took one step down, then another, and the door slammed shut behind them, plunging them into darkness. The lock clicked, a pin drop in the silence.

"Keep going," instructed Gideon.

Just as Carmer was about to protest that he couldn't see where he was going, a dim silver light emanated from somewhere behind him; the band around Gideon's wrist was glowing, and it provided just enough light to see the edges of the stairs beneath his feet. They creaked with every step the boys took.

After what seemed like an eternity, they finally reached the bottom. Carmer nearly lost his balance, expecting there to be another step. The light moved and the air shifted behind him. Gideon strode away from Carmer, leaving him momentarily unguarded. Carmer watched Gideon's light zigzag around in the dark, dodging unseen obstacles. Carmer considered running back up the stairs but didn't think much of his chances down here in the pitch-black with an adversary who clearly knew the territory.

Somewhere, Gideon flipped a switch, and half a dozen arc lights stuttered on — big, unflattering bulbs usually reserved for factories. Carmer shielded his eyes until they grew adjusted to the light.

They were in the basement of the Orbicle, and it was an explosion of organized chaos. Bits of set pieces, old costumes, spotlights, mannequins, spools of rope and wire, even old stage curtains, cluttered every bit of the cavernous space. The ceilings were surprisingly high for a basement, and Carmer knew they must be deep underground. Here, a piece of Juliet's balcony leaned against a Roman chariot. There, giant sheets of glass in every color of the rainbow lined up like soldiers at attention. Above Carmer's head, six pairs of angel wings hung from a wire rack suspended from the ceiling, a macabre mobile. One of the feathers brushed against his cheek.

"It won't do to run," said Gideon. He placed a pale hand on a black silk–covered birdcage on the workbench next to him. "I've locked us in, and no one will hear you down here."

"What are you *doing*?" asked Carmer. He knew the rival apprentice didn't like him, but kidnapping him and dragging him into a deserted, locked basement seemed a little severe.

"Even for an idiot," observed Gideon, "I didn't think you'd be quite so gullible." He reached into the folds of his cloak and took out the knife—but it wasn't a knife at all. It was a magic wand with a pointed silver tip.

Carmer *did* feel like an idiot then. "What do you want from me?"

"Please don't play dumb, Carmer. It won't get you anywhere. Tell me where the faeries are, and my master will let you crawl back into whatever hole you came from."

"The faeries," said Carmer. Clearly, Gideon Sharpe was toying with him. "The *faeries*?"

"Yes, Carmer, the faeries," spat Gideon. "Surely you didn't think we wouldn't notice such a flagrant use of fae power, even at the pedestrian levels of *your* magic act."

"Listen, I have no idea what you're talking about—"

"I don't have time for this," muttered Gideon. "You refused to join us willingly, but you *will* lead us to your little friends." He swept the black cloth away from the birdcage. Inside was not a real bird, but an automaton even more complex than Carmer's soldier. It was a completely clockwork crow, all of its parts painted jet-black except for a swirling silver orb under its breast where its heart should have been. It spread its wings and cawed, beady glass eyes fixing themselves on Carmer.

Carmer remembered the Mechanist's mechanical doves dive-bombing the Orbicle's stage and gulped.

"I will be the one to bring the rest of Skemantis's faeries to my master," said Gideon, red spots rising on his pale cheekbones. The crow stepped out of the cage and flew onto Gideon's shoulder.

"Find any faeries hiding on him," Gideon told the bird. "And if he won't tell us how to find the rest, peck at his eyes until he does."

"What the—" Carmer had just enough time to duck before the crow dove at his head. Its talons raked against the fabric of his coat. He swatted at it with all his might, but the crow kept coming, pecking at his pockets, his sleeves, even the turn-ups of his socks.

"I don't have any faeries!" Carmer yelled and turned to run, but the crow sank its talons into his collar and dragged him back with much more strength than it should have had. "I don't know what you're talking about!"

"Save it!" yelled Gideon. His cool attitude from earlier abandoned, he leapt over the workbench toward Carmer. "I know a Friend of the Fae when I see one!"

He pushed Carmer, hard, but Carmer knocked Gideon across the face in one of his attempts to throw off the crow. They fell into the ring of hanging angel wings, accidentally pulling one pair off its hook and onto the ground with them, oversized white feathers floating around them like snow. Gideon pinned Carmer beneath him.

"You think you're so special?" asked Gideon, panting. His hat had fallen off in the fray and strands of blond hair were escaping his neat braid. "You think you're the only lonely child those creatures have ever preyed on?"

The crow flew back to Gideon's shoulder. They both looked down at Carmer with wild eyes. Carmer had no idea what this insane boy was talking about, but he knew one thing: if he had any hope of getting out of this place, he had to destroy that bird.

With his last ounce of strength, Carmer reached up, grabbed the bird around the middle, and smashed it as hard as he could against the concrete floor.

"No!" gasped Gideon. He released Carmer, just for a second, but that was all Carmer needed. He scooted out

269

from under Gideon and crawled backward until his back collided painfully with something behind him.

The crow still flew, but haltingly. Its left wing was bent at an odd angle, and the fine silver powder that seemed to operate it was leaking out of its side. Both boys watched as it dipped and weaved around the room; they couldn't look away. Odd things happened to the objects where the glittery dust fell. Spots of peeling paint on set pieces looked suddenly brand new. A demon's mask mounted on the wall started moving, lips spreading open in a grin with a frightening cackle. A fake Christmas tree in one corner started *growing*, actually growing, green silk boughs stretching outward and upward, its wrought iron stand bending and twisting into roots that dug furrows in the concrete floor.

The bird shuddered back toward them, weaving in and out of the angel wings still hanging above, scattering the glittering dust on them. The wings sprang to life at once, leaving their wire perches behind and flapping with utter abandon, careening into each other, soaring over the boys' heads. Carmer looked around wildly; a fake gold-painted tree caught his eye. He broke off one of the branches and waited for the moment when the broken crow tried to return to its master.

Gideon saw Carmer raise the branch and was about to stop him when one of the rogue angel wings buffeted him across the face, blocking Carmer from view. Carmer swung with all his might and smacked the crow into the wall. It met the stone with a sickening crunch, and its silver heart shattered.

The shimmering dust exploded from the bird's body. Carmer instinctively threw his hands up in front of his face, dropping the branch. But he wasn't fast enough; it was as if the powder *wanted* to find him. The specks of silver turned to gold as they hit the air. They flew into his eyes, blinding him, and all he saw was light.

Somewhere, a door inside of him opened.

Carmer remembered everything. He remembered Titus Archer, and the Autocats, and his deal with Grit. He remembered lying to protect the Amazifier, his Friendship with the fae, and his fateful encounter with Ombrienne.

Grit. Carmer had to find her. But first he had to get out of here.

The magic in the room faded with the shattering of the crystal heart. The mask stopped cackling, the tree stopped growing, and angel wings dropped to the floor, inanimate once more. His eyes still full of faerie dust, Carmer turned on Gideon Sharpe, who crouched down at his ruined bird's side.

"No," said Gideon again. The word was a sob in his throat. He stroked the bent metal wing and looked up at Carmer, eyes fearful for the first time. His silver wristband with its curious stone lay a few feet away, the clasp snapped in the struggle. Carmer picked it up and pocketed it.

"I need to get out of here," Carmer said, mostly to

himself. A place this big couldn't have just one door. How did they get the set pieces up into the theater? There had to be some sort of lift or ramp—he just had to find it.

Carmer's eyes were still burning from the faerie dust, and he looked at the world through a golden haze, but something told him not to rub it out just yet. One of the pairs of angel wings rose from the floor, flew over to him, and batted itself helpfully.

Carmer shrugged. It was turning out to be that kind of day.

He pulled the straps attached to the wings over his shoulders. They beat once, twice, and his feet were off the floor.

"Maybe your experience was different from mine," conceded Carmer. "I don't know what the faeries did to make you feel like this, but you have to trust me. They're not all bad. And I'm sure when they named you Friend, they didn't have this in mind."

"Wait!" cried Gideon. "You don't—"

But Carmer was already flying away, his wings scraping the ceiling as they carried him through the underbelly of the old theater, up and away through the freight elevator shaft, and back to the friend he'd promised to protect.

GRIT COULDN'T BELIEVE her eyes. She'd called in every favor, summoned every skittering creature that ran on four legs that would pay her heed, even hitched a ride with a surly, smelly garden gnome in a farmer's cart full of pumpkins—all of it to reach the Orbicle before the night's performance. All of it for the small chance that she might worm her way into the Mechanist's domain and see something, anything that might help her stop him. She'd already sabotaged one magic act, after all. How hard could it be to slip in a few well-placed jabs of her sword and ruin another?

As it turned out, she did see something—and as so often happens, it wasn't what she wanted to see: Carmer, whole and unharmed, walking arm in arm into the Orbicle with Gideon Sharpe.

It was like the first time she fell off Dusten, back when he was no more than a ball of fluff with wings, but still very much a wild thing. Something spooked him while they practiced loops around the frog pond, and before Grit knew it, there was suddenly nothing between her and the ground but open air. Her stomach sank down to her knees while her heart leapt up into her throat. She didn't even have time to make a sound. One moment, there was something holding her aloft, strong and powerful and alive; the next, nothing. Only rushing air and the futile flapping of her lonely wing that made her twist and tumble as she fell down, down, and down some more.

Fortunately, a sylph—a faerie of the air—happened to be flying by that day, and quickly summoned a stiff wind to slow her fall and nudge her over the pond. She fell facedown into the water, a brutal slap that she was lucky didn't break her bones, though it left her sore for a week. Sore, but alive.

This felt like that, but there was no one there to break her fall this time. There was only Carmer's disappearing back and the hideous blinking marquees and the choking smog and the deafening noise of the city. There were only heavy boots to dodge and steam carriage wheels to run out from under before they crushed her. It didn't matter that she'd once wanted to be a part of it all. It didn't matter that this was the world where she'd felt the thrill of combining her magic with Carmer's, where she discovered that just because her fire was different didn't mean it couldn't burn just as bright.

What mattered was that, yet again, she was alone. A small part of her had dared to think—no, dared to *hope*—that something had happened to Carmer. That there was a plausible explanation for his sudden disappearance right after being named Friend of the Fae. The Carmer Grit thought she knew could mess up royally sometimes, it was true, but when he made a promise, he kept it with a stubbornness that rivaled her own (and that was *really* saying something). Only an army of Autocats could have kept him from seeing this thing through, for both of their sakes.

Or so Grit had thought. But there Carmer was, running right back to his old life, putting on cheap tricks for money and taking meetings with the Mechanist himself, as if his Friendship meant nothing—or worse, as if he'd been waiting to use it for the Mechanist's ends all along. Grit felt sick.

She stumbled behind the theater and rubbed at her eyes, fighting back the sob threatening to burst out of her throat. Two fat black rats rummaging through the trash cans paused in their squabble over a rotten apple to stare at her. She almost stuck her tongue out at them, but it hardly seemed worth the effort.

They ran squeaking back under the trash cans and Grit sighed. Not even *rats* wanted her around.

If she'd been paying better attention, she would have noticed the real reason for the rats' flight. Luckily, Grit saw the shadow move just in time: a skulking Autocat just about to spring. For half a second, she hesitated, knowing she could never outrun the cat and feeling almost relieved that at least, finally, she could just stop running all the time.

But then Grit remembered Carmer's observation after their first encounter with an Autocat.

Everything is less scary when you know how it works. The next time we meet the Autocats, we know there's a good chance of disabling them if we go for the heart. We'll be ready for them.

The Autocat pounced; Grit skidded under its outstretched claws by a hair's breadth and vaulted upward, grabbing onto its thigh. The cat's body flailed this way and that as Grit swung herself around to its more vulnerable underside and climbed quickly toward its crystal heart, just visible under a mess of wiring. The cat rolled onto its back and tried to swat at her, but it couldn't reach Grit without tearing at itself. The Autocat lurched into the street.

Grit hung on for dear life as the cat rolled again, this time to dodge a speeding carriage that nearly crushed them under its wheels. By the time the Autocat righted itself again, Grit was firmly enmeshed in its metal insides. It shook itself in the shadows of the Orbicle, meowing and growling, but Grit held on tight. The Autocat would have to claw out its own heart to get to her now.

Messing up the Mechanist's magic show would make him angry, that was certain, but it wouldn't stop the Hyperion for good. If Grit wanted to find the missing faeries, she needed to go into the *real* belly of the beast: Theian Foundry.

"Okay, kitty," Grit said to her unwilling ride, "run along home."

20.

UNLIKELY ALLIANCES

THE FIRST REAL FROST OF THE SEASON SETTLED over Oldtown Arboretum like a prickly blanket. If the townspeople thought its sudden appearance odd, they soon forgot about it as they turned away from the Arboretum. And turn away they did, forgoing their usual afternoon stroll or shortcut through the gardens because of an inexplicable desire to go the long way around.

Carmer felt the faeries' magic working against him as his feet crunched over icy grass. He barely noticed the new streetlamp or the freshly laid cobblestones. Thoughts encouraging him to turn back, to go find a nice cup of hot chocolate instead of tramping around in the cold, sprang up in his mind. But he was wise enough to ignore them, and when he approached the North Gate, it swung open before he had so much as raised a finger. He kept his head low, well aware that his eyes were still flashing with golden light.

Carmer shouldn't have kept the magic inside of him this long, but he'd needed to get to the Arboretum as soon as possible. His eyes burned, and it was getting harder to see; red spots dotted his vision, already compromised by the golden haze the faerie dust cast over everything. There was a dull, throbbing pressure in his skull that was only getting worse, and yet he was so full of energy he was practically shaking. He was thankful for the boost, but Friend of the Fae or not, he needed to get this stuff out of his eyes.

For a second time, the path seemed to know where he wanted to go. It wove around a trail of bare tulip trees and lindens that turned slowly into pockmarked corks and a trio of frozen frog ponds, finally spitting him out in the midst of a birdhouse village. Birdhouses of every shape and size dotted the clearing, some mounted on wooden poles, others seeming to grow out of the trees themselves. There were small cottages with thatched roofs, long log cabins, stately colonials—he even spotted a replica of City Hall that he was surprised could stay upright on its own. All of it was rendered in exquisite, miniature detail.

There were few birds about. It was cold, that was true,

but there was something else. The whole Arboretum was too quiet, like it was holding its breath.

In the center of the village was a stone fountain. The statue in the middle was a siren with the head of a beautiful woman and the body of a bird of prey, and the talons that gripped the jagged rock she perched on looked deadly. Carmer approached cautiously; he hadn't had the best luck with beautiful women lately.

But the siren remained as still as stone should be. Water trickled from holes at the end of each carved feather in her outstretched wings, out of her mouth and her eyes. The surface of the pool was half frozen, thin films of ice bumping against one another in the faint ripples.

Carmer's vision flashed red and gold, blinding him, and pain seared through his head. He leaned against the edge of the fountain for support.

"I'd get it over with, if I were you," advised the siren.

Carmer was shaking so badly he could hardly muster surprise. He plunged his head into the fountain, eyes open as far as they would go.

The cold was shocking. Carmer gasped in surprise and got a breath full of freezing water in his lungs for his trouble. He came up coughing and sputtering, but his vision and his head were clear again.

"Well, that looked bracing," commented the siren.

Shivering, Carmer sat down on the edge of the fountain

and shook the water out of his ears. He tried not to think about his eyelashes, already freezing into icicles. "Yes, ma'am," agreed Carmer.

"It's a bit of an overkill with the frost and the doom and gloom, I know," said the siren pleasantly.

Carmer wondered if she had anyone but the birds to talk to.

"But I suppose, without a princess, we *are* all in for it anyway . . ."

"What do you mean, without a princess?" asked Carmer sharply.

"Oh, haven't you heard?" asked the siren. She looked a little too happy to be the bringer of bad news. "The queen's daughter's been taken by the Wingsnatchers. It's all anyone's been talking about. Or rather, *not* talking about. We'd better not let Her Majesty hear us gossiping, she's in a dreadful mood. Well, obviously—"

"I have to talk to the queen!" interrupted Carmer, already running down the path. "Thanks for your help!"

"Oh! Well," huffed the siren. "The next time you need another refreshing dip, you know who to call!"

CARMER FOUND THE Great Willow within minutes—this Friend of the Fae thing was starting to come in handy—though it wasn't a willow today, but an ancient yew with a trunk wide enough to fit several Carmers inside. The frost that covered the rest of the Arboretum grew thicker as he approached; every bough of the tree was covered in a layer of ice. Carmer could see his breath in the unseasonably cold air. It felt more like the dead of winter than autumn.

"Your Majesty?"

Queen Ombrienne knelt in a gaping knot in the center of the yew, staring straight ahead. Her dark red hair pooled around her feet and her wings beat listlessly. There was no face in the willow, no glowing woman clothed in leaves this time—just a tiny faerie sitting in a giant tree, utterly alone.

Carmer walked right up to the queen. He didn't have the time to be afraid.

"They took her," said Ombrienne dully. "They took my daughter."

"I heard," said Carmer.

"Do you know what will happen to this kingdom without a royal heir, when I move on?"

Carmer shook his head.

"Neither do I."

"Queen Ombrienne . . ." Talking to queens wasn't something Carmer was accustomed to, and Grit wasn't here to break the ice for him—literally or figuratively. "Even if you just did it to get me out of the way, you still made me a Friend of the Fae. I made a promise to help—took a *vow* to help. I think I can get past the Mechanist, but we need to work together."

The queen stared ahead, barely acknowledging that Carmer had spoken, but then something in her eyes hardened. She took a deep breath.

"I cannot leave the Arboretum myself."

"I understand that."

"But . . ." She hesitated, then made a decision. "Consider all of the fae at your disposal."

Carmer thought for a moment.

"*All* of the fae?"

"I DON'T THINK I like him," said Abby Absinthe critically. "He's got knobby knees. I don't trust little boys with knobby knees."

She took a long draw from her pipe and blew three smoke rings that hit Carmer square in the face. They smelled like rotten eggs. He coughed and would have backed away, but there was nowhere for him to go. He took up most of the room in the tunnel near the Green Goddess, and it was hard enough being careful not to sit on any faeries as it was.

"But, how do you know I've got knobby knees?" wondered Carmer. "You're . . ."

Abby Absinthe cackled. "Blind?" she asked. "You don't say! No one's bothered to tell me."

"This is hardly the time for jokes," said Ombrienne, and the assembled fae turned to face her—or rather, her image—once more. They were gathered around an underground waterfall created by the meeting of multiple pipes, and a projection of Queen Ombrienne flickered across the falling water. Ombrienne regarded them through her own waterfall from somewhere in the Arboretum. She paced back and forth, warrior hornets shadowing her every step.

"My apologies, my Queen," corrected Abby with a sarcastic attempt at a curtsy. Carmer thought Ombrienne scowled, but it was difficult to make out her exact expression in the rippling water. "But the Free Folk have already lost many of our kind to this Mechanist, and our pleas for help fell on deaf ears. It's only now that your own daughter's been taken you're singing a different tune, and all you send to help is a boy who knows nothing of the fae."

"Well, I wouldn't say—"

"You know nothing, Felix Carmer," said the old faerie.

Carmer snapped his mouth shut.

"If you are unwilling to help, then I will not beg," sniffed the queen.

Carmer was starting to see where Grit got her stubbornness.

Abby Absinthe snorted and took another puff from her pipe.

"She shouldn't have to," said a soft voice from the back of the crowd of Free Folk. A skinny, frail-looking street faerie with a worn felt wrap around her shoulders stepped forward. Carmer could only see the tip of one wing poking out from underneath it. Whispers sprang up around her; this must be Echolaken, the water faerie who survived the Autocats.

"Grit saved my life," said Echolaken. Her voice shook, and she looked down at her feet. "She's one of us, too, and we owe her a debt."

A ripple of unease went through the crowd. (Carmer would later learn that life debts carried strong weight among the fae, and one did not speak of them lightly.) A debt was power in another person's (or faerie's) hands, and it must be repaid when called upon. That was the way of things.

"Echolaken is right," said a dark-haired faerie Carmer recognized as Ravene. "How many revels has Grit joined us for? How many scavenging missions has she helped complete? She may be of the court, but we are all fae."

Many of the other faeries nodded in agreement. The corners of Abby Absinthe's wrinkled lips turned up, and Carmer had a sneaking suspicion the old faerie had planned the course of the discussion from the very start. The street fae began talking among themselves, small groups animatedly debating whether to lend their help or not.

After a few moments, Abby raised her dandelion staff and the tunnel fell silent.

"We of the stone streets of this city—tamers of the iron world—are beholden to no one," Abby Absinthe said, addressing the crowd. "We answer to no queen. I cannot and will not command any of these folk to fight these Wingsnatchers."

Ombrienne's face fell.

"But I also cannot stop anyone who wishes to try," Abby finished.

Silence filled the hall. Only the rushing sound of the water echoed through the tunnel.

"I will help you, Carmer," said Ravene. She turned her light on and hovered in front of him. "The Free Folk are no strangers to iron."

"As will I," said another faerie, a young man with thick brown hair. He was the first male faerie Carmer had seen. He added his light to Ravene's.

"And I," said a fierce-looking fire faerie nearby, flicking her wrist to produce a small torch of flame.

"And I!" said another.

"Me, too!"

"Might as well go down fighting!"

Soon, more lights were shining than not. Determined little faces surrounded Carmer and Abby.

"I think I have a plan," Carmer said to Ombrienne. "But there's no telling what will happen when we get inside the foundry."

"What do you say, Queen Ombrienne? Can the Free and Fair Folk play nicely together for one night?" asked Abby with a sandpapery chuckle.

"Well," huffed the queen, her hornets already flying into formation around her. "I suppose one night couldn't hurt."

THE AUTOCAT HAD enough of an instinct for self-preservation not to throw itself off a bridge or self-destruct, for which Grit was grateful. She endured the bumpy ride to the laboratory in silence. Neither she nor the cat were keen to draw attention to themselves, it seemed. The Autocat kept to the shadows of the busy streets; the crowds thinned out as they approached what Grit assumed was Theian Foundry.

The cat padded to the back of a main building. It was quieter here; the sun would set soon and the workday was ending. A group of studious-looking young men passed, comparing notes and sounding almost disappointed they'd been sent home early for the day. Of course, the Mechanist would be busy preparing for that evening's performance.

Grit could feel the crawling cables—she thought the workmen outside the Arboretum called them "power lines"—running through the freshly disturbed earth all the way to the theater district. Stolen faerie magic made that power possible, and if the Mechanist got his way, the whole city would soon be using it.

The Autocat pressed its nose against a metal cat flap in the back door, which sprang open at its touch. It slipped inside, meowing for attention. Grit reached up and pulled at random at one of the levers in the cat's throat. It fell silent with a strangled gurgle and hissed, a few sparks shooting out of its nostrils.

Grit concentrated with all her might on remaining invisible as they passed lab tables still occupied by a few Titan Industries employees. The Autocat tried to approach one of the men packing up for the evening, but Grit gave another one of its wire muscles a yank, and it listed to one side, nearly toppling over.

"Oh no you don't," Grit hissed, but one of the workers had already spotted the cat. She froze. If he decided to examine it, the jig was up.

But the short, brown-bearded man only shuddered and turned away.

"Those things still give me the creeps," he said to a nearby coworker. "Couldn't they make a little more noise when they walk?" Both men turned to leave.

The Autocat stalked to a plain black door where another cat flap she hadn't even seen sprang open. It shut behind them, edges melting back into the smooth surface of the door. They descended a wide flight of stairs, buzzing bulbs lighting their way on both sides, into the basement of Theian Foundry. The Hyperion was waiting for them.

Grit realized it was time to take action. She slunk down a few inches, as close to the Autocat's crystal heart as she could get, and zapped it with the strongest spark she could muster.

There was a flash of light and the crystal exploded. Faerie dust propelled outward, but Grit turned it to ash with a flick of her wrist. The Autocat collapsed in a heap, its insides a warped and melted nest of metal. Grit fell with it and knocked her head on the hinge at its shoulder. She came up seeing stars and clutched the cat's remains for support, extricating herself with difficulty. She fell onto the floor with a sigh of relief, hardly caring if anyone saw her. But there were no men down here.

Grit slowly raised her head, noticing for the first time how much noisier it was than on the ground floor. Then she saw the source of the low rumbling and scrambled to her feet.

A massive machine took up nearly half the room. Three times the width of the Great Willow and taller than a man, it was surrounded by a complicated framework of pipes and wires and had two great pillars extending almost to the ceiling. Grit could feel the pull of the giant magnets that made up the bulk of it. She could feel something else, too—the pain of nearly a hundred faeries who were trapped inside.

Grit ran up to the base of the machine, heedless of any Autocats that might be on her tail, where a multilayered cylinder—the dynamo, Carmer had called it—spun round and round. The imprisoned faeries were inside one of the compartments. But how could she get to them? The dynamo was a fortress of iron; even standing next to it made Grit feel sick and unsteady on her feet. (Although taking a knock to the head couldn't have helped matters much, either.)

Her best chance was to approach from above. If she could climb the many shelves lining the walls, hop onto the exposed piping for the sprinkler system, get her hands on some wire or twine or *something*, then rappel down between the two pillars—

Oh, for fae's sake, she thought just as an iron cage suspended from the ceiling fell down around her with a deafening clang.

"You made me scratch my floor," said a petulant voice.

Grit turned to see Titus Archer standing behind her. He was dressed as the Mechanist, his sickening cloak of faerie wings draped across his shoulders, but he wasn't wearing his trademark clockwork mask. Grit supposed he didn't much care whether his prisoners knew his true identity.

The Mechanist surveyed the broken Autocat at his feet and gave it a nudge with his toe. "You killed my cat." His face was calm, but he kicked the corpse of the Autocat so hard it ricocheted off the wall.

Grit jumped back in surprise and hissed in pain as her bare skin made contact with the iron bars of the cage. Just one more reason to hate her mother's stupid flower petal dresses.

The Mechanist ambled toward her, his black leather boots twin monsters from every young faerie's nightmares, ready to stomp the life out of any tiny being in their path.

"*And* you and your little Friend seem quite intent on exposing my identity to the people of this fine city."

289

He surprised Grit, then, and sat down on the floor, crossing his legs like a child and resting his elbows on his knees. He peered into the cage with genuine curiosity.

"If you weren't so very important, I'd be very cross with you," the Mechanist scolded.

Grit glared at him.

He shrugged. "Do you know why I perform as the Mechanist?"

She shook her head.

"Because the only time people will accept real magic in their midst is when they are a hundred percent certain it is fake. This is the mistake too many others have made in introducing magic to the general populace. My dynamo merely builds on existing theory. The electricity it creates is an extraordinary phenomenon, to be sure, but electricity can be produced by other means. My method just propels it more sustainably into the future.

"But the limits of possibility with this kind of real magic—or, as I prefer to call it, real *science*—can never be explored in the usual channels. How many witches burned at the stake are proof of that? The Mechanist's performances, safely couched in anonymity, are my true laboratory, the real testing ground to stretch the limits of my power."

"You mean the power you stole," spat Grit.

The Mechanist frowned. "Do you not have an arrangement with the humans of this city already?" he asked. "For over a century, your kind provided shelter and light in the

Arboretum. You cared for it and made it your home, but you opened that home to Skemantis."

"We didn't *make* it our home," countered Grit. "It was always ours. And we let you humans in on the condition that you leave us be."

"Yes, you did at that," said the Mechanist. "But in case you haven't noticed, Princess Grettifrida, your bargaining power has been decreasing steadily for centuries. A hundred years ago, your people consolidated their territory to conserve their power. They made a deal to ensure their survival. I propose it's time for a new one."

"To be your slaves."

"To work *with* humanity, with progress, instead of against it!" insisted the Mechanist. He shimmied a metal sheet under the cage until Grit was forced to hop on top of it or lose her toes. She was truly trapped on all sides now.

The Mechanist picked up the cage, holding it firmly from the bottom, and stood up. "It is time the fae adapted to the modern world," he said. "This is merely an extension of the relationship some of your kind have already cultivated with humans."

"I'm sure the faeries forced to spin your wheel until they drop are big fans of your 'relationship.'"

"I provide incentive, Princess. No one works well without a little pressure." The Mechanist ducked around the interconnected pipes and wires in front of the dynamo. "And I am hardly a cruel man." He paused. "Well, perhaps I am, but not to the extent that it hinders my business. I would never let these faeries work themselves to *death*—what would be the point in that?"

Grit snorted.

"Did you see the third floor of my humble establishment here?" asked the Mechanist. "It's a greenhouse. A faerie paradise utterly protected from the outside world."

"But not from you," muttered Grit.

The Mechanist stopped in front of a steel box with a door made of bars suspended in the center of his pipe maze. A direct line went from the dynamo to the box, with more wires feeding out in every direction toward the tower in the ceiling. He opened the door.

"No," the Mechanist admitted. "Not from me." He tossed Grit in the box.

"No, no! What are you doing?" demanded Grit. The box was surrounded by iron that made her head pound and her breath come in gasps. Tendrils of gold wire snaked out of nowhere and wrapped themselves around Grit's wrists and ankles. The iron's effect dulled somewhat as she found herself suspended in a web of golden wires in between two magnets wound tightly with coils.

The Mechanist's face was inches from her own. He fiddled with various knobs on top of the box, and the wires around Grit tightened. "Do you know what a transformer does, Grit?"

"No! Let me go!"

"Let me see if I can explain it in terms you'll understand. Simply put, it does exactly what it says—it *transforms* the power generated by a dynamo, either increasing or decreasing it, in preparation for distribution across the power system—to my lights in this lab, or to the theater district, for instance. I find fire faeries make particularly good transformers, perhaps because fire is one of the oldest sources of energy there is. But my system still has its limitations. One dynamo can only power a few city blocks. But with a *royal* fire faerie's magic . . ."

"I'll never help power your stupid machine," spat Grit. "You'll have to kill me first."

"Or I could just kill all the others," said the Mechanist.

"No, you can't—"

"My Autocats can always find more. Your cooperation is entirely up to you." The Mechanist actually smiled.

Grit hung her head.

"That's better," he said. A long, gloved finger chucked her under the chin and she turned her head away. "You're learning already. Now, I want you to watch these gauges here." He reached into the box and tapped inside the top, just above Grit's head, where circular displays like tiny clocks were attached to the machine. Each had a red hand that moved up and down across a scale.

"It's very important you use your power to amplify each volt of power as it passes through the transformer, and make those little red arrows point as far as they can to the right," instructed the Mechanist. "If you don't, your little friends will suffer the consequences."

"No. No. No no no no —"

"This might sting a bit the first time," warned the Mechanist. He flipped a switch inside the box and slammed the grill shut.

The power of the entire dynamo rushed into her at once, and Grit heard someone screaming like their insides were on fire.

It took her a moment to realize the screaming was coming from her.

21.

BREAKING
AND ENTERING

"THIS IS THE STRANGEST THING I'VE EVER DONE!" shouted Carmer above the sound of roaring rapids around him. He clung to the slimy mane of the kelpie propelling him along the shores of the Bevel River. Lieutenant Axel Hudspeth, his automaton soldier, stood at attention in a weather-sealed leather case strapped to his back.

You and me both, mon ami, whinnied the kelpie with a frothy toss of his head. Carmer could hear its deep, lolling voice inside his mind.

Giving a ride to a boy and *a Friend of the Seelie Court! How times have changed. I usually prefer . . . guests of a more feminine persuasion,* explained the kelpie with a chilly chuckle.

"Are you from the Unseelie Court, then?" asked Carmer as he rocked back and forth on the rapids. His legs were submerged in icy water, but the kelpie's magic kept him from feeling the worst of the cold.

Mon dieu, how the time does fly, said the water horse, sidestepping the question. His pace slowed, his body dissolving into the foaming breakers with each step toward the rocky shoreline. A few seconds later, only his shaggy blue head remained solid and visible above the water.

You give those Wingsnatchers hell from us, Carmer III, said the kelpie.

Before Carmer could reply, the kelpie disappeared completely in the gently lapping waves, and Carmer felt the horse's weight go out from underneath him. Carmer staggered up the shore and headed for the cover of the trees. He looked down and was only a little surprised to find himself completely dry.

Hiding as best he could in a thicket of birches near the river, he removed his bag and unpacked Lieutenant Axel Hudspeth. The automaton soldier had gotten a hasty makeover, Madame Euphemia-style, and could now follow simple commands and move on his own without being wound.

"Stay close to me for now," Carmer whispered.

Lieutenant Hudspeth saluted him.

They darted from the tree line, the lieutenant's brass joints creaking a little as he ran. With the kelpie's help,

Carmer had approached from the north, looping around in the Bevel River, as he was certain he wouldn't be a welcome sight waltzing up to the front door at Theian Foundry. He hoped the faeries were in place and that Madame Euphemia hadn't encountered unplanned trouble on the road.

As if on cue, a bang and a splintering crunch rent the air. *This* was the trouble on the road he'd been hoping for. Carmer's distraction had arrived.

The front corner of Madame Euphemia's vardo was smashed into the cobblestones directly in front of Theian Foundry. The remains of one of its front wheels spun uselessly on the ground, spokes splintered. The wagon looked ready to fall on its side at any moment.

"Oh, goodness!" cried Madame Euphemia. She thrust open a lace curtain and peered out one of the tiny square windows.

The driver, dressed like a small boy but with a hat pulled suspiciously low over his face, hopped down from his seat. A few curious faces poked out of the foundry's front door.

"Well, what are you standing there for, boy?" said the old woman to the little driver. "Go and fetch help!"

The puppet scampered away.

Madame Euphemia caught the eyes of the assistants watching her from the doorway. "And you!" she shouted at them. "What are you gawping at? Aren't you going to help an old lady in need, or should I resign myself to a long, cold winter out here in the middle of the street?"

Men in white lab coats hurried out at once, leaving the door behind them wide open, and three marionettes slid silently out of the back of the vardo and slipped out of sight.

"It's about time," groused Madame Euphemia.

Half a dozen air faeries—Carmer thought they were called sylphs—circled the top of the factory, unnoticed by human eyes. Two ugly smokestacks and a brick chimney protruded up through the glass-walled greenhouse on the roof. They weren't much in use today—the Mechanist had less need for burning coal now that his faerie-powered dynamo was up and running—but a few steady streams of black smoke still curled up into the sky. The sylphs sang to the air around each vent, binding it to their will until it spun in tiny whirlwinds, and then with shrill little laughs sent the twisting air crashing back down the way it came.

Poof. Poof. Poof. The ash and smoke went soaring back down the chimneys and into the laboratories, scaring the remaining Titus Industry employees out of their wits. They ran coughing from the polluted clouds billowing from the flues and out into the cold, fresh air of the grounds with their goggles still on and their coats pulled over their mouths.

Carmer and the lieutenant took advantage of the chaos. They ran alongside the foundry wall and slipped past the marble pillars into the open front door. Meanwhile,

Madame Euphemia kept the three employees assisting her occupied, supervising the moving of the vardo toward the stables while they waited for the "help" that would never come. The men staggered underneath the weight of the wagon while Madame Euphemia urged them on.

"That's it, boys! Put your backs into it! I'm not getting any younger!"

Madame Euphemia's puppets cut through the stables to get closer to the lab without being seen. The horses snorted and whinnied as the puppets wove in and out of their legs and over the walls of their pens.

"I say, where's all that smoke coming from?" asked one of the employees.

"I have some potentially volatile chemicals inside—"

"Should we wire Mr. Archer?"

"He said he was not to be disturbed!"

"Well, that was before . . ."

Two puppets wearing Japanese hannya masks and wielding curved blades, along with the little French maid Carmer thought was named Whoseywhatsy, met Carmer and the lieutenant just inside the front door of Theian Foundry. Carmer took a quick head count, looked around for witnesses, and shut the door behind them.

Carmer didn't think the Mechanist would keep Grit on the first floor of the laboratory where anyone could see her. The black door marked AUTHORIZED PERSONNEL ONLY seemed the most likely candidate—especially since

Gideon's wristband was practically humming in Carmer's pocket, as if the doorknob were calling to it—but they had to make it there first.

"Let's split up," Carmer said decisively.

Whoseywhatsy and one of the demon-masked puppets took the lab's rightmost aisle, Madame Euphemia's third puppet took the center, and Carmer and the lieutenant took the left. They proceeded cautiously. Autocats could be hiding anywhere.

Sure enough, two ruby- and emerald-eyed monsters pounced into the aisles as soon as Carmer and the others stepped forward. Carmer had a smoke bomb at the ready, but he didn't want to use it if he didn't have to.

Fortunately, water faeries were waiting and they sprang into action. They'd flown in through the chimneys after all of the humans fled, braving soot and ash and smoke, and worked their magic on the sprinkler system. Water streamed from the pipes suspended above them, and Carmer was delighted to see that automaton cats hated water just as much as their living, breathing counterparts, if not more.

The Autocats yowled and tried to run for cover, but the water faeries were faster. With a flick of the faeries' wrists, the water covering the cats froze as hard as a rock, immobilizing them.

"Go for their hearts!" Carmer instructed, and the wooden hannya puppets leapt forward, blades flashing. The Autocats' hearts exploded in blinding clouds of faerie dust; Carmer made sure to cover his eyes and shield the lieutenant, but Madame Euphemia's marionettes were not so lucky. The instant the faerie dust hit them, its magic seemed to fight Madame Euphemia's, and they crumpled to the ground in twitching piles of wood and string.

Carmer knew faerie dust could be unpredictable, but he wasn't prepared for a reaction like this. While the faerie dust incapacitated Madame Euphemia's puppets, it had the opposite effect on nearly everything else. Glass bulbs burst at its touch. Model dynamos spun frantically in the wrong direction, sending sparks flying. The machines still running went haywire, smoking and gurgling.

"Get out of here!" he said to the frightened water faeries still hovering up above. He ran to the black door and shoved Gideon's wristband at the doorknob; it sprang open with a silver flash. The lieutenant went down the stairs first, sweeping his rifle back and forth.

The first thing Carmer saw was the remains of a tourmaline-eyed Autocat lying in a heap against the wall. He ran to it and examined the insides; the crystal heart was empty, its faerie dust turned to harmless ash.

"Grit," he breathed. He recognized her handiwork. She had to be here.

Carmer looked up to see the towering Hyperion, this one nearly twice the size of the machine he'd seen only a few days ago at the expo. It was crackling and thundering and making a noise that sounded like a stampede. Carmer could see the spinning rotor from here and knew the enslaved faeries must be inside. In front was a makeshift transmission substation with a box-shaped transformer that connected the whole system to underground conduits spreading out from the dynamo like a spider's web. It took the electricity up and away to the rest of the compound and, Carmer guessed, any parts of the city now using Hyperiopower.

Carmer bolted for the Hyperion, but two new Autocats were hot on his trail. The lieutenant fired a few shots, but they merely pinged off the Autocats' armor. An orange-eyed cat pounced on him, and Carmer left them wrestling by the stairwell. Carmer brandished Gideon's wristband at the remaining cat and it backed away slightly, but he had little time to waste. Where were the street faeries?

"Sorry!" called Remus, one of the faeries from the Green Goddess, suddenly fluttering above Carmer's head. He brandished a lock pick and a razor mounted like an axe in each hand. "The cat flap nearly took our heads off!"

A dozen street fae streamed down the staircase, screaming war cries, and launched themselves at the Autocats. Some carried hatpin swords and other weapons, like Grit, and all wore armor to protect themselves from the iron in the factory.

"Get at their insides, if you can!" Carmer said to Remus, who nodded and joined the others. Carmer lowered Gideon's wristband and ran to the dynamo, dodging around the pipes and wires of the substation with care.

"Grit!" he called. "Grit, where are you?"

The machine was so loud he could hardly have heard a normal person shouting above the din, never mind a five-inch-tall faerie. But he heard the trapped faeries calling loud and clear as if they were standing right next to his ear.

"Who's there?"

"Don't answer, it's probably just one of his tricks!"

"Help us, please!"

"I'm a Friend, I promise!" said Carmer, crouching as close as he dared to the spinning rotor. He looked down into one of the few air vents cut into the cylinder, but all he could see was a rush of silver and the occasional glimpse of a tiny upturned face or a wing tangled in gold wire.

"How do I get you out?" Carmer asked. "How do I turn this thing off?"

"You need the key!" one faerie's voice cried, carrying above the others. "It's a faerie heart. He wears them around his wrists."

Carmer looked down at the silver wristband with a new sense of revulsion. Sure enough, when he crouched down low enough, he saw a small indentation the exact size of the stone at the very bottom of the outer shell. He pressed the stone into the hole and cursed when a jolt of electricity ran through it, strong enough to nearly knock him off his feet. The wristband jolted from his grasp. His skin crackled with static and his hair stood on end.

"What the—" Carmer bent down and poked at the

wristband with the edge of his coat. A thin tendril of smoke rose from the blackened, cracked surface of the stone; it no longer glowed.

It had been foolish to think Gideon's band would work as a key for the most sensitive part of the Hyperion. Of course, Titus Archer would never trust a mere apprentice with access to the machine itself.

"I'll get you out," Carmer said with more certainty than he felt. "I will."

" . . . Carmer?" The voice was faint, so quiet he almost missed it underneath the thundering of the dynamo.

"Grit! Where are you?"

"Carmer . . . I thought . . ." Her voice echoed in his head, fading in and out. He looked around wildly—he didn't think she was with the other faeries—until his eyes came to rest on the transformer. Of course.

He knew better than to touch the live box without thinking it through, but he couldn't stand to do nothing. Yowls, hisses, and scratching sounds came from the stairwell where the Free Folk still battled the Autocats. They were trying to get inside the beasts, but the cats were warier now and kept the faeries at a distance with swipes of their sharp claws. Carmer wasn't sure how long the faeries could hold them off.

He navigated through the substation as cautiously and quickly as he could until he faced the grilled front of the transformer. Through all the glowing sparks, he could just make out Grit's silhouette on the inside. He slipped on the pair of safety gloves he'd had the sense to pack and reached out a hand to test how tightly it was sealed—

"No!" Grit said.

Carmer froze.

Her voice was taut with pain. "If you try to tamper with it, the iron will crush them all."

"There's got to be a way," insisted Carmer. He examined every inch of the box, but it was sealed tight. "What's he done to you?"

"Th-thought . . . you would know . . ."

"Wait, *what*?" asked Carmer. "How would I know? Oh, no. Did I forget something else?" Carmer paced back and forth in front of the transformer. "I thought I remembered everything I forgot!" he exclaimed. "But then again, I wouldn't remember it if I'd forgotten it, would I?"

"Carmer, stop. *Stop*," ordered Grit.

He stopped.

"What . . . what are you talking about?"

Behind them, Carmer heard glass breaking and faeries yelling. "Your mother," he said, leaning as close as he could without getting burned. Grit groaned, whether from pain or realization of what he was about to say, he wasn't sure. "She made me forget, and—"

"Honestly," she said, "'your mother' was all you had to—*argh.*" Grit's body arched as another wave of energy tore through her.

"We'll worry about it later," said Carmer firmly. "What's happening here?"

"I . . . I have to amplify the dynamo's power," explained Grit. "He said only my magic can channel it. But Carmer . . . the magic competition . . . with all this power, I don't know what he could do."

Neither did Carmer, and that was what worried him most of all.

22.

HOW THINGS WORK

GIDEON SHARPE DIDN'T OFTEN VENTURE TOO close to nature these days. He preferred the ordered sterility of his master's lab, the crowded but purposeful city streets, or even the dusty grandeur of the Orbicle. He kept his horses and his birds close, lest they get any ideas from . . . outside influences. He took the long way around the Arboretum, if he could, or only cut through it in daylight. There had been a time when a place like the Arboretum would have been his sole refuge, but those days were long gone.

There were things waiting for Gideon in the wilder parts of the city, things that were very unhappy about how he had used and abused his connection to them. It was in his best interest to avoid them. How long he could do so, Gideon didn't know, but as long as he stayed well within the realm of the Mechanist's protection, he was safe.

Or so he liked to tell himself.

But sometimes Gideon couldn't help it. Sometimes the old ache came back to him, and he found himself here at the back of the Orbicle, staring toward the North Gate of the Arboretum with a mixture of longing and revulsion.

"I don't know what the faeries did to make you feel like this, but you have to trust me. They're not all bad. And I'm sure when they named you Friend, they didn't have this in mind."

No, they certainly didn't. The faeries of the Unseelie Court hadn't expected their frail little changeling boy to rebel with a will of his own, to use his Friendship to ensnare enough magic to break free of their hold and turn it against them, to attract the attention of a man with enough power and vision to bring them all to heel.

Gideon remembered his life before the Mechanist, when he was nothing but a plaything for the amusement of the fae, and thought of how far he'd come since then. Now he was the assistant to the top industrialist and most famous illusionist in the country! Felix Carmer knew nothing. The boy could keep his lousy Friendship and see where it got him. Soon enough, there would be no faeries, Seelie or Unseelie, free of the Mechanist's grip.

And Gideon had been the first one to bring the magic to him.

The North Gate knew his secret. No matter how many lights they installed, how many airships and flashing marquees cluttered the skies, there was only so much one could do to keep the darkness at bay. The wild things were still there, even in the heart of a city like Skemantis, waiting for the sun to go down.

Perhaps Carmer was right, and the faeries hadn't always been creatures of darkness. But the iron world outside had changed them, was changing them still—surely the darkened lights of the Arboretum were proof enough of that. Though Gideon knew the Seelie Court held the Arboretum, it gave him no comfort now.

It was nearly time to get onstage. He should go inside, make sure his master was ready, and check the props one last time. But as he watched the blanket of frost creep closer and closer across the other side of the gate, chilly fingers caressing everything they touched, he could not look away. Like so much of that realm, it was beautiful—beautiful and terrible.

The back door of the Orbicle slammed open, and Gideon had to jump out of the way. The Mechanist stood in the doorway, his clockwork silver mask already adhered to his skull.

"There you are," Titus Archer said. "Where have you been? It's nearly time."

"I was just—"

"Never mind," snapped the Mechanist. "Stable your horses. We will have no need of them tonight."

"Sir?" Gideon's trained horses were essential to their final performance—an Indian rope trick variation—especially now that the water tank escapology act hadn't come to fruition. (Gideon could still feel the bruises from the Mechanist's displeasure about *that*.) To change it now . . .

"Despite your lackluster efforts," said the Mechanist, and Gideon recalled his encounter with Carmer with embarrassment, "we are now in the presence of *royalty*."

Gideon's eyes widened. If the Mechanist had gotten his hands on the faerie princess rumored to be roaming the city, his power could increase exponentially. He finally had the amplifier he so desired.

"Tomorrow, we'll be powering half the city," said the Mechanist with a smile. "But tonight, we will perform miracles." He clapped Gideon on the back, a rare gesture of affection. "Just try not to look too surprised, my boy." The Mechanist winked, and his silver mask winked with him. With the Mechanist in command of royal faerie magic, there was no telling what he'd do. Gideon just hoped he had the sense to rein in some of his more outlandish impulses for the masses.

"Yes, sir," Gideon said.

That explained the frost. A royal faerie had been taken, and the shadows knew it. They licked at Gideon's heels as he followed his master inside. The royal faerie's magic would only make them more powerful, Gideon knew, but he couldn't shake the feeling of unease that was his constant ball and chain.

The things in the dark had given Gideon life, and now they wanted it back.

"I DON'T KNOW what to do, Carmer."

It was probably the first time Grit had ever said those words in her life, or at least admitted them to another person. But with every part of her hooked up to the Mechanist's infernal device, with electricity running through her veins and pounding in her skull and racing outward to fuel the Mechanist's evil magic, it was true. It took nearly every ounce of her strength and concentration to keep the dials level; if she didn't, she knew the Mechanist would make good on his threat. Somehow, the Hyperion was designed to keep every faerie working at the risk of endangering the others. If they stopped producing faerie dust to power the dynamo, the outer mechanisms of the rotor stopped protecting *them* from the oppressive iron. It was a perfect prison.

Grit could just make out Carmer's worried face through the metal grille in front of her. She wanted to tell him to run, to take the remaining faeries and find somewhere, anywhere to hide, but a great pull from the outer edges of the Hyperion's web left her gasping for breath. Cold crept into her bones, despite the immense heat she was generating. The Mechanist's performance had begun.

"Grit!"

But Grit was far away. Parts of her were soaring over the city; she watched it from above and from below, from the miraculous wires that carried her from Theian Foundry to the heart of the theater district, around the North Gate and into the Orbicle itself—into the outstretched palm of the Mechanist.

So this is what it's like to fly, thought Grit deliriously. The irony wasn't lost on her. A hysterical giggle rose up out of her throat, but the sound of applause drowned it out. People were clapping . . .

"GRIT!" Carmer rapped the side of the transformer with something.

The pinging rang in her ears and brought Grit crashing back to the present—or rather, her *own* present. "Stop!" she yelled. "I said not to touch anything! Are you crazy?!"

Carmer sighed in relief. "There you are."

Grit didn't have the energy to be annoyed at him. Although, strictly speaking, she had too *much* energy . . . another strangled giggle nearly escaped her, but she caught Carmer's gaze, and it died on her lips.

"Look at me," he said firmly. "You don't need to look at the dials. Your output's been steady since I got here, except for the surge just now."

"But—"

"No," he insisted. "Stay right here with me."

"The show started," Grit murmured. "There's nothing . . ."

"There's always something," said Carmer. He reached up to adjust his top hat, frowned when it wasn't there, and ran a hand through his disheveled hair. "Remember the night we first talked, really talked, about the Autocats? I told you that . . . that things are only scary if we don't know how they work. Or at least, a lot scarier than they have to be. Do you remember?"

Grit wanted to nod, but she was so tired . . .

"Answer me!" demanded Carmer.

"I remember, I remember!" she said. Why did he have to keep bothering her, when it was getting harder and harder to believe there was a *her* to bother?

"You told me yourself," said Carmer. "Fire is the purest form of energy there is. There's fire in you, Grit, and it's what makes you part of this machine. It's a part of you, and you're a part of it. I've seen you drive a steam engine, make fountains out of flames . . . You blew that Autocat's heart to smithereens! And . . . and if you can learn that much about your own power in such a short time, then you can figure out how this machine works. You took the cat down from the inside, Grit. I saw what's left of it. Now do the same to the Hyperion."

"Wh-what?" stammered Grit. "I can't, I . . . Carmer, there are too many . . . oh, what do you call them . . . variables! There's too much that can change, Carmer, too much that can go wrong."

"And what will happen if you don't even try?" asked Carmer.

They both knew the answer, and it wasn't good. Grit wondered how much time had passed, how much time they even had left until someone discovered them. If they were going to try anything, it would have to be now.

"I wish I'd never met you," groused Grit. She just managed to meet his eyes through the grate.

"I'm afraid I can't say the same," said Carmer. He ducked his head and looked down at his toes, turning once more into the shuffling, shy boy she'd saved only a few days ago. And it was enough.

Grit closed her eyes, took a deep breath, and became the Hyperion. She reached out with her magic, tentatively at first, sending little sparks like messenger birds down the wires and tubes around her, reading the pulsing energy and taking in everything they saw along the way. It was a great, thrumming energy, this was true, but every wave was different. The currents that tore through her weren't singular, powerful jolts, but multiple smaller ones that ebbed and flowed like the tides. She saw them, their apartness, a spidery web of red across her eyelids, and separated them even more. She took some—just enough—for herself.

Carmer watched the golden sparks spread outward, crawling and buzzing over the machinery like curious bees, inspecting every corner of the machine. He followed their path, though the light was so bright it hurt to keep his eyes on them. The sparks halted at the last of the interconnected tubes.

"You're reaching the end of the substation," he explained, keeping one eye on the transformer. "The dynamo is coming up. You'll want to keep with the current and wind around the armature—the big pillars—to get back to the center . . ."

Carmer guided her as best he could, his voice standing out sure and soothing against the grinding mess of the rotor. Grit's energy went farther, hitting iron walls and doubling back, yes, but also finding cracks. She made them bigger.

She saw the other faeries chained like her, the forced fluttering of their wings producing a boiling cloud of faerie dust. The dust was curious, exploring parts of the machine it had never seen before, but Grit held it in her sway. *Not yet,* the fire inside her said, and the fire in the dust listened.

It was getting hotter. *Grit* was getting hotter, which was impossible, because fire faeries didn't get hot. Gold sparks wrapped around the entire Hyperion, lighting it up like a Christmas tree. The little pieces of power she'd snuck away were impatient, boiling and building up inside of her. They wanted out, and she barely had time to tell them where to go before they got their wish.

"Carmer, get back!" she yelled. She opened her eyes and the power streamed out of her in a wave.

The rotor ejected itself from the iron base with such force that the very air around it sizzled with heat. It skidded across the middle of the lab, taking out the pipes of the transmission substation and sending Grit's transformer soaring into the air and crashing to the ground. Black scorch marks trailed all the way to the stairwell. The electric lightbulbs mounted on the walls exploded. Shards of glass rained down, crunching and clinking on the concrete floor.

Carmer and the street faeries had just enough time to duck out of the way. The Autocats had not been so lucky, and the sole surviving cat was crushed underneath the now-still rotor. The lock at the rotor's base sprang open, each layer of metal raggedly pulling back like an onion as gold sparks tugged at the edges. The sparks fizzled out one by one and utter silence fell.

Carmer extricated himself from the tangle of tubes that had fallen down around him, his ears ringing. The Free Folk turned their lights on as bright as they could to fill the fresh darkness of the basement. They waited with baited breath until a tiny, bony hand reached up from the metal ruin of the dynamo.

"A little help here!" called the faerie inside, and the Free Folk rushed to her aid. More lights turned on inside the empty shell of the machine, hesitantly at first, others flickering from injury or fatigue. Carmer left the street fae to help the faeries inside.

He ran to the ruined transformer, a blackened, twisted hunk of metal in the midst of the destroyed substation. He picked his way over downed wires and pipes carefully, but with little fear they were still active. Only faerie light illuminated his way now, and Carmer had the feeling the rest of Skemantis that relied on Hyperiopower would be in the dark, along with the Mechanist.

He pulled his safety gloves on tighter, turned the box over, and opened the still-smoking hatch with ease. Grit lay inside, tangled in a mess of gold wire—some of which, Carmer was horrified to note, had melted into her skin. She was barely conscious and her eyelids flickered weakly. Carmer peeled the wire away as gently as he could, stopping once to grab a pair of pliers, but he couldn't stop his hands shaking at Grit's whimpers of pain.

He lifted her out of the transformer and held her in his cupped hands. Her light flickered once, then went out, and she shivered. Her skin was freezing to the touch and tinged with blue, which Carmer knew was never a good sign, even for faeries.

"Grit," Carmer whispered to her. He leaned in so close, he could see his breath in the cold air around her. "Grit, can you hear me?"

Her eyes flickered open, just for a moment. "I'm sorry, Carmer . . ." she murmured. She shivered harder in his hands.

"Sorry?" said Carmer incredulously. "What do you have to be sorry about?"

"I don't think I have enough magic to help the Amazifier tonight."

Carmer almost laughed, but the sound caught in his throat. He bent his head to touch Grit's.

"Actually," he said, "I think you just did."

317

23.

THE SHOW GOES ON

THIS IS HOW I DIE, THOUGHT GIDEON SHARPE. HE was past panicking, past wasting effort pounding ineffectually at the heavy glass that trapped him in his watery grave. The burning in his lungs had reached its peak, and it was perfectly clear there was no use fighting it. The Mechanist was not going to let him out.

The so-called "water torture cell" was his master's newest endeavor in escapology, and he was keen to show off his new power, even if only Gideon could appreciate it. Imagine, using fire-based magic to pull off a watery escape-or-die stunt! They had never successfully performed it yet, but the Mechanist had decided that with the power of the royal faerie at his disposal, tonight was the night.

So Gideon was bound hand and foot, wrapped in chains tested and tugged by various audience members, and lowered into a cylindrical glass tank filled with water. The Mechanist would throw his cloak over the tank and remove it mere seconds later, revealing it to be empty. After the first round of applause died down, he would cover the tank again and walk behind it. This time, however, *Gideon* would walk out from the other side, completely dry, and remove the cloak. The Mechanist would now be chained inside the tank. Another round of applause, another flourish of the cloak, and the Mechanist would emerge, completely unscathed.

Would, would, would. All of this would have happened if they'd been able to channel the fresh power in the Mechanist's wristbands to cut their bonds, if their flow of magic hadn't been suddenly and swiftly cut off. Gideon felt its retreat just as his head sank under the water, like all the oxygen being sucked out of the room. The presence that he'd felt as a boy, which he'd been building on for years, vanished to almost nothing.

Just as the top of the tank clicked shut, the entire theater plunged into darkness. The electric lights, robbed of their faerie power generator, failed. Submerged in water behind two-inch-thick glass and distracted by his own thorny predicament, Gideon didn't hear the screams of alarm from the crowd, didn't see them fumbling in the dark for the exits. He didn't see the Mechanist's silver mask crack right down the middle and fall from his pale, shocked face.

It took less than a minute for the stagehands to have some lanterns lit, but that was already many seconds longer than Gideon was prepared to stay in the tank. He managed to get his hands free, but somewhere in the process of untangling the chains at his feet, panic took over, and he could only struggle and fling himself uselessly against the glass. Surely, someone would remember him in the chaos. Surely, the Mechanist would realize the trick was doomed and destroy the glass.

Conan Mesmer, lantern in hand, finally did approach the Mechanist. Gideon watched the flamboyant host gesturing wildly at him, even shaking the Mechanist by the shoulders. But the Mechanist fell to his knees, desperately holding the cracked pieces of his clockwork mask to his face. When he finally did look up at Gideon, the boy knew his master would not be freeing him that night. Gideon had brought this magic to the Mechanist, and now it had failed. Gideon had failed.

In Titus Archer's world, failure was not tolerated. His master would stand there, watch him drown, and consider it too small a punishment.

Just as Gideon was about to take his first breath full of water, Conan Mesmer swung an axe at him. Someone must have found it strapped in its hiding place at the base of the tank. It cracked the glass cylinder on the first strike and smashed the top on the second. The metal lid fell down and crushed what little air remained out of Gideon's lungs, mingling with a scream as a falling glass shard stabbed through his right arm.

The rest of the tank collapsed around him. He found himself gasping and shivering on the stage floor, covered in cuts from the breaking glass and clutching at his arm. The blood flowed freely down into the crook of his elbow, sticky and hot. He stared at the shard embedded there and couldn't bring himself to look away.

" . . . no need to panic, ladies and gentlemen!" Conan Mesmer pleaded with the audience. "Please, everyone, stay in your seats!"

But they hardly needed the encouragement now; the sight of the Mechanist's face stopped them in their tracks.

"Is that Titus Archer?"

"The inventor?"

"It is, it is!"

"Someone help that boy!"

The ushers herded the crowd back. Someone put the Mechanist's cloak over Gideon's shoulders and Gideon shuddered at the touch of the faerie wings, picked from tiny creatures long dead at his own hands. It was a relic from the earlier days of their experiments, before the Mechanist had found more use in keeping his faeries alive, but his master had insisted on keeping it—like a grim trophy from a hunt. Black spots danced in front of Gideon's vision.

"The curtain, the curtain!" hissed Mesmer to the stage manager, a man in black with a door-knocker beard. The crew pulled on the ropes and the thick velvet curtain closed in front of them. Titus Archer stood as still as a statue, but Mesmer was at Gideon's side at once.

"Easy, boy," said the announcer. He took Gideon by the shoulders and let the boy sag into him. Blood and water stained the sparkling fabric of Mesmer's flashy jacket.

"But your suit," Gideon protested nonsensically. He was already slipping into blackness when Titus Archer finally let out a long, desperate howl of fury. It cut through the hisses and boos coming from the disappointed crowd on the other side of the curtain and carried out over the Orbicle, and some even swore they heard it in the street beyond.

The Mechanist was unmasked at last.

CARMER RACED TO the Orbicle on Madame Euphemia's horse. His last sight of Grit, unconscious and being carried away to the Arboretum by Bressel and the other faeries, weighed heavily on his mind. But they had waved him off with assurances that Grit would get the proper care she needed at home, that the queen would surely contact him when all the faeries were safe. Even Madame Euphemia had insisted he leave before the authorities descended on the ruined laboratory. He hoped the street faeries had managed to escort all the former captives to safety.

The theater district was embroiled in thinly disguised chaos when he arrived. Confused show goers were pouring out of the theaters, shouting for cabs in the dark streets. City watchmen were scattered every few yards, controlling the crowds, patrolling for any ruffians attempting to take advantage of the blackout, and directing traffic. So many people were trying to get *out* of the Orbicle, the doormen didn't spare a glance for a small boy trying to get *in*.

Where was the Mechanist? Had the Amazifier even had a chance to perform? Questions upon questions rose in Carmer's mind as he darted through the exiting crowds. The usher he passed on the way in merely shrugged as Carmer edged inside and didn't even ask for a ticket. Carmer supposed there was hardly any need. The house was nearly empty.

But there is an old show business adage that says, "The show must go on," and against all odds, it seemed to be doing just that. There were hardly fifty people left in the audience, but they had all been ushered forward to fill in the first few rows. The only light came from oil lamps set on the stage, and the curtain was already half closed.

The Amazifier sat on the edge of the stage, Kitty crosslegged beside him with her elbows on her knees. She and the remaining audience members watched him fan a plain deck of cards from hand to hand. He spoke at a near normal volume; there was little need to project for the crowd here. Carmer hung back in the shadows.

"I'd like to thank you all for staying tonight," the Amazifier said. The cards danced around his hands, appearing in one and then the other, twisting in and around themselves in complicated patterns. He made it look effortless.

"Though we magicians like to pretend we are infallible, that our illusions are airtight and each trick goes off without a hitch, there are always mistakes. Unfortunately, tonight you witnessed a particularly dire one. And as we try to one-up each other, to make each trick grander than the last—to be bigger, flashier, more dangerous than our competitors—the risks also increase."

The Amazifier rubbed his hands together and threw his fingers outward. The cards burst from his hands in confetti-sized pieces; Carmer heard a collective intake of breath from the audience. But the Amazifier didn't milk the moment. He scooped up the card pieces off the stage and into his hands.

"Perhaps, as the devices get more complicated, as the stakes get higher—and as our egos grow larger—we lose sight of the simple wonder that drew us to magic in the first place. I would like to believe that wonder can still exist, even in competition with shock and awe."

He cupped his confetti-filled palms together and blew on them. The cards, whole once more, peeked out from

324

between his fingers. He spread out his palms to show the entire deck before throwing them up in the air, where they vanished. Another collective breath.

"I would like to think we can still be amazed," said the Amazifier, almost shyly. He exchanged a look with Kitty, who smiled.

"Check under your seats, folks," she suggested.

Tentatively—Carmer couldn't blame them, at this point—people did. Every one of the fifty people sitting in the front rows reached under their seat and came up grasping a single playing card. There were a few gasps and exclamations, but mostly just that slight intake of breath, the small moment of "How did he do that?" before smiles of delight broke across their faces.

It reminded Carmer of the first time the Amazifier came to his orphanage—what felt like a lifetime ago. The magician had put on a small show in their shabby hall, simply because he was "passing through" and thought the children might like to see something new. He was a welcome bright spot in their gray lives, and Carmer was instantly entranced. He was ever curious even about everyday phenomena, and the Amazifier's magic tricks proved even more fascinating for him. He knew there was a plausible explanation lying beneath the surface of every disappearing dove, every coin plucked from behind a little girl's ear, and he resolved to figure it out. The Amazifier had noticed Carmer's intense attention, and the rest was history.

Until now. Now, all was changed again. He was no longer the Amazifier's apprentice. He knew the secrets behind one kind of magic, but now the real thing was knocking on his door. Carmer didn't think he could ever make sense of it all. Perhaps he wasn't meant to.

While the audience clapped, Kitty Delphine rolled out a cart with a black cloth draped over it to the center of the stage. She and the Amazifier lifted the drape to reveal three model buildings, each about two feet tall. The one in the center was an exact replica of the Moto-Manse, complete with a leaning attic tower. On the right was a big top circus tent, and on the left, a simple farmhouse with a windmill.

"Many years ago," explained the Amazifier as he and Kitty wound the mechanisms attached to the back of each model, "these devices were all the rage. We're all much more accustomed to machines now, and clockwork creations are not nearly as impressive as, say, electric lighting." He gave a sly smile, and a few of the audience members chuckled.

"I admit, these have been collecting dust in my attic for a long time," said the Amazifier, "but as I have little else to offer you today, I think they'll do. Ladies and gentlemen, please sit back, relax, and enjoy the show."

Kitty and the Amazifier pulled levers behind each of the automatons. Gears whirred to life inside them, and for a moment, the only sound in the theater was the soft clicking and grinding emanating from the stage. Then the automatons began to move.

A tiny farmer walked out of the farmhouse to lasso a horse trotting toward him. The tower of the Manse swayed back and forth. There was a pop and a puff of smoke, and a gray-haired figure opened the tower window to wave at the audience as if to say, "It's all right here, nothing to see!" The figure bore such a resemblance to the Amazifier, even viewed far from the stage, that the crowd had to laugh. The circus tent opened and lengthened, revealing little trapeze artists in bright silk costumes swinging back and forth.

The few remaining members of the orchestra struck up a simple tune, and soon the audience was clapping along as the farmer chased his runaway horse, the little Amazifier turned the wheel of the Manse, and jugglers took the place of the trapeze artists.

The Amazifier and Kitty wound the automatons again and the scene changed.

All three buildings folded in on themselves. The farmhouse flattened, disappearing into the heavy base of the machine, with only the spinning windmill remaining. The circus tent furled upward like a blossom. The Moto-Manse appeared to be turning itself inside out, panels of the house flipping backward to reveal a dark, bark-like texture on their other side.

That was when Carmer noticed the change in the air.

It was slow, at first, but he sensed it all the same. Then, one by one, the stage lights began to turn on, bathing Kitty and the Amazifier and the metamorphosing automatons in bright golden light.

"Ah," the Amazifier noted, "it seems our power issues are being resolved as we speak."

For a moment, Carmer feared the Mechanist had somehow restored the Hyperion, but that would've been impossible in such a short time. And this didn't feel like the light produced by the Hyperion. It felt warmer, somehow. Right.

Where there was once a farmhouse, a mobile mansion, and a circus tent, there now stood three small trees. Carmer knew these machines well. He'd spent hours and hours studying their many parts, the chain reactions that turned each windmill spoke into a tree branch, each wall of the Manse into a thick trunk. He knew the hundreds of components that went into every movement, how it was timed just so, and found himself—well, amazed—by his mentor's skill.

The audience clapped, but the show wasn't over. The trees blossomed—small white buds, at first, and then into real oranges, apples, and pears. At smaller dinner party performances, the Amazifier often plucked them from the trees and presented them to the guests to taste and confirm their authenticity. The blooming orange tree was by now a famous and well-worn device, but the Amazifier had built an entire garden.

With each tree in full bloom, the old magician smiled at the applauding audience and took a bow. Even the judges, who miraculously had not abandoned their posts in the first row, clapped only a little grudgingly.

"Thank you, ladies and gentlemen," said the Amazifier, "once again—"

But someone gasped and pointed at the center apple tree that had once been the Moto-Manse. The Amazifier stopped short.

Glittering golden powder fell from the stage lights like snow. It hit the trees and they shuddered, leaves suddenly turning silkier, fruit glinting in the light, blossoms growing bigger and more colorful. Shades of blue, red, purple, and orange seeped into the white flowers. Vines sprouted from the bases of the trees and danced across the stage floor to cheery pipe music that overtook the surprised orchestra. People looked around but saw no instruments, and when they heard the singing, they didn't care.

Carmer couldn't help the huge grin that spread across his face. The faeries were here, and they were saying thank you the best way they knew how.

Water spilled from the bases of the trees and streamed out in purposeful rivulets to connect all three of them. It froze over in the blink of an eye, and the tiny figurines—the farmer, the Amazifier, the jugglers and the acrobats—all emerged from the multicolored blossoms. They skated and danced on the ice, sliding from one tree to the other in figure eights and loop-de-loops.

The trees grew even taller, their branches stretching toward the golden light above them. Kitty and the Amazifier's eyes were as wide as saucers, but fortunately, no one was paying them any mind. Doves burst out of the trees and soared overhead, their cooing harmonizing with the otherworldly music that filled the theater. The pears, apples, and oranges grew bigger, too, shimmering and pulsing, until they exploded in showers of golden sparks in different shapes—snowflakes, starbursts, sun rays, and even laughing faces.

The Amazifier reached out his hands to touch the sparks nearest him and the rest responded in kind, swirling around the old man from head to foot. He laughed, sounding like a boy again. His hands, still capable of grace after all these years, gathered the sparks to his palms. He sent them shooting out over the audience, where they rained down on the awed crowd and disappeared with a harmless crackle.

The little figures skated back to their places, the water retreated and dried up, and the blossoms shrank back down to normal size, though they still retained their brilliant colors. The trees lowered away from the stage lights to their normal height, folding and contracting with metallic clicks, until the three original buildings took their place. The farmhouse, the Manse, and the circus tent stood whole once more, and if it was the machine turning the windmill, or something else entirely, well, who can really say?

Carmer left the Amazifier and Kitty bowing and curt-sying and basking in adoring applause, but not before he stepped out into the aisle and caught the Amazifier's eye. The old man looked surprised—but not surprised enough, Carmer thought—to see him there. The Amazifier winked at him and bowed again, and relief swept over Carmer, more powerful than any magic he'd seen that night. There would definitely be time to talk later.

24.

BOYS OF FIRE AND IRON

DAWN REDWOODS WEREN'T NATIVE TO THAT PART of the country, but it seemed fitting that the Arboretum put on a good show after the faeries' safe return. Fair Folk and Free Folk alike reveled together late into the night in the grand ballrooms of those giant trunks, singing thanks for those returned to them and raising toasts to a speedy recovery for the princess who saved them all.

For the first time since Carmer had been to the Arboretum, there were other humans there as well. The faeries lit the lanterns and opened the gates again — hesitantly to be sure, but also willing to extend the olive branch. Today there were children playing hide-and-seek in the maze of shrubs, making crowns out of pinecones and chains of cattails, climbing trees and scraping their knees and getting dirty enough to be scolded at home, as all children should every now and again. It was cold—winter was still on its way, after all—but the atmosphere in the Arboretum was anything but chilly.

Carmer took the time to walk it from end to end before he reached the redwoods. He climbed Widdershinner's Hill, watched a few locals repairing a section of the Whispering Wall, visited the birdhouse village, and even said hello to the siren in the fountain, who filled him in on all the latest gossip. He walked through paths of porous gray cork trees from Japan, the ever-blooming blue roses, and maples whose leaves were still bright and bigger than his hand. Autumn crunched beneath his feet and filled his nostrils, crisp and clean.

When he reached the redwoods, he simply stood there for a moment, taking in their beauty. Manipulating the elements and making automatons come to life were all very fine things, but there was something magical here, too, about knowing that spaces like the Arboretum still existed in the world. Skemantis was a beautiful city, but its beauty without Oldtown Arboretum would be incomplete.

Carmer stepped carefully up and over the giant roots of the largest redwood on the path, lest he step on anything or anyone living under them. He climbed into an opening at the very base of the trunk and was not surprised when it widened to accommodate him. He sat down, crossed his legs, and waited.

"I know I was supposed to wait," Carmer said, "but I wanted to make sure you were all right."

A split in the bark in front of him yawned open, glowing from within. Grit sat inside, looking tired but otherwise fine.

"You're a ninny," she said. "I'm fine."

"Are you?" Carmer pressed.

"On my way there." She shrugged and smiled. "How is the Amazifier handling his rediscovered fame?"

"Oh, pretty well," said Carmer. The celebration in the circus camp had lasted long into the night. "But he knows he can't count on it forever."

"What did you tell him?"

"As much as I could without sounding insane," Carmer said, "which wasn't very much. But I think he might be more in the loop than we suspected."

Grit raised an eyebrow.

"He's retiring and going on the road with Madame Euphemia," explained Carmer. "Apparently, they knew each other from the old days. And if he hasn't noticed that those puppets of hers are beyond natural, I'll eat my hat."

Grit laughed. "You have a new one, I see."

Carmer tipped his new black top hat in her direction. "Courtesy of the Amazifier."

"But Carmer," Grit said, suddenly worried, "if the Amazifier is retiring, what will happen to you and Kitty?"

"I wouldn't worry about Kitty," said Carmer. He explained how she'd already had half a dozen job offers from the various dress shops and theaters she had applied to.

"But she's going to stay in costumes at the Orbicle, at least for their next show," explained Carmer. "They're doing *A Midsummer Night's Dream*, and she says she can't miss a chance to make faerie costumes."

"You'll have to be her consultant."

"I'll insist that hatpins and leather really are essentials for every outfit," Carmer agreed.

Friendly silence fell between them.

"And you?" Grit prodded gently. "Are you . . . staying behind as well?"

Carmer avoided her gaze. "I thought about it," he said honestly. "Someone still has to find a way to stop the Mechanist from just building a new machine, and there's still so much I don't know about faeries, and there are amazing places to study here—the Academy of Science, for one thing. I'm a little young, and my schooling hasn't been the most consistent, but my portfolio—"

"Carmer," Grit interrupted. "Just say yes or no."

Carmer sighed. "No."

"Oh." The light in Grit's hollow seemed to shrink a little.

"The Amazifier left me the Moto-Manse," Carmer explained, "and it feels right to keep it moving. Ever since he first took me on as his apprentice, I've been on the road. Something's telling me I can learn more out there than stuck behind a desk here." Carmer shrugged. "Plus, I've never really . . . done well in groups. With people my age."

"Well, I can relate to that." Grit laughed.

Carmer blushed before he next spoke. "I know," he said. "And so that's why I thought . . . maybe you'd like to come with me?"

His words hung in the air, and he could see Grit's pleasure at being asked—and then her disappointment. "I want to, Carmer," she said. "I do. I want to see the world more than anything."

"But?"

"But—and I can't believe I'm saying this—I have a duty to the faeries here," Grit said, sighing. "What happened with the Mechanist showed me that. My mother won't be around forever, and when she's gone, I need to be ready. I need to know about the world, but I need to know about *them*, too."

"I understand," said Carmer. He did, even if he was disappointed. But it was Grit's choice to make—as was what to do with the object he was about to pull out of his pocket.

Carmer fumbled around in his coat and produced a bundle wrapped in handkerchiefs. "But I wanted to leave you with something before I go." He carefully undid the wrappings and held the delicate mechanical faerie wing in an outstretched palm.

"You were right to be angry with me for not asking your permission," said Carmer. "And I know I can't succeed where, as you put it, generations of faerie magic didn't. But maybe, with a little of your magic *and* a little of mine, this might just work." He placed the wing in front of her.

"I'll think about it." Grit nodded. "Thanks. For everything, Carmer."

"You're welcome. And—"

"Help!"

A familiar figure crashed through the trees. His blond hair was streaming out behind him and his arm was in a sling, but Carmer would have recognized Gideon Sharpe anywhere.

Gideon circled the trees in a panic, eyes darting behind him every few seconds, like he was running from something. The redwood holding Carmer and Grit started to close protectively around them.

"Help!" Gideon said to the trees. "As a Friend of the Fae, I claim sanctuary in this place from those who would do me harm!"

Gideon Sharpe, a Friend of the Fae? Carmer had suspected as much, but it still surprised him to hear the words aloud.

"Wait," Carmer said to the redwood. "I know him."

Carmer started to climb out of the tree, when a flurry of hornets buzzed past his ear. He shrank back against the trunk. There must have been hundreds of them, buzzing angrily; they morphed into the shape of a face Carmer was getting to know all too well.

"It was not my court who named you Friend, changeling," said Ombrienne. Her voice vibrated with the buzzing of the bees that now formed her likeness. "And the stench of your betrayal clings to you like the foul cloak of your master. Leave this place."

"But I—I just made a mistake, please. They'll kill me!"

"LEAVE. NOW."

The hornets burst apart and zoomed straight toward Gideon.

Carmer couldn't believe what he was about to say, but he said it anyway.

"Wait!"

Much to his surprise, the hornets paused. Gideon, who'd lifted his good arm to cover his face from the oncoming onslaught, lowered it cautiously. The hornets reformed into Ombrienne's face.

"Yes?" she hissed, as if she already regretted not stinging the other boy to death.

"I don't know exactly what Gideon's done," Carmer admitted. "And I don't know anything about how these courts you keep talking about work. But . . . the Arboretum did let him in, right?"

The hornets crawled over each other, and their outline of Ombrienne's eyes narrowed.

"It let me in when you weren't . . ." Carmer trailed off. "Well, when you weren't in the best of moods with me. And that ended up being a good thing."

Even Grit was looking at Carmer like she couldn't believe what he was saying, but she didn't disagree.

"So maybe you should hear him out," Carmer finished. "Or, um, not. It's up to you, Your Highness."

The hornets took flight in a tight whirlwind, flying closer and closer together, until they disappeared with a pop. Queen Ombrienne, in regular faerie form, hovered in their place.

"This boy taunted you, kidnapped you, beat you, and nearly had your eyes pecked out, and yet you plead for his life?" Ombrienne asked in disbelief. She rolled her eyes, reminding Carmer very much of Grit. "You humans have the strangest moral qualms."

"She has a point," conceded Grit, poking her head out from inside the redwood.

Carmer frowned.

"And yet, as the boy notes," Ombrienne said, turning to Gideon, "my realm did admit you. It would perhaps be unwise to ignore such a sign."

Carmer watched the queen in amazement. That was probably the closest to saying "I might be wrong" she was ever going to get.

"But I cannot obstruct the laws of the Unseelie Court," she continued. "To do so, especially for the sake of a human boy I know to be guilty of crimes against the fae, would mean an end to an eternally fragile peace."

Carmer expected Grit to speak up, to once again protest her mother's aversion to risk, but she was silent.

"Please, just convince them to give me a chance to explain," Gideon pleaded. "I know I can't run forever."

"No, you cannot," agreed the queen. "But it is clear you've severed your ties with your master. My realm can sense it. And fortunately for you, I am in a forgiving mood." She looked at Carmer shrewdly. "I'm willing to negotiate with the Unseelie Court on your behalf," she continued. "But we shall have to meet on neutral ground. Grit will be my representative."

Carmer and Grit exchanged surprised looks. Since when did Queen Ombrienne trust Grit to be her representative? The queen *must* be in a good mood. They should save her entire kingdom from extinction more often.

"Neutral ground," repeated Carmer. "Where's neutral ground for the Unseelie Court?"

Queen Ombrienne smirked, but there was no real amusement in her eyes. "It is a place where the fae do not tread," she explained. "And I believe you're acquainted with a perfect spot already."

Carmer felt a sinking feeling in his gut.

"How would you like to escort Mr. Sharpe to the Vallows?"

"CAN SOMEONE PLEASE explain to me what the Unseelie Court actually is?" Carmer whispered as they crept along a crumbling side street in a decidedly unsavory neighborhood on their way to the abandoned mining town. Carmer supposed there wasn't as much need for secrecy this time, but the Hollow Valley was the kind of place where sneaking glances behind you every few feet didn't seem like such a silly idea.

It was less creepy in the late afternoon than in complete darkness, but Carmer could feel the unease in the air emanating from Grit and the other faeries from the queen's retinue. The latter faeries hovered on either side of Carmer and their princess, hidden from view but ready to both protect Grit and keep Gideon from escaping, if the need arose.

From Eduardo's back, Gideon Sharpe snorted. Carmer was starting to regret his offer to let the other boy ride, even if he was injured.

"They named you Friend, and you didn't even know which court you were serving?" scoffed Gideon.

Grit turned around to glare at him from her seat between Eduardo's ears.

"Did you?" asked Carmer pointedly, and Gideon fell silent. Carmer led them on.

"It's not like there's a hard and fast distinction," explained Grit. "And the Free Folk who don't travel in troops or live in kingdoms aren't aligned with a court at all."

"But?" asked Carmer.

"But generally, the Unseelie Court's attitude toward humans is not as . . . benevolent as ours."

"Your mother is *benevolent*?" asked Carmer.

Grit shrugged. "Compared to some other creatures out there? Yes."

"Wait a minute," said Carmer. "The . . . water horse thing—"

"Kelpie."

"Kelpie. He mentioned it was funny that he was helping the Seelie Court and letting me ride him. Why was that funny?"

Gideon snorted again. Carmer ignored him.

"Well . . ." hedged Grit. "Kelpies don't have the best reputations."

"And why is that?"

"They usually lure young maidens into the water to, um, drown them," confessed Grit in a rush.

"Oh," said Carmer. Despite his best intentions, he was starting to see how Gideon Sharpe's experience as a Friend of the Unseelie Court really could have been wildly different from his own.

"Queen Ombrienne seems positively rosy in comparison, doesn't she?" noted Gideon.

"But not all the Unseelie want to hurt humans," Grit said. "They're just more solitary, more comfortable in the shadows."

"And graveyards, and bogs, and raging seas, and old abandoned houses," added Gideon cheerfully.

"Why are we helping him, again?" Grit asked.

Carmer wasn't sure, to be honest, but he didn't have time to dwell on the decision.

"We're here," Gideon said.

Gideon struggled to get down from the horse with one arm and stumbled a little when he dismounted. Carmer almost asked if he was all right, but stopped himself. What should *he* care if evil, faerie-enslaving Gideon Sharpe was all right or not?

And they weren't even close to the Vallows. Carmer could just see the lonely dirt road that led to the abandoned town a few blocks away, where the claustrophobic tenements and warehouses started to thin out. Grit, however, seemed to agree with Gideon's assessment. She followed his gaze down to a poorly covered manhole that split the street in front of them.

The queen's faeries flew over the manhole and spun around it counterclockwise, shedding faerie dust and singing their eerie song. The lid twisted off with a groan and hovered a few inches in the air. Carmer took hold of an edge, and together he and the faeries lowered it carefully to the ground.

Carmer expected the hole beneath to be a sheer drop into darkness, but found a surprisingly smooth concrete stairway in their path instead.

"We can't meet *in* the Vallows, exactly," Grit explained. "Official exchanges between the courts have to take place at the crossroads between realms."

"The crossroads *between realms*?" asked Carmer.

"It's symbolic, you imbecile," drawled Gideon.

"Shut it, Sharpe," snapped Grit. "Let's go. We don't want to be late."

They left Eduardo in the care of a few of the queen's faeries and began their descent into the tunnel.

"What is this place?" Carmer asked Grit, but it was Gideon who answered.

"Before the Relerail, the city tried to build an underground railway, like the Met in London," he said as they crept down the stairs. "But Skemantis wasn't the hub it is now even a few decades ago, and between poor planning and budget cuts, the project was abandoned. This is one of the test stations that was nearly completed."

They reached the bottom of the stairs and found themselves on a deserted railway platform. The faeries' lights were barely enough to see over the edge and into the gaping tunnels running in either direction. Carmer had expected some trace of the people who once worked here to remain—some rusted construction equipment or rubbish heaps or abandoned lunch pails—but there was nothing. Even the floor was startlingly clean, as if it had been swept that day. A half-finished tile mosaic on one wall was the only indication that the station wasn't perfectly operational.

"We're not alone here," said Carmer.

"A brilliant deduction," sneered Gideon, but Carmer heard the fear creep into his voice.

At Grit's instruction they hopped down onto the track and picked their way along the rails. Thick black vines ran under their feet and along the walls, though how anything grew down here in the utter darkness, Carmer couldn't guess. Water from the street had drained into the tunnel, and now and then they were forced to wade through inches of damp muck.

It seemed hours later that they finally stopped at a cross section of tunnels. It was impossible to tell which ones actually led anywhere and which ones simply faded into the bedrock around them. The temperature dropped steadily. Carmer felt gooseflesh rise on his arms, and Grit drew a shuddering breath.

Her keen ears heard the approach of the Unseelie Court before the rest of them.

"They brought the Wild Hunt," said Grit. For the first time, she looked actually worried.

Then Carmer heard it—the echo of a screaming whistle, growing louder and louder. The churning, rumbling growl of an approaching engine followed. Loose pebbles rained down from the ceiling, and dust clouded the tracks ahead. A wind whipped up out of nowhere—which Carmer was quickly learning was never a good sign.

Roaring filled Carmer's ears. He thought it must be the noise of the train whistle and the howling wind, but then he realized it was *actual* howling. Battle cries, yowls, hammering fists, the clash of metal on metal, and eerie ululations all came from the unseen approaching onslaught. The mud along the tracks morphed into grasping hands, long brown fingers dripping ooze and squelching as they crawled toward the Seelie retinue. Rats the size of cats skittered in and out of the shadows. Only glimpses of their silky black backs and red eyes were visible in the faerie light.

Carmer never saw the train round the corner, but it screeched to a stop mere feet from him and Gideon, smoking and hissing like a living, breathing monster.

A skeletal three-eyed man in a tattered navy blue conductor's outfit leaned out the window and grinned at them, revealing rotted yellow teeth filed into points. His cap was a dark, damp-looking red that Carmer didn't want to think too closely about. The ghostly outlines of other men—or what looked like men—were just visible behind the cloudy windows.

"All aboard!" he called.

Howls, hoots, and banging noises came from inside the train.

He pointed a papery-skinned hand with black finger-nails at Gideon. "I believe one of you's got a train to catch."

The hands in the mud seized Gideon by the ankles and dragged him to the ground. Gideon yelped with pain as the movement jarred his arm. His clothes were soaked through with muck in seconds.

"Wait!" said Grit. She stood on Carmer's shoulder. "My name is Princess Grettifrida of Oldtown Arboretum. I come as a representative of Queen—"

"Yeah, yeah, I know who you are," said the three-eyed man. He opened his door and swung down from the train. "Question is, why should I care? My king wants his head. Maybe his liver, too. The old man does enjoy a handsome cut of liver."

The conductor licked his lips with a forked tongue, but the muddy hands stopped trying to drag Gideon any farther toward the train.

"As a Friend of the Fae, he's entitled to a fair trial under his own court," said Grit.

The conductor fumbled in his coat pockets and plucked out a dingy-looking pack of cigarettes and a lighter. He took a long moment to light one and take a drag before he spoke.

"Well, darling, you're lookin' at judge, jury, and executioner."

The shadows in the darkness hissed and giggled their approval.

"Mister Moon, at your service." He doffed his red

cap—it was *definitely* stained with blood—and leaned forward in a mocking bow.

"The Wild Hunt's keeping up with the times, I see." Grit nodded to the train.

"Well, you know, lots of lost souls to gobble up on the platforms these days, even topside," said Moon, grinning. "And a surprising number of jumpers, too."

"Just take me and get on with it," spat Gideon Sharpe, huddled against the wall. "I've seen enough of faerie justice to know what's in store for me."

"With pleasure, boy," snarled Moon. His third eye flashed, and he looked beyond Carmer and Grit to the tunnel behind them. "But first it seems we should welcome an uninvited guest. Why don't you come out them shadows, Mr. Archer?"

There was a wet thud and brief sounds of a struggle before the black vines creeping along the tunnel walls dragged a nearly unrecognizable Mechanist into their midst. The Seelie faeries shrank back in alarm, and even Carmer took a step away. Titus Archer was filthy and disheveled in his Mechanist costume, ghastly cloak of faerie wings hanging half off his shoulders.

He spotted Carmer first.

"You!" Archer lunged toward the boy, but the vines tightened around his wrists and ankles and forced him into a kneel. The train's light shone straight into his face.

He breathed hard through his nose and squinted up at Mr. Moon's three black-rimmed eyes.

"*This* is the man you sold our secrets to?" Mr. Moon asked Gideon incredulously. "For what? A warm bed at night? Learning your ABC's?"

Gideon turned his head away.

"I hate to be the one to break it to you, chap, but you've got pretty poor taste in father figures."

Carmer looked at Gideon then, and he wondered exactly how Gideon had ended up covered in cuts with his arm in a sling. Carmer had an educated guess.

"He made me do it," said Gideon. "He made me lead him to the faeries. He stole the Unseelie hearts that were entrusted to me, they're on him right now—"

"Why, you lying little—"

SMACK. A length of train track broke off from the ground, a snapping snake of metal, and struck the Mechanist across the face. The blow sent him sprawling to the earth. When he struggled to a sitting position, blood was pouring out of his nose.

Carmer gasped: the tracks, like much of the train, had to be made of iron, but these faeries were manipulating them all the same.

"I would have saved all of you," Archer growled at Mr. Moon. "A new order, a new way for the fae to *contribute* to the world again. What are you now? Forgotten gods and dying spirits, scraping out your meager existence while you hide in the shadows."

"Really quite an unpleasant fellow, ain't he?" Moon commented to Gideon. Then Moon's eyes turned hard, and in one fluid motion he was nearly on top of the Mechanist, the human man's chin gripped in his sharp black nails. "Did it ever occur to you, *Mr.* Archer," hissed the conductor, "that some of us might *prefer* the dark?"

The Mechanist's eyes widened in fear.

Mister Moon bent closer and flicked his forked tongue over Archer's bleeding face. He wrenched the silver bands from Archer's wrists and pushed him back down into the mud. Mister Moon caressed the stones—the faerie hearts, Carmer knew now—with surprising gentleness and slid them over his own bony hands.

"It should have." Mr. Moon patted the front of his train as if it were the nose of a faithful steed, and the engine roared to life. He snapped his fingers, and one of the train's doors slid open. Gideon Sharpe flew through the air like a rag doll and into the car. The door slammed shut behind him.

"What are you doing?" demanded Carmer. He ran to the window where Gideon Sharpe stood pounding on the glass as disembodied, skeletal hands grabbed at him from all sides.

"It talks," smirked Moon with surprise. "Oh, don't worry about him, little Friend!" Mister Moon swung up back into the driver's seat. The hands grabbed at Gideon's face, his hair, his neck, until he was obscured from view and dragged back into the murky gray smoke that filled the compartment. The roaring of the engine barely covered the sound of his screams.

Carmer banged on the window, but the mere touch of the car burned him like a brand, and he snatched his hand away.

"He rides with the Hunt!" shouted Mister Moon.

Battle cries, wails, and the pounding of spears and shields met his words.

"For how long?" Grit yelled at him.

"Until I decide he's paid off his debts," Moon replied with a savage grin. "LAST CALLLLLLL." His voice boomed through the tunnel until it shook. Bits of dirt and pebbles fell down on Carmer and the faeries.

"Carmer, run," ordered Grit from his shoulder.

Carmer looked to the Mechanist, who was still shackled to the tracks, struggling in vain against the viselike grip of the vines and the wires twisting themselves around him. "But — but what about him?" he asked above the din of the engine and the shrieking of the Unseelie faeries.

"Carmer, we need to move NOW!"

Carmer ran. His last glimpse of Titus Archer was of black vines growing out of the magician's mouth, choking back even his screams.

Being chased by the Wild Hunt was like being chased by a tornado. Carmer ducked into a service doorway in the nick of time. He sucked himself in, holding on to the short emergency ladder with all of his might as the train roared past. He opened his eyes, just for a split second, and thought he glimpsed a terrified face staring back at him.

And then all was quiet. Only the scurrying of rats and the soft *drip, drip, drip* of dirty water disturbed the silence. The queen's faeries' lights shivered around Carmer's head; they looked at him with concern, bobbing anxiously up and down.

Carmer placed Grit safely on one of the rungs of the ladder, sank to the ground, and promptly vomited all over his shoes.

25.

WINGS TO FLY

GRIT SAT ATOP THE WHISPERING WALL AND AB-
sentmindedly picked at loose pebbles with the spurs of her
heels. Dusten's saddle was in her lap, and the owl himself
wasn't too far away, happily munching on a cluster of fat
worms she'd unearthed for him that morning. He deserved
a treat after the upheaval of the past few days. They all did.

She was supposed to be fixing the straps of his saddle—
all that time around Carmer's inventions had given her
a few ideas for improvements—but she found her gaze
wandering. For the first time, she didn't just look beyond
the wall to the South Gate and the city outside, but back
into the Arboretum. It was a chilly, overcast day, but there
were still people strolling through the trees, sweethearts

stealing away for a moment under the kissing bridge, a group of young factory workers tossing a ball around on their lunch break. They couldn't see the faeries that lived and breathed right beside them, but Grit saw everything: the Sprout Mothers leading fall cleanup lessons in the vegetable patch, the mice and squirrels putting the finishing touches on their homes for the winter, the water faeries tending the fountains and streams, the lamplighters resting in their glassy domes until sundown.

Just a few days ago, Grit would have thought it impossible that her magic could one day tie them all together. Now she could feel her power coursing through her veins, connecting her to the kingdom and every faerie in it. But she was still gaining back her strength from dismantling the Hyperion. She hadn't been able to do any magic since then, and it bothered her like an itch she couldn't scratch.

Grit gave up on Dusten's saddle for the moment and set it aside. She closed her eyes and rubbed her hands together, reaching deep down for the spark that was always there, waiting to be lit. She blew on her hands and opened her palms; a small flame flickered there for a few seconds and fizzled out.

Grit lurched forward, dizzy and tired from even that simple effort. She forced herself to take deep breaths. Dusten waddled over to her and nudged her gently with his beak.

"It's all right, Dusten," she assured him, but she turned

her face into his feathers to wipe a few tears away all the same.

"It will come back, you know."

Grit's mother was suddenly beside her, looking beautiful as usual in a gown of soft gray cobwebs and baby's breath.

"It just takes time," said Queen Ombrienne. Her iridescent wings shimmered, even in the overcast light, in shades of brown, purple, and blue. "Your magic is incredibly powerful, Grettifrida. More so than I ever expected."

"So I get advice now?" scoffed Grit. "I had to figure it all out on my own, Mother. I had to *bribe* Free Folk to teach me. I had to catch salamanders in strangers' fires with my bare hands, because I didn't know how to sing to them. I spent years trying to hide what I was really good at, because nobody told me it was worth anything! A *human boy* saw power in me when you were too scared to let me light a single spark."

"And I was wrong," admitted Ombrienne.

Grit let go of Dusten's feathers in surprise and stared at her.

"You have your own unique power, Grettifrida, and I hope you continue to use it well. I will teach you what I can, if that is what you desire." Ombrienne stepped forward and cupped her daughter's cheek. "Without you and your knowledge of the outside world, we would have never been able to stop the Mechanist."

"Thank you," said Grit stiffly, resisting the urge to duck

out from under her mother's touch. But after a few seconds, she turned away and looked out toward the South Gate. She imagined Carmer and the rest of the circus camp packing up and moving on now that the Seminal Symposium of Magickal Arts was over. He could barely speak to her when they parted the other night, after the Unseelie Court had unleashed their wrath on the Mechanist. It would be years before the next Symposium, and she wasn't sure he would come back. Perhaps he'd had enough of the faeries of Skemantis.

"Which is why I've been thinking," continued Ombrienne, "that you should leave us for a while."

"What?" Grit gaped at her mother, who looked out past the Arboretum gates with a critical eye.

"You *are* different from the rest of us, Grettifrida," acknowledged the queen, "but your curiosity about the world outside these walls is what saved us all. Perhaps, in the years to come, that knowledge will be more valuable. It may even be the key to our survival."

Grit couldn't believe what she was hearing.

"So you . . . you *want* me to go with Carmer?"

"Believe it or not, my dear, I want you to do what makes you happy," said Ombrienne. "If you had asked me before all of this nonsense with the Mechanist, I would have said no. But I know that you understand your responsibility to your people now. I know you will return when they have need of you."

"I will," insisted Grit. She flung herself at her mother and threw her arms around the queen, taking them both by surprise. "I promise, I will. Thank you, Mother."

Ombrienne squeezed her daughter tightly. She stood back and placed her hands on Grit's shoulders. "If you're to be a woman of the road, dear, you're going to need more dependable transportation."

Ombrienne waved her hand, and the mechanical wing appeared in the air before them. The queen began to sing, the same haunting melody that opened the door to Faerie, and gold sparks wove in and out of the gears and pulleys and along the paper-thin glass. The wing spun in a tiny twister of shimmering gold, the glass changing to the iridescent membrane of a real faerie wing while the metal stayed intact. The brass glinted in the sunlight.

The wing made its way toward Grit and hovered near her back. Ombrienne's eyes met Grit's, awaiting her approval; Grit took a deep breath, nodded, and put her arm through the strap. There was a pulley system that extended to a knob she was meant to hold in her hand to control it, but there was no need of pulleys when the whole thing was animated by faerie magic, and it disappeared in the spinning gold sparks. An electric shudder went through her and she felt the wing connect with her back with a stinging zap of power. It burned sharply for a moment; she cried out in surprise and fell hard on her knees.

The sparks disappeared, and the pain along with them.

Grit took a shaky breath and looked over her shoulder. For the first time in her life, she saw two fluttering wings behind her.

Ombrienne took a tentative step forward, face filled with concern. "Are you all right? I didn't think—"

Grit held up a hand. "Give me a minute." She lurched to her feet, mechanical wing fluttering alongside the real one. Faerie magic alone hadn't been enough to help her, but paired with Carmer's model, it might just work. Grit closed her eyes, wishing as hard as she could, just daring to hope—

"Darling, open your eyes," said her mother gently.

Grit did.

Her feet were no longer on the ground. She hovered over the Whispering Wall, looking down at her mother smiling up at her. She was a faerie with one wing—an impossible thing, she'd once thought—and she was flying.

CARMER DECIDED TO go south. Winter in New England was not a good time for those who made their living on the road. He would be more likely to find receptive audiences in smaller towns with warmer climes. Such was the life of the traveling magician.

He stood at the wheel of the Moto-Manse as it chugged down the road out of Skemantis, windows thrown open to the crisp fall breeze. Madame Euphemia and the Amazifier were headed west with her vardo, the puppets, and Eduardo.

The Amazifier was planning a study of desert plants; in retirement, he hoped to continue his contributions to academia more seriously.

When they bid each other good-bye at the circus camp, the Amazifier pulled Carmer into a gruff embrace.

"The next time you get an inkling to muck about with faerie magic," whispered the Amazifier as he patted Carmer on the back, "you might want to let an old man in on the joke."

He winked, tipped his hat, and rode off with a cackling Madame Euphemia before Carmer could even think of a reply.

Kitty was settling in quite well at the Orbicle. Carmer had to pry her away from her work amidst a gaggle of equally impressively dressed women to say good-bye. She'd tried hard to stay angry with him, but failed miserably, and nearly suffocated him in a bone-crushing hug.

"Spirits and zits, I'm glad all this nonsense is over with," she said with a sigh. "But I'm sure gonna miss you, Carmer. We had some good times."

"You'll have to tell me your secret for getting tomato stains out of our clothes," said Carmer.

Kitty laughed, but wrote it down for him just the same. She was always a practical girl. "You be careful now," she said. "Try to stay out of trouble for once!"

That time, Carmer laughed, but it didn't quite reach his eyes.

Bumping along the road, he couldn't help but feel that trouble was closer than ever before. He glanced at the woods on either side of him. He knew what kinds of things waited out there now, and he wasn't sure if it made him feel better or worse. Every time he closed his eyes, he saw Gideon Sharpe's face in the train car, or the Mechanist's last struggles before meeting his brutal end. His world had gotten bigger, but for the first time, he wasn't sure if he wanted it to.

And then something smacked into his head.

He slammed on the Moto-Manse's brakes and the house jerked to a halt, top floors swaying from the impact. He reached up to grab his new hat and felt familiar tiny hands bat him away.

It seemed trouble wasn't done with him just yet.

"Hey, where's the door on this one?"

Carmer just smiled, put his foot on the accelerator, and kept on driving.

Acknowledgments

There are many wonderful people who helped *Carmer and Grit* make the journey from a sparkly idea knocking around in my head to the book you now hold in your hands. I would like to thank:

My parents, for not blinking an eye when I told them my first project after graduating *film* school, was—wait for it—a novel, and for always keeping their door open.

My partner, David, for listening to me ramble about my life *and* the lives of fictional people for hours on end. Also, for hugs and ice cream.

Brooke Mills, best friend and writing soul mate. We

speak troll, and it's great. FLAIL. (Also-also, I know you're Baelfire.)

Harvard John, for invaluable feedback as the first pair of human eyeballs to read this whole book.

Eric Bogosian, Alice Daken, David Kociemba, and all of the mentors and teachers I've had the privilege to learn about storytelling from. You make me want to do better every day.

Victoria Marini, agent extraordinaire, for fierce advocacy and sage advice.

My editor, Krestyna Lypen, and the whole team at Algonquin Young Readers. I am so happy that my first book can call Algonquin home. Thank you for taking a chance on Carmer, Grit, and me.